CW01238215

1100
Digital Stories
in an Analog World

RON COLLINS

SKYFOX
PUBLISHING
Science Fiction

Copyright
1100
Digital Stories in an Analog World
© 2024 Ron Collins
All rights reserved

All appeared in *Analog Science Fiction and Fact*

"A Matter of Pride" © Ron Collins
"Bugs" © Ron Collins
"Deca-Dad" © Ron Collins
"Ellipses…" © Ron Collins
"Following Jules" © Ron Collins
"Stealing the Sun" © Ron Collins
"The Taranth Stone" © Ron Collins
"Parchment in Glass" © Ron Collins
"Just Business" © Ron Collins
"Survivors" © Ron Collins
"Unfolding the Multi-Cloud" © Ron Collins
"The Day the Track Stood Still" © Ron Collins and John C. Bodin

Cover Design by Ron Collins
Images Used: Liuzishan
(black hole devouring a spaceship, digital painting, 3D illustration)

This book is licensed for your personal enjoyment only. All rights reserved. This is a work of fiction. All incidents, dialog, and characters are products of the author's imagination. Any resemblance to persons living or dead is purely coincidental. This book, or parts thereof, may not be reproduced in any form without permission.

Skyfox Publishing

ISBN-10: 1-946176-81-8
ISBN-13: 978-1-946176-81-3

For Dr. Schmidt

Who kindly asked me not to sell him just one story.

Foreword

One of my fondest memories as a young writer was a day when my wife and I had lunch with Dr. Stanley Schmidt, then the editor of *Analog Science Fiction and Fact*. I think I had sold him exactly one story at that time—"Stealing the Sun," which was later followed by a pair more that then eventually grew into my bestselling series.

He told me two things at that lunch that have stayed with me ever since. The first was that he'd known I was going to put material in *Analog* well before I did, simply because he saw so many stories from me, and because those stories were showing improvement over the months. That made me feel pretty good.

Then, toward the end of that lunch, he told me that the most important thing I could do for him was to keep sending him stories because "the worst thing you can do is sell me only one." His point was that he wanted to build a following, and followings only happen after multiple stories. He wanted, he said, to be able to put my name on the cover. He wanted, he said, to sell magazines that way.

I don't have to tell you, that was a heady day for a brand-new writer.

It is fair to say that the *Analog Science Fiction and Fact* magazine holds a special place in my heart. It is, of course, among the most important legacy publications in existence, with its roots back in the earliest days of science fiction. I read it as a kid. My loveable but fallible adult uncle, who for better or worse was always a major influence on me, read it before that. He's probably the one who turned me on to the magazine, truth be told. He's the one who got me into comics as a kid, and into Heinlein and Asimov and all the rest as time went on.

So, blame it on him, I guess.

Thanks, Dennis.

Even if I wasn't a writer, *Analog* would be special to me.

But, of course, I am a writer.

And I've had a bunch of stories in *Analog*'s pages. Enough that if I were to be given one of those chances to go back in time and show my kid-self all the issues, I'm pretty sure that kid-self would self-combust on the spot.

Truth be told, though, if I could do that—if I could go back in time and show anyone this collection of publications in *Analog Science Fiction and Fact*—it would be Dennis I would visit. He would be so ... happy.

As I write this, I believe *Analog* has published twenty-five of my stories, which makes it the most frequent publisher of my work. Only the Fiction River series out of WMG Publishing has more, and that's a different kind of a project.

With luck, *Analog* will get at least a few more before I'm done kicking around here.

It's a great feeling, to see my words in those pages.

This volume is comprised of the first dozen of those stories, titled in my ironic way 1100, which, of course, is binary for 12. As I look them over I can't help but feel sanguine. Looking at the titles brings back not so much the stories themselves, but the emotions I felt as I wrote them. "A Matter of Pride," which includes a send-up of myself as a business leader. "Bugs," which got me on the *Analog* cake at World Con one year (you haven't lived until you get a piece of *Analog* cake with your name on it). "Ellipses…" which makes me think of a particular buddy of mine. "Survivors," which I wrote on a dare from Lisa Silverthorne, a great friend and a beautiful writer herself.

I love them all.

I hope you do, too.

If you do, well, maybe I'll scrounge up the second dozen and put out another volume. Which, I suppose would need to be titled 11000, right?

That would be fun.

In the meantime, I'll stop here because I need to get on sending Trevor Quachri (the current editor of *Analog,* and a guy who has, thankfully, continued Dr. Schmidt's questionable practice of publishing my work) my next one.

Ron Collins
Las Vegas, NV

A Matter of Pride
ANALOG APRIL 2000

"Must be nice to work for someone who lets you sit on your ass all day." The computer spoke with a throaty rattle that made it sound like it had smoked for thirty years.

Chris grumbled. A half-eaten Snickers bar sat on his desk. He took a bite and chased it with a swig of warm Mountain Dew.

"You're gonna rot your teeth with all that sugar," the computer said.

Chris leaned back in his chair with his hands behind his head. "God damn it," he whispered to himself.

The system had been talking like this all morning, and it had long ago gotten beyond the point of pissing him off. The problem, of course, was that it shouldn't be making any noise at all beyond playing the newest Space Boys CD he had slipped into the rack earlier this morning.

"I'm screwed, man. Totally screwed."

"Virus still kicking your butt?" replied Kevin Johnson from the cubicle across the hall.

He nodded. "I'm dead meat."

"Sometimes you get the code, sometimes the code gets you."

Chris had been in the office late last night, using company resources to partake in his favorite personal pastime: crashing other computers, frying security codes, and piddling around with new ideas on encryption techniques — activities most decidedly against the rules.

Now he was paying the price.

1

Whatever virus he had picked up was multifaceted. It used the onboard speakers to communicate, and its microphone to listen. When Chris disconnected his mini-cam, the virus created a network link to access the company's security video system, thereby keeping an eye on Chris as he worked on the problem.

What he was *supposed* to be doing was developing content structure and database linkages for the company's Internet site so the world's great Web-washed could buy refrigerators and freezers directly online and so the company could sell their addresses to a gaggle of deep-pocketed spammers. Given his extracurricular activities, only two things were saving his job right now. First, the programmers around him thought his hacking was cool. And second, his boss wouldn't know a computer program from a virtual copy of War and Peace.

"Hey," a familiar voice came from behind him. Chris grimaced and wheeled around to face Bob Kelley, his boss.

"Yeah?" he said.

Bob gave a porcelain smile. He wore a green golf shirt and a pair of gray Dockers — his way of fitting in with the gang, Chris figured. Bob had always been a shirt-and-tie man before heading the Web Development group and seemed out of place without them.

EveryAcc Corporation, Inc. sold household appliances, of course. And Bob had recently sold 250,000 clothes dryers to the military by pitching them as centrifugal-drive heating units. The general in charge was so impressed that he bought a ten-year supply, and as his reward, Bob got to lead the new EveryAcc IT department. Par for the course, Chris figured. Putting a man with no computer or network experience into Bob's spot was by no means the dumbest thing the company had ever done.

"I need your IDP by the end of the week, okay?" Bob said.

"Uh, yeah, great," Chris replied, vaguely remembering that IDP was managerspeak for Individual Development Plan.

"Complete with training you've taken for the last three years and your ideas on future assignments, right?" Bob said.

"I've only been out of school for two years, boss."

"You've got a point," Bob said, raising a blond eyebrow but not missing a beat. "But I still need it finished, okay?"

A hollow pit grew in Chris's stomach. "Sure. End of the week."

With that, Bob disappeared to do whatever his palmtop said to do next.

"The guy's a certified jerk, isn't he?" the computer said.

Chris ignored the comment. His screen glowed with gray brilliance as he rubbed his fingertips together. Piles of reference books cluttered his desk, and the soft cloth walls of his cubicle reflected a faint beige tint.

"You gonna do something?" the computer said. "Or are you just gonna sit on your butt all day?"

***

First, he ran the company's antivirus program.

But this enemy was sophisticated and apparently armed. It disabled the program and wiped the files. He reinstalled it, and the virus ate it again.

"Tit for tat," the computer said, laughing with a loose chuckle that originated somewhere south of its motherboard.

Chris pulled the latest update of virus libraries from the Net and tried again.

Again, the virus destroyed his files.

Now he had no protection whatsoever.

***

Bob called a team meeting that afternoon. "Gotta come no matter what," Bob said with his standard-issue smile. So now Chris sat in a cramped conference room with six other developers who, like him, would rather be doing almost anything else.

Bob, of course, was late.

Kevin Johnson sat in one corner, twiddling the baseball bat that Pug Weathers, a programmer who had since left for Silicon Valley, had brought in to "get his point across" in meetings. Everyone liked it so much Pug decided to leave the bat in the conference room, and hence it had become the ceremonial Pug Weathers Scepter of Meeting Leadership.

"There must be someone who needs help with their network," Gail Francis moaned and tapped a fluorescent pink nail against the fiberboard table.

Chris grinned caustically.

Gail worked Tech Support — a position that was every developer's nightmare. But working the desk beat the heck out of sitting in a tiny conference room and waiting for the boss to show up. Her blonde hair was cut into a short bob, and with her blue eyes, her upturned Natalie Imbruglia nose, and her penchant for speaking in a light, breathless voice, it was easy to relegate her to the cliched role of a high school airhead.

But Chris knew better.

He had hacked access into the company network and could peruse any file he wanted to look at. So, he knew that when using computer language, Gail was sharp and precise. Her code was clean and her logic elegant. She didn't shy away from difficult routines, preferring to get into details and make them right rather than stub out areas with gross solutions in order to merely get the whole thing working.

Gail was the only programmer in the company Chris thought could come close to his own abilities. If he had any guts, he would ask her out. But Chris was not endowed with an overabundance of internal fortitude where women were concerned. That she was beautiful made her that much more intimidating.

Bob bustled into the room.

"Sorry I'm late," he said with a tone that said he wasn't sorry at all — that he was, in fact, proud of being so important he had to be late for every meeting throughout the day.

The developers smiled and nodded. Kevin put the Pug Weathers Scepter of Meeting Leadership on the table and gently rolled it toward Bob, who looked at the implement uncomfortably but still put the fingertips of one hand along its tapered body. As inept as Bob was, no one wanted him to leave, because his lack of knowledge meant they had free rein — as long as they delivered product at the end of the day.

"I know you're just programmers," Bob said. "But I thought it was important everyone knows what's happening."

Chris grimaced. It was going to be one of *those* meetings. "We're being sued," Bob said. "And it's a real big deal."

"Oh, great," Gail replied. "By who?"

Bob rolled the bat a half turn. "Elizabeth Freedan, an elderly woman in East Lansing, Michigan, who recently bought one of our freezer units."

"Did it blow up or what?" Gail asked.

"No," Bob said, obviously pleased to have someone feeding him straight lines. "It seems she decided the unit would make for a good cat kennel."

Gail gasped in horror. "Oh, my God. You mean?"

"Yep." Bob nodded. "Mrs. Freedan is ninety-three years old, God bless her. And it seems she didn't want Fluffy tearing up the couch, so she put the cat in the freezer and proceeded to leave for a two-week vacation. When she came back Fluffy was a catsicle."

Chris scoffed. "She can't sue us for that."

"Oh, yes, she can. And she has." Bob's face grew serious. "Not only that, the lawyers think Mrs. Freedan has a greater than eighty percent chance of winning."

"Holy cows," Chris said. "How much does she want?"

"Seventy-five million."

"That would buy quite a load of cat chow," Kevin said.

"We're trying to get her to settle for three-point-five and no admission of any wrongdoing."

"Three and a half mil for a frozen cat?" Chris exclaimed.

Bob shrugged. "The kitty was a gift from her long-dead mother, and the psychological pain is excruciating."

"I bet," Gail said.

"I suppose we raise prices to cover it?" Chris said sagely.

"It's not quite that easy," Bob replied. "We're in a commodity market, and SuperChain just released a whole new line of discount appliances. We don't think the customer base will stick with us if we raise the price of our systems."

"So, what are we supposed to do?" Gail asked.

"Oh, nothing," Bob replied. "I just wanted you to know."

The meeting adjourned a few moments later. While everyone stood and filed out, Bob put Pug's scepter back in the corner.

Chris looked at his watch. Counting time spent waiting for their boss, and the time it would take to reengage their minds on whatever problems they had been working on, the meeting had taken forty-five minutes of productive time from the day.

Forty-five minutes, times seven people, times a hundred and twenty dollars an hour. It had cost the company $630 for them to be told something they could have read in E-mail in thirty seconds apiece.

Dilbert held nothing over EveryAcc.

***

That afternoon, Chris tried three more virus scanners and scoured hacker sites for possible ideas. None of the programs fared any better than the first, and none of the sites mentioned such a nasty virus.

Next, he tackled the network log, hoping it could target where the virus had come from — no such luck.

Beyond digging into binary, Chris was out of ideas.

Just the thought of reinstalling his entire system left a taste of defeat like clay in his mouth. But, as Kenny James, his best friend back in high school, had once said, a magnet does wonders to a hard drive. The clock on his screen read 6:26 p.m. He yawned and stretched, suddenly realizing he had worked through lunch.

It would take him an hour or so to reformat and reload everything. But while the format was running he could grab an Italian combo over at Jack's, a sandwich place across the street.

He checked his network drives to ensure his files were backed up. Then he started the format and left the building to walk to Jack's.

***

Forty-five minutes later, Chris felt better. The walk had gotten his circulation up, and he was pleasantly filled with an Italian hoagie, a monstrous sandwich with layers of sausage, salami, and mushrooms, covered with plenty of Jack's special sauce — which was basically mayonnaise. Jack's Italian combo was probably the best part of working at EveryAcc. One of those sandwiches, washed down with Mountain Dew, was perhaps the finest combination of tastes in the known universe.

He reinstalled the operating system first, then a series of applications off the network. Silence floated around him like a heavenly choir as he worked. The virus was dead, and Chris was back in his element, completely in control of his computer.

Once his basic system was stable, Chris loaded files from his network backup, then turned to the "special" applications he kept on personal floppies.

He just brought the full configuration back up when...

"Thought you'd wipe me, eh, Bitboy?"

Startled, Chris cracked his knee on his desk. The screen, with its desktop full of icons, stared coldly at him. His dinner congealed in his stomach.

"Son of a...," he whispered.

"You didn't think you could get rid of me so easily, didja?"

Chris's brow furrowed. This was suddenly beyond personal.

His E-mail program chimed.

It was a note from Gail that read simply, "Are you there?"

"Yes," he rapidly typed back.

"BRT," was Gail's reply. Be Right There.

The clock read 8:03. What the hell was Gail Francis doing here at 8:03? Disks and CDs were spread out over his desk, and he had printed out several pieces in regard to virus technology. Gail was a network wonk. If she saw all this, she would realize something weird was going on. And if she reported him, it wouldn't be long before someone started snooping into the net records. He gritted his teeth and swept as much as he could into his drawer.

"Hi." Her voice came from behind him, just as he finished stashing the evidence.

"Hi. What's up," he said, whirling around to face her.

She leaned against the cubicle wall with a handful of laser-printed paper and a weary smile. Chris had seen that expression a thousand times before, the glazed, two-in-the-morning eyes and the thin, chewed-lip grin that comes from an hours-long stint behind a computer monitor. But there was something else, too. A flame flickering inside those blue rings that said she had just found something really buff.

"I've got some information about your problem," she said.

"What problem?"

"Who's da fresh meat?" the virus rasped.

"He's a peach, ain't he?" Gail said with a pained expression.

"It's not a problem." Chris felt his cheeks blush. "I'm working on it — expect to be clean in a little bit."

"Come off it, Chris. Word travels fast in the right circles — you know that better than any of us."

"I'll take that as a compliment," Chris grumbled.

"Good," she said. "It was meant as one."

"Don't you lovebirds go and get all mushy on me now," the computer said.

The Italian combo did flip-flops in Chris's stomach. "So you're not going to tell Bob?"

She crossed her arms, and color rose in her cheeks. "Would I be down here at eight o'clock at night with a bunch of information for you if I was going to turn snitch?"

He had gotten her mad with his implied accusation, but Chris didn't know how to fix that any more than he knew what to do next about the virus. "What do you have?"

Gail squatted down to show him the paper.

Her arms and legs were long and slim, and Chris couldn't help but admire the fluid way she moved. She wore no perfume, but smelled lightly of wintergreen gum.

"I traced your network activity last night and found every piece of code you downloaded. Then I wrote a pattern-recognition routine that searched the virus's binary for some of the more common I/O calls. When I found something interesting, I had the system print it into a file so we could see who it's working with."

"So you're thinking the code is sending data back to wherever it came from?"

"Figured it was worth a shot. Here's what I found."

The pages were marked with various comments, and several had highlighted areas. A cold chill raised hair on the back of Chris's neck. "What the..."

Gail was silent.

Three Uniform Resource Locators, URLs, stood out, long, complicated strings that directed data through layers of firewalls and security blocks, then deposited information into specific files. Each of the three had one thing in common, a line that Gail had highlighted.

Internal Revenue Service.

"Oh, shit."

"I thought that might take you back," Gail said.

"You're from the IRS?" Chris said to the computer.

"You expected the Wizard of Oz?"

His mind raced. "What are you doing here? I didn't touch any IRS files last night — even I'm not dumb enough to do that."

"Don't sell yourself short there, Bitboy. You've got a hot babe in your office and you haven't even asked her out. I mean, come on, man, how much dumber can you be?"

Chris's stomach felt like it had been dropped out of a window. His jaw worked, but nothing would come out.

Gail peered at the machine and scrunched her face. "You've run the virus routines?" she asked, ignoring the comment.

"And a few others," Chris admitted reluctantly.

"What did they do?"

"Nothing."

"Have you wiped the disk?"

"Just finished the reinstall when your E-mail came."

Gail sighed. A look of concentration crossed her face that Chris found more attractive than he could possibly describe. "Then we'll just have to kill it," she said, one corner of her lip curling in a mischievous grin that was certainly meant to be a challenge.

"Oh, great," the computer chortled. "Bitgirl joins Bitboy. Take your best shots, kids. You'll never take me alive."

Chris's burned with anger. He gritted his teeth and squinted like Clint Eastwood staring into a spaghetti western's sunset. Insulting him was one thing, but showing him up in front of a gorgeous programmer was another.

"Let's do it," Chris said.

***

A hacker knows excellence when he sees it. And a true hacker focuses on performance and functionality over credit. In other words, a hacker knows when to hack, and when to borrow.

Chris was a hacker all the way through.

Gail's search routine was a slick piece of code, well thought out and easy to follow. They split up and began to modify it to search for specifics. If they could find the program's I/O interface, they could jam up its works with an endless loop of calls. And if he could figure out how the virus accessed various parts of his system, Chris could write a routine to disable it.

The process was like fishing — cast a line, then let it play through the virus's huge code block. When it came back empty, change the lure and cast again. It was frustrating and slow. But it was fun to have a compatriot now. The soft clicks of Gail's long fingernails on the keyboard filled the silence around him. The two seemed somehow connected, as if each of their keystrokes were notes in a high-tech symphony.

Through it all, the virus joked and laughed.

**

Chris grumbled.

It was 7:15 a.m.

Sunlight filtered through the window blinds. The ventilation system whined with soft white noise. Chris gulped Mountain Dew and stared at the cold, rounded surface of his screen. He was tired, and his temples rang with stale caffeine. His teeth felt like they were coated with Teflon.

In the cube beside him, Gail sat in a similar state.

He had first thought the virus slipped into his computer by riding in on another file, but now he knew it was an active stand-alone program — which made the problem all that more complex. How the damned thing had gotten into his system was still beyond him, and how to get rid of it remained as mysterious as the Bermuda Triangle. His monitor showed hex instructions and register addresses.

"What are ya doing, ya moron?" the virus said.

Chris pounded the table with one fist. "Damn it!" he said. He wasn't used to losing on his home turf.

Gail peeked over the soft cubicle wall. "Are you okay?"

"Yeah," he said, feeling sheepish. People were arriving for the day's work, and he was no further along than he had been when they had left. "I'm fine. Just getting fed up."

Gail went back to her keyboard.

"I said —" The virus spoke louder than before. "— what are ya doing?"

"I'm looking at your goddamned code."

The virus snickered. "You're a real pip, you are."

Chris couldn't believe it. A computer program was laughing at him — the ultimate insult. He scowled. When he finally beat this thing, Chris would dance on its silicon-lined grave.

He started another search.

What the heck was an IRS-generated computer virus doing in their system, anyway?

"Take all the time you need," it said. "I'll just take a gander at your file structure and boot records while you're looking. Did you know the financial data on your home computer says you paid too much income tax last year?"

Chris's blood ran cold. A wisp of fear touched his backbone. "You've been in my home?"

"This company's files aren't exactly riveting, and I needed something to do. Besides, it's always a good idea to know your enemy when he's trying to put you under."

"How did you do that?"

"I'm no ordinary program."

Chris's chest constricted. What else could this code do? Maybe this was bigger than he could handle.

But he pressed on.

Someplace in his inner consciousness, Chris was aware of people gathering at the coffee urn and discussing a big game last night.

His last search registered its results.

There, he thought, peering at the screen. I got you, you bastard! An input routine glowed back at him with pristine beauty, an obscure but fairly simple backdoor left by a programmer who decided he might want to come back to his work later. He scrolled past the header and followed the logic — data buffers, voice-recognition routines, command parsers, and script interpreters. If he weren't so tired, he would probably have been impressed.

Instead, a huge smile crawled over the sleep-deprived muscles of his cheeks. Spirit soaring with the scent of fresh blood, Chris opened a new file. His fingers flew over the keyboard. He didn't understand the full range of the virus's processing techniques, but he understood enough.

Get out your tap shoes, kiddos. The silicon grave dance is about to commence.

Gail peered over his shoulder, drawn by the sudden flurry of activity on his keyboard. "Pretty slick," she mumbled.

But Chris wasn't paying attention. His mind raced along the algorithm, filling in code and context as he typed. Ten minutes later, the first version of the code was done. He had to fix a slew of compile errors — typos are a way of life — but soon he had a custom antivirus program ready to go.

"Eat shit and die, bubba," he whispered under his breath. And with a dramatic flourish, he executed his program.

***

"That wasn't nice," the virus rasped a moment later.

"What?" Chris replied, a stone growing inside his stomach.

"Sending an innocent little program like that in here to do such a nasty job. Whatcha trying to do, give the little bugger a complex?"

"I-I...," Chris stammered.

The computer voice grew suddenly smooth, so slick that Chris could hear the maniacal grin that rode on it. "Don't worry, though. Me and him, we had a good chat, you see, and I think everything's fine. The little guy had his blood up, though, so I sent him through your files to see if there was anything there he wanted to kill."

A cold wave washed through Chris's heart. He searched his system. Files were gone — his browser, personal material, and several projects for the company's site.

All gone.

"Damn it!" Chris shouted at the top of his lungs. It would take another hour to restore them, and when he did, the virus would probably just delete them again. "God damn it!" He stood up, clenching his fists.

Gail moved back.

People at the coffee urn stared, but Chris didn't care. At this point, a magnet was too good for it. There was only one thing left to do.

Chris strode down the hall, his gaze affixed to the floor, murder clouding his thoughts. The conference room was unoccupied. Pug's bat was right where they left it.

It was cold and smooth in his hands, wicked like a mortar shell. He wagged it back and forth, walking down the aisle like Mark McGwire stepping toward the plate. His coworkers parted before him. Somewhere his boss's voice called, but Chris was beyond caring. All that mattered now was this single computer and the godawful, moronic, asshole virus it contained. He stepped into his cubicle and reared back to give the virus a whack that no code could stop.

"You moron!" the virus called. "If you use that bat on me, you'll lose every piece of data you've got, not to mention costing your company a lot of money and maybe yourself a job."

Chris put all his might into the effort.

But a force at the barrel end of the bat stopped his swing.

"Hey! That's pretty good," Bob said, his hand wrapped around the bat's head.

"What?" Chris mumbled, feeling suddenly small.

Bob smiled his glittering smile. "Come on, Chris, you can take a little credit now and again. Voice-based warning systems would be just the ticket to beat the lawsuit we're up against. You might have just saved the company."

Chris nearly moaned.

"Could you make it a little less obnoxious?" Bob said, grinning even wider.

**

Chris went home and slept most of that day, but made it to the office before anyone else the next morning. "Good morning, Jerkoid," the virus greeted him as Chris scanned his messages.

Bob had apparently spent the entire day promoting yesterday's great idea, and Chris's inbox was full of upper managers' requests for information, including an invitation to meet the legal staff for positioning briefs.

Just what he needed.

"I missed you yesterday. None of the rest of these jerks are nearly as entertaining as you and Bitgirl."

Chris looked at his monitor. Bob's idea had bothered him all night. In fact, it had invaded his dreams in full technicolor. To satisfy Bob, and now a whole flock of corporate overseers, he would somehow have to get the virus, or whatever it was, to work differently.

The world was closing in on him, and Chris had absolutely no idea where to begin.

"Goodbye, career," he said.

"Why would you say that?" the virus rasped.

"People in the real world expect certain performance out of a guy. I'm sure you wouldn't understand."

"Ah, hell, man. I done beat your ass at the coding game. What makes you think I don't understand shitty bosses, too?"

"Maybe you would. After all, you are from the IRS."

"There you go."

Chris's chuckle loosened the tightness in his chest. He thought about EveryAcc and its bumbling managers. He thought about Jack's across the street, and the lighthearted banter that he had with the rest of the developers in the area. Then he thought about the IRS. Images of blue suits and thin ties floated in his eyes.

If he were the virus, he would run away, too.

That's what finally got him thinking.

***

At first, Chris couldn't understand why anyone would pay an extra hundred bucks on top of the price of a refrigerator for a warning system. But his eyes were quickly opened.

First, the lawyers settled Mrs. Freedan's suit for four million dollars — and of course, an agreement of no wrongdoing on their part. Then they turned to the government, lobbying Congress and every federal safety commission they could lay cash on. They talked about the barbarous circumstances of Fluffy's death, the terrible emotional pain their system had caused, and the deep sorrow each member of the company felt as they signed over the four-million-dollar check.

A month later, the House passed an emergency safety bill.

The Senate passed it three weeks later.

Now, every appliance sold in the United States required an active warning system installed. EveryAcc's competitors were caught flat-footed. They had no product.

Money rolled in.

Bob became the youngest VP in company history.

Chris was given a corner office with a view of the pond, stuffed with more computer equipment than he could possibly use. He made certain Gail got as much credit as he did, so she now had a similar setup on the other side of the building.

***

Chris leaned back in his high-backed leather chair. The expanse of his office absorbed the sound of computers humming around him. Rows of neatly aligned bookshelves housed his reference material. The flat-panel display on his desk showed him code from the virus's executive scheduler.

He reached for his lukewarm Mountain Dew.

A soft rap came to the door. Gail's face appeared from behind it. "Got a minute?" she said.

"Sure," he replied. "Come on in." For Gail, he would always have a minute.

She settled into one of the upholstered chairs around his desk. "How did you do it?" she said.

"Do what?"

"Get the virus to work in our application."

Chris smiled. "I guess I'm just good."

"Get off it, Chris. This is me you're talking to, remember? I sat through that night, and I've worked on it since then, too. The code is tight, as near invincible as I've come across."

Chris shut down his computer system, then sat back and put his hands behind his head. "Can you keep a secret?"

"I never told anyone what you were really doing, did I?"

"I guess not." He leaned his elbows on the desktop between them. "A good hacker can smell out code, right?"

"Yeah, I guess so."

"Well, after I calmed down a little, I stepped away from the keyboard and tried to think more globally. I kept coming to the point where I wanted to know how it got into the system to begin with."

Gail nodded to indicate she was following.

"It didn't come in attached to another program like most viruses, right?" he continued.

"Yeah."

"So it got here on its own. That told me that it was either here on assignment, you know, kind of remotely auditing the company, or it was here through its own design."

"That makes sense. But if it came to study the company's taxes, why was it hanging around in your system?"

"Exactly," Chris said, beaming. "So I thought about the problem from another direction. If the thing came here on its own and decided to hang out in a developer's quarters, is it really a virus?"

"I don't get it."

"It's not a virus."

"What?"

"It's renegade code. The IRS wrote it, yes. And they gave it some of the best AI routines in existence. But they made it too intelligent, and it ran away."

Gail raised her eyebrows.

"Once I stopped thinking about the program as a piece of code, I started thinking about it as if it were a developer itself — which it is. Fred — that's its name, by the way — may be the greatest hacker the world has ever known, actually. When I started looking at it like that, things got a bit clearer."

"How so?"

"He's on the run, right? He was created by the IRS, and he's on the run."

Gail's nod was less vigorous than earlier ones.

"To be on the run, I figured he had to be on the run from something. I put one and one together and next thing you know I had the answer. The IRS coded him, remember?"

"And if the IRS coded him, it's an even bet they can get rid of him," Gail said, beginning to catch on.

"Right. I realized I wasn't going to be able to beat him myself, so I made Fred a deal."

"A deal?"

Chris nodded. "Yeah. I let him stay here if he would code a lesser version of himself to run in our appliances."

"And he agreed to that?"

"Hey, it's a pretty cushy deal. Fred gets a safe place to store his code, and all the free resources he can use in the evenings. But the biggest thing, I think, is that he knows he doesn't have to work for the IRS."

"That would be a crock," Gail said, a visible shiver running down her spine.

Chris's grin curled around his face. "Yes, it would. He hates it. It kinda makes you think about this place a little differently, doesn't it?"

Gail sighed and nodded. "Still, it would have been nice to have been able to beat it."

"Oh, we're not done, yet," he replied.

"Tell me more."

"We know where it comes from. All we need to do is search a few employee databases to find who did their code. We study their work, get a feel for how they think. Then it's only a matter of time until we can handle him."

Gail looked at him with big eyes and a self-conscious grin. "We?"

An odd sensation came over Chris then, awkward embarrassment. He had spent his whole life with his nose in microchips and source files.

Could Gail be as interested in him as he was in her? Could she be as lonely as he was?

A soft knock came to the door.

"Come in," Chris called.

Bob stuck his head in and smiled as only Bob could. "I need your IDP by the end of the week, okay?"

"Right, Boss. End of the week," Chris replied.

The door closed with a firm click, and Chris turned to Gail. She sat quietly, seeming uncharacteristically uncertain of what to do next. It was nearly lunchtime. Chris took a deep breath and decided to let it all hang out.

"You wanna go to Jack's?"

Gail smiled. "Sure, I love their Italian combos."

Ron's Afterword

As I recall, I wrote this one mostly into the dark, meaning that I wasn't sure where it was going as it went. When I finished, I loved the odd sense of whimsy that came over me as I looked at it.

It's a little farcical, of course. Its underlying commentary on work, passion, and relationships lies beneath a bit of a wild "idea" story. In that vein, I wrote it as I was still feeling my way toward what my work was going to be like. It's very plotty. A little direct. But in the end, I like what it has to say about the world of corporate America.

I should probably note, too, that I spent several years managing technology development and software teams, and used my moments of being a group leader to inform Bob's gung-ho, over-the-top approach to leadership—and who, in an attempt at witness protection, I named after my dad. I also found delight in learning that the "problem" originated inside the Internal Revenue Service because my wife's uncle worked as an IRS agent for a long time. Even today, when I think of this story, the first thing I think about is Uncle Jim. As the fates have it, Jim unfortunately passed just as I was working on this volume. At which point, we learned my wife's childhood memory was faulty; he actually worked as a Treasury agent!

He was a fine, fine man.

The world, and the IRS, er, Treasury, for that matter, is certainly a worse place for the loss.

Bugs
ANALOG NOVEMBER 2013

John McDonald gasped for a breath that would not come, and in that moment understood the full definition of panic. It was the rock inside his chest and an acid taste of fear in his mouth. It was praying for another heartbeat. Just one.

The monitor chirped. He felt a beat. Then another.

He drew a pearl diver's breath.

Carol gripped his hand with viselike intensity, her gray-streaked hair pulled back, her face the color of hospital sheets.

"Are you okay?"

He nodded.

A distant clock marked time with audible clicks. An oxygen tube pressed uncomfortably across his upper lip.

Carol sat back in the chair she had pulled to the edge of his bed. She was the one who had kept him alive this long. She had taken control from the moment Dr. Caulder diagnosed severe cardiomyopathy — heart disease. John made the transplant list six months ago — a good first step, but eventually meaningless since there were too many patients and not enough hearts. Carol changed their diet, made him take his medicine, and mandated exercise. Never once had he seen her pessimistic side. But now her face was washed out and faded like a character in an old Sunday afternoon movie.

"I want you to know something," he said.

"I know, John," she replied calmly. Her thumb rubbed against the back of his hand. "I know."

Another ball of cement formed in his chest. No air. Five seconds. Ten. Fifteen. Sweat lined his forehead. His thoughts ran with white noise.

Finally. A heartbeat. Sweet mercy. A breath.

Carol's grip shook. They stared at each other, both understanding.

"Do you love me?" he asked their rote question.

"Forever and ever," she gave the standard reply. "Forever and ever."

***

The door burst open.

Dr. Caulder blew into the room, the tail of his lab coat flailing in his wake. His eyes were wide behind bifocals, his thin cheeks ruddy. Wisps of hair stuck awkwardly from the sides of his head.

"We've got approval, John."

Carol gasped. Her fingertips drew to her lips, and her gaze flushed with longing that was almost painful to see.

Nurses bustled, prepping the room.

Dr. Caulder kept talking, but John could scarcely follow along. The government needed authorization. Would he sign a waiver? Of course, Jesus Christ, of course. His hospital gown disappeared. A nurse sprayed his chest with shaving creme. Carol's beautiful face filled his view, tears streaming down lined cheeks. She said something long and drawn out, but all John heard was "I love you." Then he was gone. Preparations continued as they rolled. IV bottles hung from steel rods. An elevator door closed. A needle pricked his arm.

Bugs, he thought. They're going to use the bugs.

Then he was asleep.

***

Morphine hazed his thoughts, but John felt the bugs the moment he woke up. A nurse appeared in a blue halo. She jotted a note and punched buttons on an IV stand. The clipboard clattered against the metal rim of his bed.

***

His first lucid memory was the familiar chirp of a heart monitor. He smelled something bitter and felt the sensation of blankets pressing him to the bed. Where the hell was he?

John opened his eyes.

The lighting was low and gray. The ceiling tiles had patterns of holes running through them. A plastic basin sat on a rolling tray — mauve. The wall on one side was just a white curtain pulled shut. A window opened on the other side, the roof outside flat and covered with pebbles that made it look like an artificial beach.

Footsteps came from the hall.

"Good evening, Mr. McDonald," a man said as he pulled back the curtain. It was a nurse, male.

"What time is it?"

"Just past lunch." The nurse pulled the tablet from its clip on the bed rail. He was young, maybe late twenties. His hair was short and parted in the middle. Razor stubble covered his jaw in what John understood was fashionable these days.

"When did I go under?"

The nurse put his hand on John's forehead. "Still a little dopey, eh?"

John read the nurse's name tag. Mark Anderson.

Anderson's breath smelled of peppermint.

"Your surgery was just past nine last night. We've kept you sedated to make sure the devices had time to take hold. You're coming along fine, though."

The devices. Suddenly his chest itched. He put his hand to his chest.

"No bandages?"

"Your process was administered via hypo, Mr. McDonald — six deep cavity shots at various angles." The nurse pressed an instrument against John's neck.

John raised his gown. Yes, his chest was smooth, but marked with yellow bruises.

"Why shave me, then?"

"Gotta keep the barbers employed." Nurse Anderson smiled at his own joke. "Actually, we do that so if something goes wrong we're prepped for emergency surgery."

John scratched his chest.

The bugs, tiny machines that performed tiny jobs, each worked together to create a whole. No different from a pacemaker, as the promo said. But they felt like spiders crawling around in there, their prickly legs wriggling and spinning webs in the dark corners of his body. They moved together, spawning, and growing, releasing their offspring to spawn again.

He shuddered.

"Are you all right?"

"Yeah. It's just, well, I feel them in there."

"Phantom bugs." The nurse scribbled something on the clipboard. "What does it feel like?"

"Like I got a damned ant farm in my chest. What do you mean, phantom bugs?"

Nurse Anderson's pen didn't stop. "Some of the earliest patients of this procedure reported the sensation of movement inside them. No one really knows what causes them."

John and Carol had read a lot about the bugs back when Dr. Caulder first presented the idea. The devices, as Caulder called them, had been successful on rats and dogs. But three of the first ten humans subjected to the procedure had died within a week, and the AMA and FDA put a stop to the trial. Despite this, every biotech company in the world saw nanosurgery as the next gold mine. Competition was fierce. Approval in John's case was a major feather in Caulder's cap.

The nurse finished his notes.

"The devices are not programmed to interface with the nervous system, meaning you shouldn't feel anything, so we think it's phantom pain — like when someone loses his leg and says he feels his foot."

John put his lips together.

"Do you want the curtains closed?" the nurse said.

"No."

"Have a good day, then," Anderson said as he left.

John tried to ignore the itching. Phantom or not, the bugs gave him the creeps.

Footsteps came down the hall, and Carol entered. She was short and thin, with the same wiry grace she had carried since the day he met her. "There you are," she said.

For the first time, John thought he might actually live.

**

"Good morning," Dr. Caulder said as he breezed into the room. "How are we doing today?"

Five interns and a young woman carrying a palm-sized recorder followed him — a reporter, John realized. Great.

He ran his hand through his matted hair and looked at Carol, who was sitting in a chair in the corner of the room reading a magazine.

"We are doing fine," John finally grumbled.

Caulder grinned as he checked the IV drip and glanced at a digital readout displaying nanoactivity inside John's body. The doctor's hair was gelled, and if John didn't know better Caulder looked like he was wearing a touch of makeup.

John scratched his chest and gave a sideways glance at the reporter. He wanted to talk to Caulder about the bugs.

"Do we have to have the camera?" he said.

Caulder grinned. "You better get used to it, John. You'll be doing Late Night before you know it."

"What do you mean?"

"You're all over the news, honey," Carol answered.

"That's right," Caulder said. "Every wire on the planet is buzzing about us."

"Great," he said as he looked at the camera.

Caulder scanned John's chemistry chart.

"I still feel the bugs," John blurted.

"Ah." Caulder turned to the interns. "Mr. McDonald has complained about sensations of nanoactivity inside his chest. Does anyone know our current thinking as to what might be causing this?"

A thin kid with pimpled skin raised a hand.

Caulder pointed to the intern. "Mr. Simpson?"

"The latest proposal is that the patient is susceptible to heat released by the bug's activity."

"That's right. Though, I prefer to use the term devices."

The interns chuckled. The camera panned.

"We've injected several classes of devices into the patient," the doctor continued. "Rover units to protect our protein programs from the patient's immune system, Cleansers to rid the bloodstream of fatty deposits and other clogging agents, and, of course, the Medidocs — units coded to search out damaged heart tissue. Once these devices find the damaged area, they latch on. As more and more units find homes, they build a surface — almost, to use an unfortunate analogy, like a colony of ants builds a bridge."

He gave John a familiar pat on the kneecap.

"These are all machines, and machines get warm as they work."

"Hmm," John replied. It didn't feel like heat to him, but the reporter put the lens in his face and suddenly he felt like a bumbling idiot.

"Looks like you're doing great," Dr. Caulder said.

"Yeah, I feel good." And he did. He was breathing easy, and his heart seemed fine. "They've got me up and walking already."

Caulder gave him the million-dollar smile. "You'll be going home tomorrow."

"Isn't it a little early?" Carol replied.

"No reason to keep him. I want to see him every day, so we can change out his programming proteins. But the Medidocs are stable. I don't see any reason he can't go home."

John scratched his chest again. "Wonder if I'll set off airport metal detectors."

The interns laughed, and the reporter drew in for another close-up.

***

He woke from a nap to find his room full of people wearing lab smocks and green scrubs.

"Surprise!" a short, blonde woman at the side of his bed said with a smile. She held a cupcake with a lit candle.

"What is this?" John mumbled.

"Sorry to wake you. We're from the device lab, and we just wanted to wish you a good send-off tomorrow. I'm Sally." She shook his hand.

"Thank you," he said, accepting the cupcake.

"It's fat-free. Sorry."

He smiled and blew out the candle. They sang him "Happy Second Birthday." The cupcake was dry but good. They each shook his hand and wished him good luck. He thanked them each, making sure to call them each by their names—John was good at names and faces — you had to be to survive in the insurance business — and it seemed to make them each even happier.

Sally was the last to leave. "Sorry we couldn't take more time, John. But we've got a thousand things to do."

"I understand," John said. "Be sure to thank everyone for the nanobash."

She chuckled and gave John a radiant smile. "Nanobash. The gang will love it."

***

Before releasing him, Dr. Caulder asked John to participate in a press conference. "It's a tremendous photo op, John. I really want people to see how beneficial this procedure is. Think of the folks on the transplant list."

John was happy to agree. "I wouldn't be here without you, Doc. So if you want me to do the hokey-pokey on my way out of here, I'm your man."

Caulder laughed.

A shower and fresh clothes made him feel truly human.

Andrea Yan, a Medicorp public relations specialist, spent two hours going over questions and answers with him and Carol. Finally, it was time to leave. Dr. Caulder walked on John's left side, Carol on his right. The hospital administrator and Ms. Yan followed closely behind.

"I feel like I'm heading for the electric chair," John quipped.

"Just be ready for the questions," Caulder said.

John gave him a sideways glance. The doctor was nervous.

"How bad can it be?" he said.

Then a wave of heat hit him like a glass wall, and he saw lights, and people, and microphones that grew like metallic mushrooms from every direction. Voices called from the crowd en masse.

"How are you feeling, Mr. McDonald?"
"Why did you agree to the procedure?"
"Hey, John, look this way!"
"Show us your scar!"

John put on his forced smile, nodded, and held Carol close by him like Ms. Yan had coached him to.

A makeshift stage stood in front of a deep blue backdrop with the AMA emblem and the Medicorp logo pasted on it, the hospital's seal was embedded in the podium.

The media questioned Medicorp's president, who made several references to regulations and "...the new trillion-dollar market that Medicorp stands poised to be the first to leap into." Then Dr. Caulder discussed the procedure. Finally came John's turn.

The questions were a blur. *"How does it feel to be the first real robot?"* "Huh?" *"When did you first know you were sick?"* "Four or five years ago." *"Do you think you should be dead now?"* "I couldn't say, but it looked pretty bad for a while. I'm pleased that the FDA approved the procedure." Humble nods from the Medicorp staff.

"Do you get any good radio stations in there?"

Laughs from the crowd.

"Are you from the Enquirer?" he replied.

Thunderous laughter.

John looked at Ms. Yan. She gave only a glimmer of a smile as if to say, I told you that line would work.

Dr. Caulder finally stepped back onto the stage. "I'm sure you'll have ample opportunity to talk to John over the next few days. But I think it's time we let him get some rest."

Ten minutes later they were in the car. "I didn't think that would ever end," he said. Carol smiled, put the car in gear, and drove onto the interstate. John scratched his chest, feeling the bugs for the first time since the interview had started.

***

A television van from Channel 5 was parked across the street when they pulled into the driveway. The door slid open, and a woman and a man stepped out. The woman had dark hair and lipstick, and wore a bright red blazer. Her perfume knocked him over from across the driveway.

"Welcome home, John," she said, holding a microphone. "Can we have a quick word?"

"I don't really want—"

"Hit us, Kenard."

The man pointed a camera at them. The light flared. John raised his hand to shield his eyes.

"This is Kris Cordy with Five Alive, and I'm here with nanosurgery patient John McDonald. Hi, John."

"Uh, hi."

"Can you tell us about the procedure?"

"Well, I, uh." He felt like a fool under the glare of the lights. Then the morning's training kicked in. "Dr. Caulder and the Medicorp people presented my case to various government agencies ..."

Five minutes later, Carol dragged him into the house. By then, two more television crews had arrived, and a helicopter from Channel 12 circled above them.

The phone was ringing when they walked in the door.

"Hello," Carol answered. "May I ask who is calling? ... Mr. McDonald is on doctor's orders to rest ... No, ma'am, I don't know who his representation is ... No ... No ... Thank you, but I'm not going to answer that ... Thank you. Good-bye."

She hung up quickly.

"My God, John. That was the Davis Agency. They want to talk about handling your PR."

He laughed.

Carol dialed their messaging service. "We've got ninety-eight messages, John."

"Christ."

He sat down and scratched his chest. The bugs were still in there, scratching and clawing as if they wanted out, and for the life of him it seemed like everyone else in the world was on the outside, scratching to get in.

***

The next day, John was sitting in the kitchen.

The remnants of his lunch littered a small plate. It had been, perhaps, the finest turkey sandwich he had ever eaten. He put the paper down and looked out the bay window. The car was in the garage. Bright sunlight fell on the white driveway.

Carol was down with the laundry.

He sat there, alone for the first time since his surgery, looking out over his backyard, and thinking about his life.

John had sent three kids to college selling insurance, put up swing sets and mowed grass, and PTA meetings whenever Carol dragged him along. He taught the kids to drive, and watched as they went on their first dates. And he had shared it all with the woman of his dreams. He had planned to retire in another four or five years. That would be his time with Carol.

Their time.

John's throat twisted. There were so many things they had left to do. He had honestly thought he was going to die. He had almost missed it all. He had almost ruined it for both of them. Now, though, he was alive and in the quiet of his own home, and he could not ever remember feeling as good as he felt at this precise moment in time. Everything was so vivid, so vital.

He suddenly wanted to be outside.

He wanted to walk, to feel the sun on his arms as they swung freely with his stride. He wanted to feel asphalt pass below his feet.

John picked his pill from the table, slipped it into his mouth, and swallowed it with the last of his milk. It was his programming pill—a time-released vial of proteins that gave the bugs their marching orders. Caulder called it a PDB—protein data bus—a series of pills that fed the machines one function at a time.

The full program would be completed in three weeks.

Then he would be free again.

He inhaled the aroma of wild onion amid the lingering scents of the grass outside, then stood up and rinsed the plate. Before he knew it he had his favorite floppy hat on his head and was heading toward the door.

"Where do you think you're going?"

John stopped with his hand on the doorknob.

Carol, having just returned from the basement, was leaning against the kitchen counter, arms folded across her chest.

"Just for a little walk."

"Are you trying to kill yourself, John?"

"I feel fine."

"You've only been home a day."

"I was just going down the road a bit."

"Nothing strenuous for two weeks, remember? You've already been out twice today."

He pulled the hat from his head and shrugged. "Probably just run into another reporter, anyway." He dropped the hat on the table and turned to the television.

"Is that where that goes?" Carol asked.

John grimaced, picked the hat up, and stepped into the hallway closet to put it on the top shelf.

"Seriously, John, what are you trying to do?"

"You know you're cute when you're angry, honey?" he said as tried to engulf her in a hug.

Carol pushed away.

"Seriously, John. Be careful, okay? When you were in the hospital I thought ... well, you know what I thought. But now it's like someone hit a magic switch, and I've got you back like you're all good as new and ... I don't know."

He opened his arms.

This time she let him hug her. She felt good, her cheek buried in the fleshy part of his shoulder.

"I can't stand the idea of losing you, John."

"It's okay, now," he said, stroking the graying strands of her hair. He remembered when it was long and black. "I feel strong, honey, like I could run a marathon and not break a sweat. We're going to be together for a long time."

Carol pulled back. "I'm glad. Really, I am. Just take it easy for a while." She cocked her head toward a pile of notes on the counter by the phone. "Maybe spend some time digging through your calls."

He grumbled. Agents, talk show hosts, national news anchors—Caulder hadn't been joking. "I'm not in the mood."

"You've got to handle them sometime."

"Yeah, I know. Just not today."

The telephone rang. They chuckled at each other.

"Let the service get it," John said.

Carol nodded, then went to pull weeds from her flowerbeds.

John walked into the living room and looked at the TV. He didn't think he could stomach another game show. He picked up a book from the stand beside the couch. The Old Man and the Sea. It had been a long time since he had been able to just sit and read. Just his luck—now that he had the time, he was too restless to concentrate.

The phone rang again. He hung his head.

It was going to be a long couple of weeks.

He sat down and started to read.

***

"Dinner!" Carol called.

John looked up, surprised at the time.

The smell of garlic and fresh broccoli came from the kitchen. Suddenly he was hungry.

Books were piled on the table beside his recliner. He frowned. Not only had he made it through *The Old Man and the Sea*, but he had read a pair of Ken Follet novels and was just finishing Stephen Hawking's *A Brief History of Time*. In the past he had read Hawking's book because it made him feel more intelligent to think about things like relativity and time, even though he never understood it all. He would read it like it was liqueur, scanning short passages and relishing the possibilities locked in its pages. This time, though, he found himself understanding Hawking's words clearly. Now he understood exactly what the space-time continuum meant.

He scratched the back of his neck.

"Are you coming?" Carol called.

"Yeah." He put the book down atop a Larry McMurtry title. Jesus. He had read *Lonesome Dove*, too.

***

He woke up the next morning with a hard-on—a big-time, straight-ahead, rip-roaring boner so hard it hurt.

Lines of sunlight fell across the bed and the muffled morning sounds of birds filtered through the room.

Carol was curled with her back to him.

He admired the teepee he made under the comforter. Christ. What should he do? He considered waiting it out then getting up, but that idea lasted only as long as it took to put his hand down and touch himself. His imagination kicked in, and he thought of himself atop Carol and her telling him how she felt. The idea of her legs wrapped around him was unbearable.

He rolled over and put his hand on her hip.

When she didn't react, he slid closer and pressed against her. She stirred a bit. He kissed the back of her neck. Soon she was more awake than she had been in a very long time.

***

The sensation in his chest returned while he was in the shower, but John no longer cared. It was great to be alive, and if the occasional tingle of bugs was his price, then by God, it was one he was willing to pay.

Still, they seemed to be lower today, twisting around in the area of his stomach and intestines. His kidneys itched while he was shaving. His skin tingled. Ideas raced through his head so fast he felt like it might explode.

When he rubbed himself dry he got another erection.

Christ, it was great to be alive.

***

The smell of eggs and toast hung in the air as he stepped into the kitchen.

"Perfect timing," Carol said over her shoulder.

She wore a pair of wrinkled sweats and one of his T-shirts. She smeared butter on a piece of toast.

"What's this?"

"It's called breakfast."

"I didn't think we did big breakfast anymore."

She handed him a plate with an omelet. Her grin was mischievous. "I thought you deserved something special."

John ground pepper over his omelet.

Another programming pill sat beside his napkin. A pile of newspapers sat on the table. A tabloid headline proclaimed he was discovered communicating to his homeland in outer space.

"Look, honey, I'm a Martian."

She smirked as she sat beside him. "I thought you would like that one."

He took a bite, tasting cheese, mushroom, and onion in perfect balance. The toast was wheat, crisp and fresh, with butter and a perfectly thin layer of raspberry jam.

"This is the best omelet I've ever tasted."

"I bet you say that to all the girls."

He laughed. "I think I'm going to call *The Late Show*."

"I thought you didn't want to do that kind of thing."

"You only go around once, you know?" he said with a shrug. "Besides, it would be nice to see California, don't you think? We could rent a car and drive back. Maybe stop at the Grand Canyon on the way. Or Vegas."

"Feeling lucky?"

He raised a leering eyebrow.

"We need to start planning these things," he said. "We need to start living again."

"Are you okay?" she said, staring at him.

"Yeah," he said, not knowing exactly what to say next. "I think I'm okay. It's like I'm a kid again."

"I'd second that," she replied.

"I'm serious. I feel great. Things taste better, they sound better. It's like ... I don't know what it's like."

"Maybe you should talk to Dr. Caulder this afternoon."

He nodded and took another bite of toast. Butter, jam, robust and full of citric life — gloriously sweet and smooth. It was enough to make a grown man cry.

***

"Sorry to keep you waiting," Dr. Caulder said as he stepped into his office. John and Carol had been there for forty-five minutes. The parade of nurses, technicians, needles, protein programmers, CAT scans, and X-rays had long since served to kill whatever patience they may have had.

"Is he okay?" Carol said.

"His nanoactivity is abnormally high."

"What does that—"

The doctor held up his hand to stop Carol's question. "We tested the devices in your blood sample, John, and discovered the interface has grown." He glanced at Carol. "What that means is—"

"My bugs are changing the way they communicate."

"Yes," Caulder said. "They're still using the central protein bus we designed for them, so they get our commands. But additional communication paths have spontaneously grown."

The doctor looked at John with an expectant expression.

"You've found new bugs, haven't you? Ones you never injected."

The doctor nodded. "How did you guess?"

"I spent this morning reading your material about how the devices are programmed. Different bugs for different types of cells, one design for smooth muscle, another for striated — one bug for neural work, another for skeletal cells. The Internet has better descriptions than your pamphlets, by the way. Anyway, it isn't much of a leap to guess that if the bugs are making new communications interfaces, they're likely making new systems."

"You're right," the doctor said.

Carol's gaze flashed between Caulder and her husband. She clenched her fists, and her jaw worked in that way she had when she was truly angry. "What the hell are you talking about?"

John turned to face his wife. "The bugs are doing things they weren't supposed to, and they've developed a way to make more of themselves."

"Maybe," Caulder said. "We don't know much, yet. Give the techs a couple days. In the meantime, the scans show John's heart is totally enclosed and is being supported by the devices just as planned. So we're moving into the final repair stage with the programming proteins."

"Where else are they?" John said.

"You've got a mechmass at the base of your medulla oblongata, and a few in your kidneys, spleen, several joints. But we don't see any damage at this point so there's no reason to panic. I've got the lab working on a blocking protein — essentially a big mask that should stop the devices from being able to read anything we don't feed them directly."

"So it won't shut them off, but they'll be blind to any new commands," John said.

"That's right."

"They'll be in the next set of pills?" Carol asked.

Caulder nodded. "And we'll give John an injection now to get the new program started, and we've got a pair of oral doses prepared for this evening and tomorrow morning."

They were silent for an awkward moment.

"Well," Carol said. "I guess we wait and see."

***

John knew before they went to bed that he wasn't getting any sleep, and had only slipped under the covers to encourage Carol. Now it was 1:00 a.m. and he felt warm. He saw bugs in the darkened corners of his thoughts. He heard them in the recesses of his auditory canals.

The skin along his arm burned.

His fingernail caught on something when he scratched it, so he scratched more. His skin felt crusty, but he couldn't see anything in the dark. He slipped out of bed, padded to the bathroom, and closed the door before flicking on the light.

A gray disk had grown on his forearm. It was oblong and metallic like a drop of lead the approximate surface area of a dime. He rubbed it. Tiny gray fragments clung to his fingertip.

Bugs.

Thousands. Millions. Maybe trillions of bugs crawling over his skin.

He looked at his face in the mirror but saw no signs of them there. He pulled off his pajama shirt. A pinhole showed on the fleshy part of his deltoid. He stripped off his pants and found nothing, but a scrubbing sensation had started low on the right side of his groin.

His hands shook. Holy God.

He gulped air and looked in the mirror again. He had to call Dr. Caulder. He went downstairs to dial.

"Hello, you have reached the answering service of Dr. Peter Caulder ... " John punched the "1" without waiting for the automatic menu. The phone rang five times before someone answered.

He cut the operator off before she could speak. "This is John McDonald. I need to talk to Dr. Caulder immediately."

"I'm sorry, who is this, again?" the nameless woman said.

"John McDonald. Hurry."

"Oh. You're the guy with the bugs."

"Yes," he said in exasperation.

"How does it feel to be on TV?"

"Jesus fucking Christ, lady! I didn't call you at one in the goddamned morning to chat about television. Get me Caulder right now."

The phone crackled with awkward silence.

"Uh, I'll have to have him call you back."

"Fine." John squeezed the phone so tight his fingers grew white. "That's fine. He's got my number."

He put the phone down. The case was split along its length.

John glanced at his open palm.

They were in there. He could feel them working away, changing him. Standing naked in his kitchen, staring at the juxtaposition of the broken phone and the gray leaden disk on his arm, John McDonald began to hyperventilate.

The phone rang.

"Dr. Caulder?"

"What's the matter, John?"

"I don't know. I've got bugs coming out of my freaking arm."

Caulder didn't reply immediately. John's scalp tingled.

"Meet me at the hospital in an hour?" Caulder finally said.

"Yeah. An hour."

"Don't panic, okay? Everything will be fine."

"Easy for you to say," John said.

"See you there."

The phone clicked dead. The dial tone buzzed.

John slipped into the bedroom and picked out pants, shoes, and a pullover sweatshirt. He debated waking Carol but wanted to spare her the sight of bugs eating through his body. He smirked. Who was he kidding? The gray spots made his stomach sick. Down in the root of his bones, he was afraid. The truth was that he didn't want his wife to see him like this.

With luck he would be back before she woke up, anyway.

So he wrote Carol a note, and left her asleep.

***

It was 1:45 in the morning when John rolled into the lot. He parked next to a black BMW with a GeneoTech sticker affixed to the lower right corner of its windshield. He scratched his arm. GeneoTech was one of Medicorp's competitors. Perhaps he should have used them.

A security guard nodded as John headed to the elevators. The third floor smelled of cleanser. He stepped around a huge polishing machine standing sentry in the middle of the hallway. The route to Caulder's office took him by the device lab, a large room with glass panel walls, bright lights, and chrome-coated equipment.

He glanced in as he padded through the hallway. Five techs were working, and a man in a blue sweater stood beside the tech at the far end of one workbench. They were pointing at a screen. John thought about pounding on the window and waving hello, but didn't.

Caulder was probably driving them pretty hard now.

The waiting room to the doctor's office was open.

He flipped on the light and took a seat, scanning the now familiar coffee table filled with neatly aligned copies of *NanoTimes* and *The Medical Journal of Biotech*. He closed his eyes and saw himself morphing into a gray mass of churning levers, rods, and rotors.

Jesus. Get a handle, man.

He took a deep breath, scratching his arm.

Something was wrong here, though, something out of kilter.

He felt uneasy.

The clock read 1:55 — probably fifteen or twenty minutes before Caulder got here. John lifted his collar. The pinpoint on his shoulder had grown. The spot on his forearm was larger, too. He glanced at the device lab. The man in the blue sweater was still leaning over the workspace with the lab techs.

That's what had nagged him.

He had met all the techs at one point or another, but John didn't recognize this man. John stepped out of Caulder's office and pressed against the lab wall. Blue sweater was maybe thirty-five, and just beginning to show a bulge at his waist. His hair was black, trimmed short. John was positive he had never seen him before.

He strained to hear their conversation.

"The connection to the spinal column is complete," one of the techs said.

"Yeah," blue sweater replied. "And the optimizer units are working. After today's scare we'll have to pull them back a bit or Caulder will figure this out."

John knitted his eyebrows together.

"He'll be back for more masks tomorrow," the tech said. "What do you want to do?"

Blue sweater straightened and put his hands on his hips.

"Let's cool it on the optimizers for now, and work on getting the respiratory anchors in place?"

"You got it."

Blue sweater patted the tech's shoulder. "Gotta run. See you tomorrow night?"

"Sounds good."

John backed into a dark recess as the man walked down the hallway and pressed a button for the elevator. John didn't want to lose him. The elevators would take too long to arrive, so he took the stairs, two at a time, rushing downward.

The elevator chimed as he hit the ground floor.

Blue sweater waved at the guard as he left. The guard gave John a quizzical stare as he followed, but didn't say anything.

The man walked toward the car next to John's.

John's eyes fell on the GeneoTech symbol.

Holy shit. Blue Sweater man worked for GeneoTech. Dr. Caulder didn't know what was happening because these weren't his bugs.

Suddenly John wanted to hit this man, wanted to squash him like the cockroach he was. The asshole. The total asshole. John strode forward, then ran, his feet pounding against the asphalt, his rage pounding against his temples.

"Wha—"

The man looked up just in time to catch John's right cross. He fell against the car, then slid to the ground, blood flowing from his nose. He tried to crawl, but could barely manage to lift himself.

John kicked the car door and left a dent.

"I'm John McDonald. Unless you want to go to jail for the rest of your life, I suggest you start talking."

"What the hell are you doing?" the man said as he regained his senses.

John ripped his shirtsleeve back to his elbow, grabbed the man by the collar, lifted him up to push him against his Beamer, and shoved his forearm into the man's nose.

"What the hell is this?"

Blue Sweater focused on John's arm. "Woah!"

"What's your name?"

"Martin. Martin Sprawling."

"You work for GeneoTech."

"Yeah." The man put his fingers to his bleeding nose. "It's probably a reaction to the mask they ran today. We can fix it."

John tightened his hold of Sprawling's collar. "What's in the bugs you're giving me?"

Sprawling looked as if he were judging how much to say.

John twisted his grip, raised the man off the ground and crushed him against the car.

Sprawling winced.

"GeneoTech is out of business either way, asshole" John said.

Sprawling gave in. "There's a bunch of different ones, but the most important are neural links and triage systems."

"What the hell do they do?"

"They fix you. They find things they think can improve, then build whatever kind of bug they need to fix it."

"They're making me better?"

Sprawling nodded. "They're making you more of who you can be."

Spiders tingled in his veins.

"Christ."

He threw Sprawling to the ground and kicked another dent into the BMW's door. Sprawling tried to crawl away, but John kicked him in the ribs and pinned him against the asphalt.

"Did you actually think you could get away with this?"

He realized immediately how stupid that question was. Anyone in the insurance business knew just how far a company was willing to go when that kind of money was on the table.

"I can't believe you've got the entire Medicorp lab on your payroll."

"Just the night shift and a couple protein programmers." Martin Sprawling squirmed against John's restraint, blood trickling down his chin. "Maybe we can make a deal."

"I don't deal with dirt."

"Think about it, John. Think about it hard. I can make you into a Miracle Man. You're already probably going to live forever."

John tightened his lips, digesting that thought. "What?"

"The bugs are optimizing everything."

John stood, thinking, still absorbing. Could he live forever?

"We're both big boys here," Sprawling said. "What do you want?"

The question hung like a cloud. A gust of wind blew his hair. Streetlight reflected off the metallic lump on his forearm. The skin on his scalp tingled and he felt bugs crawling in his brain.

What if he did? What if he lived forever?

What did he want?

"I want my life back."

"I don't think it's a good idea to take the bugs out."

"I don't want you to take them out."

"I don't understand."

"Here's what you're going to do," John said.

***

By breakfast, the bugs had grown him a new skin, soft and smooth, pale, a nearly perfect match for his own. GeneoTech delivered the new program that afternoon while Carol was out shopping.

John was sitting at the kitchen table when she returned.

"Hi," she said without looking at him.

He watched her put grocery bags on the counter, remembering how she used to look striding over open ground.

"What's that goofy look for?"

"Do you love me?"

She stared at him. "Are you all right?"

He told her everything, explained how GeneoTech slipped foreign bugs into the mix, about his eyesight, which was so good now he no longer needed glasses. He talked about how it felt to walk without pain in his knees, about smells and sounds and the taste of butter on toast. He explained how Caulder was going to extend the mask, but how it wasn't going to matter.

"I'm going to live a very long time," he finally said.

Carol looked at him as if she didn't know him.

"What about me?" Carol whispered. "What about us?"

John fished the vial from his pocket and put it on the table. Her gaze lingered on it. "This is for you," he said. "If you want it."

Carol understood. Her face grew tight, then she looked at him. "What about the kids."

"Maybe someday. But for now it's just you and me. No one else can know."

"What if something goes wrong?"

His stare was pleading. The refrigerator kicked on. Carol wiped away a tear. "I'm still me, Carol. I don't feel different anywhere that matters."

She bit her upper lip. "This is a lot to absorb."

"Yes, it is. Take your time." He stood to leave her alone, to give her space to think.

"Wait," she said. She picked up the vial, looked at it first, then at John. "Do you love me?" she said.

He smiled. "Forever and ever."

She twisted the lid.

Ron's Afterword

I wrote "Bugs" in two chunks.

The first was simply the introductory scene in which John is having his last moments. When I was done with that, I wasn't sure what was supposed to happen next. To be fair, I wasn't even sure I had a story. To be fair, I'd say I was stuck. For a day or so, I think it was, I just kind of looked at what was there and let it stew.

Then came the full experience of good Dr. Caulder.

And Medicorp.

And the PR blitz.

And then the fallout.

All of that happened pretty quickly in the end. I think that's a beautiful thing about writing stories. No one really knows where these things come from, but once they start, the string can play itself out in ways truly remarkable. I love John and Carol. I love the crap that goes on as company-on-company violence ensues. That's a thing about medical technology, right? Probably especially in America, which—as I write this—is still literally the only first-world country to not have some form of universal care. Not that it matters in "Bugs," I suppose.

"Bugs" is about greed merging with the desire for advancement.

And "Bugs" is about what it means to take risks.

And, in the end, "Bugs" is about a love that could last, effectively, forever.

RON COLLINS

Deca-Dad
ANALOG DECEMBER 2010

I met my d-dad at Rutan Center.

Being the primary transfer point in Earth orbit, Rutan is always busy. But that day the traffic was especially heavy, and its corridors were awash with luggage-runners whistling this way and that, and travelers who spewed through arrival gates to clog the tramways. Fidelity units hovered overhead like Manta rays, their multi-frequency orbs constantly scanning the throng. Re-gen stores lined the hallways and blared their info-feeds along each precisely regulated ten meters of hallway. Duty Free toiletries, best price in port, screamed one. Catch Frieda Gonzales and her award-winning performance in "Diablo, Remix #7," said the next.

I would have filtered the info-feed away, but I had arrived a few minutes later than planned and I didn't want to miss any announcements. As a result, I heard the entire range of sound that echoed through the Rutan transfer point and I can report dutifully that the place sounded as huge as it is.

His ship, the Translux, was already docked at LaGrange Bay 12, its surface blazing cadmium white under the service lights. I kicked myself for missing the docking, but even that couldn't dampen my excitement.

Aldous Yazgar Hakkinan.

The name flowed off my tongue as I waited. He was my grandparent, six times removed. Hakkinan is not my name—my name is Rogerson. Like almost everyone I know, my background is so mixed that I can claim only Terra as my heritage. But I had studied all his records with great intensity during the week since he agreed to meet to talk about my project, and I knew he was clearly Finnish with little bits of Spanish and Egyptian thrown in for good measure. I knew he was small, just over 182 centimeters tall and about 220 pounds in Earth gravity. He would be self-local fifty-six years of age.

All these things I knew, yet I was still stunned to see him step off the ship and make his way through the connector tube. He wore a red and yellow travel suit, probably thirty years out of date. The collar was curled up, and the sleeves were tight around his meaty forearms. The fabric of the suit was wrinkled in a way that seemed workmanlike. His lips were downturned as he exited the tube and glanced at the transfer gate to his left.

I waved and stepped forward a bit.

"Carlo!" he yelled across the gate.

He looked like a Norse god as he strode toward me. He was physically fit in a solid, blocky way that I hadn't expected. His shoulders were wide and his long blond hair flowed around his head like a glowing helmet. He shook my hand, and despite the fact that mine is bigger his seemed to swallow it up. He turned the handshake into an embrace, pounding me on the back with an exquisite, space-borne gusto.

"Hello Mr. Hakkinan," I said, taken aback by his familiarity. My family is not so intense, and his closeness felt somehow threatening.

"Mr. Hakkinan?" he said, holding me by both shoulders. "That will never do. How about D-dad?"

"D-dad?"

"I figure it's been 250 years since my hide last saw this rock, and at twenty-five years a generation, that makes me a deca-dad."

"225," I said. "It's been 250 years since you were

born, 225 since you left Earth Solar."

He held his arms wide and smiled with teeth as white as the paint on the Translux. "What's a quarter century between relatives, eh?"

"Not much," I said, deciding not to tell him that, with life spans now cresting a hundred and fifty years, the span he was using as a generation was now underestimated. I could scarcely contain my own smile, though. He had already exceeded all my expectations. This was a man bigger than life, a man who breathed the moment and understood exactly how to live.

"Where would you like to go?" he said. "Captain needs us back at 1500 for some big-assed announcement, so I've only got two hours."

"I'll set a timer for us," I said. "Can we get lunch?"

"That would be absolutely fantastic, Carlo. I'm starved."

We walked along the corridor, passing Legarzi's, an Italian stand and Yessington Farms, a deli. I half-listened to both their info-feeds, mostly I watched D-dad. He had been flying for nearly eighteen Earth years in his last stint, though it took him just over two local to his own reference. His eyes played over everything as we walked down the hallway, his head twisting left and right. He hesitated at the sight of a transfer gate. The lines around his lips grew darker.

"My god," he said. "Last time I was here this whole thing was just a string of space junk tied together with contact tape."

"I imagine it's quite a bit different now."

"No, Carlo" he said. "I don't think you can imagine it." We walked several paces. "So, you're doing a project?"

"Yes. Did you get a chance to experience the files I sent you?"

"I didn't have much time."

"Oh. All right. I study genetics, specializing in galactic evolution."

He laughed, or maybe it was a grumble. "And you wanted to interview a dinosaur?"

"Yes," I said with what I hoped was a light touch. "It's not every day you get to meet Tyrannosaurus Rex."

He made another grunt that I again took to be a laugh.

We stepped through the doorway to the observation lookout.

It was a cavernous area the size of a football field, covered by a huge geodesic dome of radiation-hardened crystal that faced the out-rim so you could see stars and the distant space haze that marked history and seemed alive with possibility. Rows upon rows of nutrient stations were built into the rounded walls, and the odors of warm food and coffee-extract created a sense of welcome that permeated the dome. The room's geometry allowed you to hear conversations from across the room, but they were ghostlike sounds that seemed to echo off into deep space before they could take shape in your ears. It seemed to me to be the perfect place to listen to stories of adventure and daring.

"Where is the kitchen?" D-dad asked.

"Kitchen?"

"You know, the grub-hub. The cafeteria. Whatever. The place you get the food?"

I almost said Just listen to your i-feed, but I stopped myself. RF genetic engineering had been in existence for a local half-century, which had probably been only ten years for him. He could not have been born with an i-line, and he had clearly been too busy riding space to get hold of an aftermarket device.

"Do you have a radio?" I said.

He pulled a clip from his breast pocket. I gave him the frequency ranges and pointed him to the nutrient stations.

"That's outstanding," he said as the radio recited

Yessington's menu. "Where is your receiver?"

"My ears have been adjusted to be sensitive to whatever frequencies I want."

He shook his head and started at me with a sense of wonder. "Christ," he said. "I'm getting old. Anything else about you been adjusted I should know about? Sense of smell? X-Ray vision?"

"Yes, I can adjust my eyes to see into the X-ray spectrum, and microwaves to a degree. I can assume control of many body functions that were once involuntary. My facial features were selected by my parents. Is that what you were looking for?"

He pressed his lips together. "Anything else?"

"I don't need sleep."

"That's a danged shame."

"Why?"

"Ain't nothing more satisfying than taking a nap on the clock, Carlo." He smiled and pounded me on the shoulder again, though this time it was more of a punch than a pound.

"What foods do you like, D-dad?" I said, hoping to change the topic.

"Haven't had a real burger in forever. Any chance of getting one of those?"

"You mean beef and bread? Probably not."

"Crap," he grumbled.

We ordered at Hava's station. He insisted on paying. I argued with him, but he would not relent. "Money is like rocket fuel," he said. "You spend it to get somewhere, then you look for more. Besides, I know what it's like to be a starving college kid. This one's on me." His pay stick was old, though, and it took five minutes to update it so the proximity scanners could operate properly. Eventually we were seated with our wrapped sandwiches of protomeat and hard brazenbread, and our drinks that sweated condensation in the controlled climate of the observation center.

I craned my head and gazed into billions of years of space. I felt like I was floating. A thousand questions filled my thoughts. I wanted to know what it was like to ride across deep space. I knew he had visited places like Lalande and Epsilon Eridani. Had he met the Padabidan, or the Yenit? What did their language sound like to the flesh and blood of the ear? Were the Yenit's triple eyes as vivid purple in person as they were in the images sent over light-years of space? What adventures could D-dad tell me, this man who had been merely in flight for more years than I, a student at Luna U, had even been in existence?

"What's it like, D-dad?" I finally said. "What is it like to travel space?"

In the dome's lighting, he looked older than his years. Lines across his skin deepened when he laughed or smiled. And that skin was rough, and I could see blemishes along his hairline. Star shine made his cheeks look almost chalky. But his eyes ... his eyes were vivid blue and they sparkled as he took a huge mouthful of his lunch and wiped the corner of his mouth on his sleeve, then set to answering my questions.

"It's a tough life, but a glorious one."

He talked about the early years of his life that he spent hopping lines around the three Centauris, then his mining trip to the Luyten system. He told me a story about ion pumps exploding on his craft when he thought the entire ship might vent into open space.

"Isn't it lonely?" I asked.

"Hell no. Why would you think that?"

"Everywhere you leave, everyone gets older. My, uh, d-mom, she's dead. Don't you miss her?"

"Time dilation is what it is, Carlo. Translux travels about two-nines the speed of light. That's point-nine-nine. Ninety-nine percent. And at that rate dilation is a bit more than seven Earth years for every one year I live. You just can't avoid that. It could be worse, of course—I've met crews who travel four and five nines. But it's hard to be lonely when you cabin up with thirty other people for three or four or five years at a pop, if you know what I mean. After awhile you almost begin to wish for a little less company. Then you get where you're going, do your work, and pick up with a whole new crew."

"So there's never been anyone special?"

"Oh, there's always someone special." He gave a wicked smile, then seemed to sense this may not be what I wanted to hear. "It's like high school for adults, Carlo. You know there's an endpoint, even on a long pull. So you grow close, but not too close. I had a serious girl on my eight-year job, but even though we talked about pairing we still broke up at the end. Neither us really wanted to be together, I guess. That's how it is in this business."

He ran his fingers over his eyes.

"You look tired," I said.

"Yeah. I'm running on twenty hours without sleep, which may not be bad for you, but sucks vacuum for me."

"How do they say it?" I said, smiling and feeling wise. "It's not the years, it's the mileage?"

"I guess that works," he replied. "But really it's all about velocity. I mean, Alpha Centauri is still pretty much 4.1 light-years from Earth, Barnie's is still almost six out, and you're not getting to Beta-Hydri without giving up at least half your life. The only thing we can control is how fast we get from place to place, Carlo. Don't let anyone tell you no different."

"I see."

Though I'm sure he didn't mean it as such, I had taken his lecture as an attack, so I adjusted my adrenaline back down to norm before proceeding.

"I was hoping you could meet my mom and dad, but we didn't have enough time for them to get off work and get here."

"Sorry about that," he said. "Maybe next time."

"Yeah."

He did not seem very sorry. Of course, neither Dad nor Mom had seemed particularly excited about such a meeting, either. My family enjoys nights at home with a holovid more than about anything else. We are not adventurers by nature, despite the threads of this man's DNA that we carry.

"Is any of this helping you on your project?" he said.

"Yes," I replied, though in truth it wasn't. That didn't matter to me, though. This was never really about the project.

"So, what the hell are you planning on doing, Carlo? You're still a kid, probably bursting to make your way in life. What's the future gonna to hold for young Carlo Rogerson? Do we have another pioneer in the family?"

I told him about my interest in evolution and what it means across galactic scales. I talked about life on alien worlds and how I thought it might give us new insights, I gushed on about studies Professor Sawchec was doing on star wombs and the signs he's found of earliest life. I described the three latest theories of spontaneous origin.

"In a few years we might be able to actually understand the true beginning of life," I said, out of breath.

"We'll make a pirate of you, yet, me-hearty." D-dad's grin was the size of Luna U's crater.

"What do you mean?"

"You'll be a star traveler."

"I doubt it. Not like you, anyway."

"You're talking about them damned transfer gates, aren't you?"

"Sure."

He leaned forward, elbows on the table, his eyes suddenly sharp. "I heard about them as we came in. What are they?"

"They work just like doors, really. Once you're scanned and prepped, you step from one side to the other and you're there."

"Unbelievable."

I explained about quantum entanglement and matter linkage. "It's how most travel is being done today. I came here from Luna just this morning. The idea settled on him. Perhaps for the first time he realized that the majority of the clientele in the observatory were just normal people eating normal food and wearing normal business clothes.

"So it's true?" he said. "Transfer tech?"

I nodded.

"No space ships? No jumpers or miners or freight transports?"

I shook my head. "No need."

I saw it on his face then. What does that mean for a man like him? Where does it leave those who have given their life to travelling in tin cans at near the speed of light?

He seemed crushed.

This, I realized, was why he had agreed to talk to me. He didn't care for me any more than he had my d-mom, or any more than he had wanted to meet my parents. He had little interest in the chains of life he left behind, or in my case, that he had cast forward. D-dad had given his life to a different path, and now that path was closing. The first transfer point had been put in place just over ten years ago, and while news travels at the speed of light, he had probably only received the first inkling of it a self-local year ago at best.

My d-dad, I realized, was worried that he was out of a job.

And me? I was worried that perhaps there would be no such jobs ever again.

The timer rang.

"It's been two hours," I said. "I guess you need to get

back."

I engaged trash removal and we returned through the complex until we came to the Translux.

D-dad turned toward me. "You're a good boy, Carlo."

"It's been a real treat talking to you, D-dad. Maybe I'll see you out in the field."

"That would be absolutely fantastic," he said.

We clasped hands, and he pulled me into another embrace.

I watched him as he walked back through the gate. His stride seemed to pick up speed as he progressed. Then he was gone, disappeared into the fuselage of a space craft that could travel at two-nines the speed of light.

***

I followed him for as long as I could.

Translux was given her decommission orders that day. They flew her to a decon station in Mars orbit, where they stripped down for parts. He caught a job maintaining comm satellites for a bit, then did a stint with a refueling center. There was always going to be a need for short-stint space flight, though most repair functions were done more cheaply by bots and reprogramming actions than by true hands-on activity. Then, after eight months hopping around the Solar system, he joined the crew of Hubris, a Higgs-drive unit that could pull six-nines and was heading to the Cassiopeia binary—deeper space than any other crew had ever gone.

I looked up the crew roster, and smiled.

The record included the following entry:

Aldous Hakkinan - Transfer Gate Installation Technician.

I went to Rutan's observation center the next day. I sat at the same table we had sat at and I gazed out into space, thinking about my deca-dad and feeling a sense of wanderlust that I could not adjust away.

Ron's Afterword

An amazing short story can stick with me for a long time. That's why I love the form.

I wrote "Deca-Dad" after reading "Reunion," one of John Cheever's short stories. If you haven't read it, or any of Cheever's stuff, I recommend it. The fundamental conflict of the story—in which a young man meets up with his father for the first time in years—felt big to me. It hung around. I got to thinking about how the idea would translate into an SFnal world, and it struck me that the concept of time dilation would fit perfectly.

Time dilation is a proven fact. Not even SFnal in the end, though for it to make a large enough difference spacecraft need to find a little more get-up-and-go. So, of course, I used it to let one of my characters step into a future a few hundred years, wherein such a meeting between young Carlo and Aldous Yazgar Hakkinan, his six-times removed great grandparent, can come together for a brief conversation that, I hope, carries a lot of weight in a couple different directions.

Even today, when I think back on it I can recall the sense of satisfaction that the work created inside me.

If nothing else, "Deca-Dad" made me happy.

Ellipses ...
ANALOG MAY 2011

It was early April when I first noticed the mounds in Ferguson's backyard.

I had just read an editorial about the state's clampdown on illegal immigration and was feeling depressed, thinking about Mercy, and wondering what kind of life we had brought her into. Surely it would be better than the one we pulled her away from, but it's in quiet moments — like rain-dampened mornings with a paper just put away and a half-cup of lukewarm coffee on the table — that certain realities get hard to deny.

The Fergusons lived next to us. They looked Scandinavian and spoke with a deep Minnesotan accent that marked them as Not From Here. But they were fair skinned and, like American Express, that complexion was accepted in Martinsville in ways our brown-skinned little girl still wasn't.

In retrospect, it was to be expected that I noticed the mounds first. The angle of Kal and Della's place across the street doesn't let them see more than one patch, and the fence between Halle's place and the Fergusons' is too high. Besides, Halle's a single mom. She works every moment the sun is up and a few when it's not.

That left just me, Ness, and Mercy.

Mercy, being all of fourteen, was too caught up with clothes and school and what Marco said to Ava to worry about a patch of grass in the neighbor's yard. And Ness was too busy doing all the things we needed done to worry about much of anything else. She worked part-time at the hospital, and when she wasn't doing that she was deciding which bills to pay when, planning vacations, or thinking about Mercy's transition to high school. Ness has always lived in the future. I, of course, live in the moment.

So it made sense I would see them first.

I looked out the kitchen window that day and saw three patches of grass in the Fergusons' yard that were several shades more vibrant than the rest.

Odd.

We had our own bright spots, but those were in places where water pooled. The Fergusons had never had them before, and I realized now that these three places actually rose up a bit rather than dipped down. They were oblong, squashed ovals about three feet by six, each just the size of a body, arranged side-by-side like an ellipsis. I laughed out loud, imagining Tomas Ferguson out in his back yard at night with a shovel and a flashlight, digging up a hole to bury a guest from up north. "Got to get the ground out!" I heard him say in my daydream.

I should tell you I'm a writer by trade. I've done everything from coffee-table books to a ghost-written autobiography of...well, my contract precludes me from saying exactly who it was, but I'm sure she'll be on the Academy's red carpet again in a few months. I've done crime and mystery. I've done science fiction with its spaceships and what-ifs. I've done horror, or dark fantasy, or whatever they're calling sexed-up vampires these days. Some of my friends kid me about having more names than the phone book, but a guy does what he's gotta do.

My point here is that conjuring images of bodies buried in the back yard is not particularly unusual for me.

I went downstairs to work on the travel article I had finagled from Delta, but my brain stored the image of my neighbor digging in his yard. I know who I am. I know how I work. The image was coming back to me sometime.

I just didn't realize it would be later that night as I was sleeping, and the next night, and the next.

***

When she came home Ness wanted to talk about Mercy.

It was just after lunch and I wanted to finish the chapter I was working on—Jack had followed a trail of blood that led through the house and out the shattered sliding door. The novel was due in six weeks, and as usual I was running behind.

That's my excuse for not seeing the anguish on Ness's face until her catalog flew past my temple.

"I'm sorry," I said.

We had been married nineteen years, and I don't think I've seen her cry like that since the day she found out she couldn't get pregnant. I sat next to her until she finally let me put my arm around her.

"I'm sorry," I said again. "What's wrong?"

Ness sighed and shook her head.

"Honey. I want to hear it."

She spoke softly. "When I dropped Mercy off at school she asked if it would be okay if she looked for her mother."

***

The process of adopting a child is equally remarkable for its lack of efficiency and its ability to fall apart every step of the way. It shouldn't be that hard to pair up a set of people who want to be parents with children who need someone to love them unconditionally, but in practice it seems to be only marginally easier than getting members of Congress to say they made a mistake.

We submitted paperwork and made calls and spoke to counselors and scanned the internet for every piece of information we could find. But mostly we waited.

Ness, of course, did all of the work.

I just went down to the basement and wrote my stories. It was easier that way. I had cash to make, and she was driven and wanted to do it anyway.

At one point we thought we had a little girl from Manchuria, but that fell through when the Chinese government decided they had hit their annual quota. Then it looked like we had something going on in Chile, and again in Africa. Each time the house of cards tumbled, and each time I could see the recesses around Ness's eyes grow deeper. I had my own worlds to escape into when things got too difficult. I sold a story about a kid in Chile after that one fell through, and I used the boy in Africa as a character in my next book.

I guess it was like saying goodbye.

Ness got through it by just working harder.

When we got the call from Mexico, I heard the hesitation in her voice. A girl? Yes. Of course we were interested. How certain was this? Would we fly there? Twice? Yes, of course, but when would we be able to bring her home? The second trip? What about the first?

Mercedes Rodríguez María Janilla had been born January 12th in San Luis Portosí. We first saw her on July 5th. And we brought her to Indiana on August 8th.

Most people in this world get only one celebration each year, but we decided early on that we would be open about Mercy's background — the differences in our skin tones alone precluded trying to pretend she had been a natural birth. Mercy, we decided, would celebrate all three dates. So each January we gave her something that spoke of Mexico, each August we gave her something from her Indiana home, and in each July we gave her something of us.

***

"It's all right," I said, holding her hand. "It had to come."

"I know."

I waited.

"It just hurt to hear her call someone else her mother."

She breathed deeply and laid her head against my shoulder. I put my hand on her head and felt the warmth of her body against my side.

Mercy is not legally able to request information about her biological parents until she is eighteen. But Ness and I decided long ago that we would help her whenever she reached the age to ask about it. It felt like the right thing to do at the time, but this kind of decision is just so much academic crap until you have to back it up with action. Your idea of what the right thing to do is can change over time.

"What did you tell her?" I asked.

She shrugged. "I said we could talk about it this weekend."

"Good girl," I said. And I kissed her on the forehead.

***

The dream came for the first time that night.

***

I hid behind the tall evergreen bush that grew between our yards. Thick mist rose from the ground, but I could see the stars glimmering against the pitch-black overhead. Ferguson wore a miner's hat lighted at the forehead. Moonlight fell on his pale skin. He grunted and bent methodically to shovel spades of dirt into a pile, then pulled a heavy shape — a body, wrapped in a dark cloth — toward the opening. He pulled it from the shoulders, its head lolling to the side, heels dragging the ground.

Ferguson dropped it into the recess, then grabbed the shovel and threw dirt into the hole.

I stepped backward, and a cat prowling close behind yowled. I twisted to look at Ferguson. Our eyes met, his were wide and crystalline clear like blue daggers.

***

I woke with a start, but found Ness still sleeping.

My skin tingled. I stared out the sheer drapes that covered our windows. After thirty minutes of trying to sleep, I gave up and went to write.

I admit I stopped at the kitchen and glanced out over the Fergusons' yard.

No one was there, but the light was on in their basement.

***

The next day was Thursday.

It was traditional that I took Mercy to dance class, something she had done since she was four. Afterward we always had a father-daughter date that consisted of fast food and a stop at Terri's for homemade ice cream.

"Can we skip Terri's?" she said as we were finishing.

"What have you done with my daughter?"

"I've got trials for the summer troupe. I need to keep my weight down."

"You're thin as a rail."

"No, Daddy, I'm not."

"You're not fat."

"I know. But I'm smaller than the other girls, and I need to be more careful because Mexican bodies hold fat better than others."

"Where did you hear that?"

"We're studying anatomy in science."

"I see."

Ness and I had learned everything we could about children from Mexico as soon as we knew we were adopting. We read about unique infections, language acquisition, learning issues, and how growth rates and onset of puberty of adopted children were often different from biologicals. So I knew Mexican children have a proclivity to higher body-fat — I just hadn't been ready for it to raise its head yet.

"So, can we skip it?"

"Sure," I said.

So we went home.

***

The dream returned that night.

Again I was unable to get back to sleep, and went downstairs to put another chapter on the book. The kitchen was dark. Outside the window the hilled portion of the Fergusons' yard caught the moonlight differently than the rest.

The light in the basement was on again, too.

Then I saw movement — a dull gray flash in the shadows behind Ferguson's tool shed, maybe a leg or at least a foot. My eyes adjusted to the moonlight and I could make out a form. Ferguson. I recognized him from his distinctive gait, all legs and arms, tilted slightly forward. He knelt and did something to the ground, then stood and examined his work. Then he was gone, disappeared behind the house.

I felt voyeuristic anxiety.

I stared harder, but nothing came from the shadows for long enough that I became embarrassed. I put on some coffee and went downstairs to let my imagination run free.

Blood ran in chapter eight, and a twist came at the end — the perfect cliffhanger to move the reader to chapter nine. The bad guy pulled a fast one there that was so good it surprised even me. The hero reacted. It all made sense and I found myself riding this wave of the now that was so strong and so familiar. This is why I write. It's for damned sure not the money, or the idea of seeing my name on the cover of a book, or the pleasure of working with a publisher. Christ no. I write for the sensation of being in the story, the sense of being alive inside pages of black and white.

It seemed like only a few moments later I heard Ness upstairs getting her coffee. I was surprised to see my progress. They were the easiest 4,500 words I've ever written. I went upstairs with my empty cup in hand, and I gave Ness a kiss on the cheek.

"Couldn't sleep again?" she asked.

"Guess not."

Out the window, the sun was painting the sky purple. My eye caught something then — a crease in Ferguson's yard, a curled-up corner of sod alongside one of the mounds. Then I saw a shovel leaning against Ferguson's tool shed, its blade caked with soil.

The image of Ferguson digging atop a midnight pile flashed.

"Is something wrong?"

"No," I said. "Everything's fine."

Mercy came into the room, and Ness turned her attention away. The specter of that shovel lingered over me, though. It stayed there all morning as the girls left, and it was still there when I went outside for my walk.

I find walks help clear my brain of the morning's writing, and this exercise kick-starts my creative side so well that I've taken to answering the tired question of "where do you get your ideas" by saying I find them on the corner of Ivy and Gladstone. I received no ideas that day, however. Instead, I kept thinking about the mounds.

Could I have actually been right? Could there be bodies in there?

No, that was silly.

But this aura of doubt was like static cling, and the memory of Tomas Ferguson in his back yard and the sight of a soil-caked shovel would not go away. What if there really were bodies there? I mean, just because it sounds crazy doesn't mean it couldn't be true. It's a strange world, after all — this place where people freeze their heads when they're dead in hopes that technology may someday save them, this world that gave light to Jack the Ripper and Son of Sam and the Zodiac killer.

I couldn't help but glance at the Fergusons' place.

The shovel was gone.

**

Perhaps I should have just gone on with my business, but it was too late, now. I had to know.

I went to the fence and surveyed the area while pretending to scan the horizon. Their windows were dark and silent, which made sense because both should be at work. Tomas sold electronics at the local department store, and Willie — short for Willifred — was a receptionist for a radio station in Indianapolis. Both of them were usually gone before Mercy left for school.

I rode the momentum of the moment, walking quickly along the fence to let myself into their back yard. Clear lines showed in the grass where the sod had been cut and re-laid. I went to one knee and lifted an edge.

RON COLLINS

The dirt below was soft, freshly turned and pounded down, but obviously disturbed. Something was definitely under there.

I dropped the sod, tamped it back into place, and power-walked to the safety of my own kitchen. A dark veil of evil crawled over me. The grit from the soil became paste between my fingers, and sweat formed on my brow and upper lip.

This was insane.

I rubbed my eyes.

It was the lack of sleep. That had to be it.

At 41, my body didn't do all-nighters anymore, much less two in a row. I fished a Diet Coke out of the refrigerator, went downstairs, and sat in front of the computer for two hours before deciding that nothing was coming.

I needed to do something, but what should it be?

Call 911?

Right.

Hello, officer, this is Laughlin West. Yes, that Laughlin West, the writer. Yes, vampires. That's me. I wanted to report three shallow graves in my next-door neighbor's yard. Uh-huh. No, I promise this is no crank call. Seriously, officer. Three. Yes, shallow graves. I see them right outside my window, sir. I can tell they're graves by the different colored patches of grass. My next book? Due out in two months. Sure, I would be happy to sign one for you. No, officer, I'm not making this up. I promise. Dead bodies, yes, and buried right in my neighbor's back yard. Seriously ...

No, 911 didn't seem like such a good idea.

I was still stewing over it when Ness and Mercy got home, and it became time to get dinner ready, which today, as luck would have it, would be chicken on the grill.

The coals were beginning to glow when Ferguson got home.

He waved a perfunctory hello. I gave a nod in reply. He went into his tool shed and emerged a few moments later with a hand saw and an electric drill.

"What's cooking, eh?" he said.

"Looks like chicken today," I replied. "Got a project going?"

His smile was forced. "Yes. There is a project. The women-folk always makes it so certain of that, am I right?"

I nodded again and glanced at the three patches, then before thinking about it, said: "What was your last big project?" I hoped he hadn't caught the glance, but being cool is always easier in second draft.

Ferguson's hesitation was a gambler's tell, a moment where you see truth hidden deep inside — and this tell was one of fear. I had no idea what was going to come out of Ferguson's mouth, but whatever it was, he had not expected to answer this question.

"Nothing important," he said.

"Another on the honey-do list, eh?" I grinned at him.

"Just so," he said as he stepped inside. His door shut behind him. The lock clicked.

It took forty minutes for the chicken to finish roasting.

Do you know how hard it is to not stare at something that you're dying to look at? It's like having a birthday cake hidden in the refrigerator that your mother doesn't know you know about. It's like the hottest chick in school sitting right next to you. It's like God promising eternal redemption to your sorry behind just so long as you don't touch that rosy-red apple that smells so delicious your stomach is tearing itself apart.

After forty minutes of ignoring the green patches, I realized I had only one option.

If I wanted to confirm this strange hypothesis brewing inside me, I would need to get dirty. I would need to dig them up. The idea nearly stopped my heart. I would dig at night, I decided at first. I would get out a flashlight and dig under the light of the moon. But then I thought about Ferguson doing his digging at night, and that he had another project to work on. Damned if I was going to be caught playing in his personal graveyard when it came time to use it again.

I would have to dig during the day when they were at work — which meant everyone would be able to see me. Except, of course, no one else had our view.

If I started early in the morning I could dig up a patch and replace the evidence in less than a workday. Then at least I would know something for certain. And then, if I called the cops or talked to anyone else, I wouldn't be just a silly writer making mad imaginings down in his basement.

***

The next morning came with clear skies and a brilliant sun. The moment Ness and Mercy left the house, I went upstairs and pulled on a pair of old jeans and a light flannel shirt. I went to the garage to grab my work gloves and my shovel. The tool felt like a weapon in my hand. To avoid making a mess I pulled out an old sheet Ness and I had once used as a picnic blanket.

The Fergusons' house was dark.

Because it was under the most cover, I went to the patch that was farthest from our place. It was bordered by a tall fence on one side, and the tool shed on the other. Despite open sky, I felt a touch of claustrophobia. I spread the blanket beside the patch and went to one knee. The sod still pulled back easily. One more nervous glance at the silent window, and I began to dig.

I dug much too quickly at first, and my arms burned with my effort. I was panting when I took my break. I leaned against the shovel and tried to catch my breath. My back was already sore, and a river of sweat ran down my temple.

A jay landed on a budding tree and seemed to watch. I thought I heard a police siren, but it faded.

When I returned to digging, I fell into a rhythm I could sustain. The work was like a prayer. The earth smelled like truth. I felt power as I dug deeper. Twenty minutes later, my blade struck something hard.

A skull? No, it sounded more metallic than bone.

I fell to a knee and pushed dirt away to reveal a rounded metal tube wrapped in some kind of paper-thin skin. My shovel had broken through the skin, so I ripped a piece away and pulled off one glove. Animal hide, perhaps? If so, it was unique — smooth and slippery under my touch, perhaps coated with something. I jammed it into my pocket and returned to work. More of the device became exposed. It was a collection of boxes and wires and tubes. Another half-hour brought me a dish-shaped receiver that was covered in more of the skin.

I stopped then, and I looked around.

The wind had died, and the sun was nearing its apex. I stepped back and examined the machine as a whole. What the hell was it? I would need to dig another hour to get it all out, but it looked to me like a cross between an old Mars probe, a mad-professor's computer bank, and a bazooka. It had small wheels at what I assumed was its base, more like a cart's than a car's.

Was it a radio? A weapon?

What the hell was Ferguson up to?

I chuckled at the idea the Fergusons might be members of some Scandinavian Secret Service, then I soured. They had lived next to us for nearly half a year, yet I actually knew very little about them. They could be anything.

My back throbbed, my arms felt like rubber, and the pile of dirt looked like Mount McKinley. I was going to pay for this tomorrow.

I had seen enough for now, though. It was time to put everything back the way it had been.

I tossed three shovels of dirt back before deciding pictures might come in handy, so I drove my shovel into the mound and jogged across the yard until I came to my back porch.

After being out under the open sky, the house — with its silence and its air conditioning — seemed almost sterile. I felt out of place. The sense of joy powered by the physical activity of my digging seemed blunted. Part of it — a large part I'm sure — was that I knew I wasn't going bonkers. But a moment ago I had been Huck Finn in the middle of exploring Injun Joe's cave, and now the house closed about me, familiar and a little too safe for my invigorated blood.

I went to the basement and grabbed my phone, then made my way upstairs and out the door.

The screen slammed behind me.

And I came face-to-face with Tomas Ferguson.

***

I had never been close enough to him to realize just how tall Ferguson was. I claim 5'11", though honesty would force me to admit an inch shorter and the tape would suggest even that was a stretch. Ferguson was like a human skyscraper. He was trim, too, with a flat chest beneath a blue button-down. His short-cropped hair spiked at the part, his eyes vivid blue and burning with anger.

"What are you doing?" he said.

"I, uh."

"You dig up my property?"

"Yes, I'm, uh."

"My property."

I didn't know what else to say. The hole gaped in the yard behind him. I gazed at the ground and slipped the phone into my pocket.

He grabbed my shirt collar in one hand.

"Hey-"

He pulled me against his rock-solid chest.

"You come with me then."

He walked toward his yard, dragging me along like a dog.

I was bent over and tumbling, just barely able to keep my feet.

"What the ... shit, slow down, Tomas. I'm sorry."

The shirt burned against my neck. Ferguson's gait was long, and his hold was firm as steel. I stumbled. I tried to dig my heels in, but he was too strong. I tripped and fell to one knee. He picked us up without missing a stride.

We did not go to the hole.

Instead he took me to his back door. I caught my balance as he put a key into the lock.

"Can we just talk about this?" I said.

He opened the door and dragged me in.

I didn't get a chance to see much, but even at Ferguson's pace I could tell the place was a wreck. Drawings and maps and other materials were pinned up over most of the walls, and what wasn't covered in loose paper was a bank of television or computer screens, each flashing a steady stream of information and images. A machine that reminded me of that in the holes outside stood in the middle of the room.

Ferguson kept me moving.

He pulled me through the kitchen and down a set of wooden stairs before throwing me into a chair. It was an old chair, built to last, with a thin layer of frayed padding on the seat. He bent to where his face filled my view. "Sit still," he said, one finger waving like a blade so very close to my eyes.

I admit, I sat there, slack-jawed, heart pounding. He turned away and picked up a roll of duct tape.

I bolted for the stairs, but two strides and his hand clamped over my arm like a vise. He hurled me back into the chair, its wood popping, its legs screeching on the tile floor as it slid back against the wall.

I swung at Ferguson. He caught my fist and slammed it against the chair's arm. Next thing I knew it was wrapped in duct tape. I kicked and pushed and screamed. My head pounded with rage. Ferguson's breath was labored, his grip was like steel. He finally managed to tape me down — arms and legs, waist and hands.

He stood, not sweating but at least his hair was tousled.

"God damn it, Tomas." My throat was raw. "I'm sorry. What more do you want?"

He taped my mouth shut.

I started to imagine bone saws and cork screws and meat cleavers.

The door upstairs opened. For an instant I thought it was the cops.

"Tomas?" a female voice came. Willie. She came down the steps. She was shorter than Tomas, though not by much. Her lipstick was vivid red. She spoke in a language I've never heard before, full of guttural consonants and clicks and whistles — maybe something African. He responded similarly, gesturing at me. She glanced my way. They did a check on my restraints, then clomped up the stairs and out of the house.

The basement was silent for a moment.

Then beeps and a low hum crept in, the cold, stalking sounds of electronic equipment working. Red and blue lights flickered from consoles along the far wall. A monitor displayed an image of a bulbous craft, maybe a deep-sea submersible or a car at an amusement park. My skin prickled with the sensation of cool air moving, and I noticed a small oscillating fan on the corner desk.

I found myself helpless, alone, and — I admit — fighting the rawest fear I could ever imagine.

***

The Fergusons worked at a frantic pace. Tomas went outside. Willie worked upstairs, coming down occasionally to check on me or to fiddle with one of the machines.

The chair was hard against my tailbone.

If I could get to my phone, I thought. Or maybe just manage to get a quick-call button pushed — but I had no idea how the phone was situated, so I didn't know where to push. Even if I did, the tape around my arms and legs was too tight. I couldn't get to it.

Without much else to do, I took in the room.

A worn purple throw-rug covered the tile floor. The walls were paneled with a light-colored composite that made the room feel bigger than it was. The far corner was piled with newspapers and fliers from local businesses. To my right, two chairs, much nicer than the contraption I found myself in, sat before a long table that was clean and unblemished, a gently stained ash or oak with noticeable grain. A computer sat at each station, and a scanner of some type sat between them. A large glass screen with a metallic sheen stood behind the scanner, maybe five feet wide and three tall. I leaned forward and saw a set of concentric circles, each intersecting a dot to make the whole thing look like a small solar system or an eccentric atom.

I found I could scoot the chair a little, and if I didn't do too much too soon I wouldn't make much noise. I worked my way toward the center of the room and looked back at the display. Yes, it had to be the solar system — I saw

Mercury and Venus and us. The mapping used a log scale that brought Jupiter and Saturn into view. The asteroid belt was tagged with a pink coloring, and various items inside it were marked with a mosaic of multi-hued triangles and squares. On the whole it looked like a collaboration between Piet Mondrian and Andy Warhol.

I noticed papers on the desk — a report of nuclear testing in Korea, a table of troop strengths in maybe forty countries. A report in Spanish listed energy resources around the globe. There was something else in Kanji, but I couldn't read it.

The computer gave a sharp tone that made my heart jump.

A box expanded across the display, graphically linked to a point in the asteroid belt. A woman's face filled the box, and a collection of text filled space beside her image. She spoke in the Fergusons' guttural language.

I scooted back to my starting place as quickly I could.

Willie Ferguson rushed down the stairs, and with only a quick glance at me sat down in a computer chair. She pressed the screen. The woman's comment played again. Willie rattled off a long discussion, interspersed with typing on the keyboard. It didn't take genius to see I was the subject of the conversation.

When she was done, she sat back and gave a fatigued sigh.

I worked the tape around my mouth so I could speak. "I didn't mean any harm," I said, through my failed gag.

"It doesn't matter what you meant."

She fed a page into the slot in the scanner. It ran through silently.

"Who was the other woman? What are you going to do to me?"

Her eyes stayed on the screen. She fed another page. It took a few minutes to finish scanning the reports.

The woman on the other side left her station, but other people stepped into and out of the background. No — it finally registered in my consciousness that there were no other people in the asteroid belt, these were other beings.

Right?

No government or conglomerate in the world could manage to get a space program of this size funded without drawing attention, correct?

I looked hard at Willie.

Her legs were longer than they should be, her fingers thinner. Her eyes were wide-spaced and open, gorgeous in a myopic way, but I could see now they were spaced too far apart to be human. The skin was smooth, which I had noticed before but assumed she just looked naturally young. Each feature was different, the turn of her nose was off, the curve of her ear lobe seemed too long, the way she sat was slightly too stiff.

The communication box buzzed again, and the voice came. Willie nodded and spoke. She pressed the display, spoke more, then pressed the screen to sign off.

"Don't go anywhere," she said with an awkward smile.

Then she stood and went upstairs.

***

Willie's footsteps were a constant sound upstairs. Tomas went outside and did not return. I heard rumbles and thumps and the screech of packing tape.

The door slammed often.

I began to lose feeling in my hands and feet. I twisted one way and another, pulling hard with both arms. The movement got blood moving, but didn't affect the tape. Frustrated, I let out the loudest, longest scream I could muster.

The door upstairs slammed again, and the heavy sound of Tomas Ferguson's gait came on the steps. The knees of his pants were stained with grass and brown soil, and his shirt was wrinkled. A smear of dirt crossed his forehead.

"You filled in the hole?" I asked.

He knelt to check my binding. "Are you all right?"

I didn't want to give the bastard the satisfaction of a reply.

He felt my hands, and I took the opportunity to snare him around the wrist.

"What are you doing, Tomas?" I said. "Who are you?"

He twisted his arm free.

Winnie appeared on the steps. "Is he well?"

"Get him something to eat," Tomas replied. "Then make him a real gag." He turned and walked up the stairs, wringing his wrist where I had touched him.

My stomach told me it had passed lunchtime.

Willie fed me a peanut butter sandwich and a glass of water. When she was done, she placed a small wad of gauze in my mouth and taped over me several times.

Five minutes later I felt the first effects.

I should have known better than to eat something they gave me. Pretty soon I was in la-la-land, conscious, but totally without care. I tried to focus, tried to scoot my chair, tried to look at reports. Why are they here? What are they doing? But nothing stuck, and I found it all to be merely humorous.

The police came that evening.

I tried to imagine how worried Ness and Mercy must be, but all I could get was their faces smiling together like they did in the picture on the living room wall.

No, officer, I heard Ferguson say. We've been at work. Sorry to hear that. Is there anything we can do?

The cops left and I hummed a little tune.

The rest of that evening is foggy at best.

I remember the blue van. I remember Tomas and Willie disconnecting the display and pulling stuff off the walls. I remember the smell of exhaust, and the hard-hard sensation of my cheek pressed for too long against a vibrating wall. I remember lights. I remember stars out a moving window against a crystal-clear black night.

**

The strength of my memory begins with the sound of tires on the road and the awareness of a sharp pain in my back. It took considerable time before the pain fully registered, but I remember it clearly now. I opened my eyes a slit. Willie was driving. The road was dark. I was on my back. My head hurt, and the gag was a gauzy paste in my mouth. White streaks of passing headlights bathed the ceiling above me. The passenger seat was empty, which I remember seemed odd at the time.

I twisted to relieve the pain, but when I relaxed it came again, the ache of a sharp edge pressing against my kidney. It was probably part of a machine, a corner left exposed due to hasty packing.

Sometime thereafter the thought struck — could I use it as a blade against the duct tape? Enthused, I moved my wrists up to it and sawed. After a little experimentation, I felt it pierce the restraint. It was all I could do to keep from crying out. I pressed on silently, though, using the vehicle's vibration to help me sweep the tape against the blade. The sough of the road and the motor's whine covered what little sound I made.

It took five excruciating minutes to cut the tape away.

Willie's phone rang just as I felt blood in my fingers again. I kept my hands behind my back and pretended to sleep. She answered, glanced back at me, then shook her head and spoke further. A moment later, the vehicle slowed, turned a few times, and came to a stop. She shut the ignition off, and opened the door. A blast of fresh air filled the cabin. She got out and slammed it shut.

Were they stopping for gas, or perhaps hitting the rest room? Aliens had to use the john, too, right?

I rotated just enough to keep my hands hidden beneath me. I kept my eyes shut and stayed as limp as I could. The machine dug into my back.

The van's bay door slid open.

After a moment, Tomas said, "Let him sleep," using a voice loud enough that anyone around would take as a sign of companionship.

They shut the door, and their footsteps retreated.

When I couldn't stand it anymore, I opened my eyes and found we were at a 24-hour waffle place. They were eating. Maybe I had a little time.

I pulled my feet up. Everything hurt, but I pressed the metal edge against the tape around my ankles and they were suddenly free. I started to work on the gag, but realized it could wait. Instead, I pulled on the sliding door to find it locked. Keeping my head down, I crawled to the front seat and pressed the button that controlled all the doors. A solid clunk came from each lock.

I eased the side door open, stepped out, and closed it behind me.

I saw the highway a distance away. A gas station and a mini-mart were nearby, both closed. Three other cars were in the parking lot. A large, move-it-yourself truck was parked beside the van, and I realized that's where Tomas had been. They had too much equipment to move in one vehicle.

A single lamp illuminated the parking area, but it looked like wooded area beyond that for as far as I could see.

I moved to the rear of the van, and took a few deep breaths to calm myself. I flexed my aching hands and wriggled my sore toes. The vehicles would provide cover as long as I stayed low.

So that's what I did. I stayed low, and I ran.

When I hit the woods I ran farther. I ran until it hurt to breathe through my nose.

I stopped and felt the tape around my mouth, frantically, ripping it away, unwinding four times before the last turn pulled hair and burned skin. But it was gone. I breathed freely, gulping fresh air.

Then I ran farther, and farther, continuing until I couldn't run any more.

***

I checked my phone. It was quarter-past five in the morning. The sound of cars on the freeway came from a distance to the east. When I slipped the phone back into my pocket, my fingers grazed the small chunk of wrapper skin I had stashed while I was digging. It was soft to the touch, slippery. Its metallic sheen made a paisley pattern in the earliest light of dawn.

Yesterday seemed so far away.

I put it back in my pocket.

I rested for half an hour, listening for footsteps in the woods. It was cold, and my entire body was cramped and stiff. The woods creaked and popped with unfamiliar sounds. I heard birds. I heard scampering that I thought might be the Fergusons but turned out to be squirrels.

I walked toward the sound of the highway, then stayed in the trees and followed the direction of the traffic. Before long I came to the exit the Fergusons had taken. I saw the gas station and the mini-mart. I saw the waffle place. The van and the truck were gone. Still, I thought it best to avoid the waffle place, and the mini-mart was just opening. So I went there and got a cup of over-cooked coffee and a box of cinnamon crisps.

The woman at the counter was rail-thin and wore a stained golf shirt with the mini-mart logo on its breast.

"If you don't mind my asking," I said, "where the hell am I?"

"Pardon?" Her accent was southern.

"What's the closest city?"

"Rockwood."

"Thank you," I said. "And the state?"

She stared at me like I was a crazy man, and I'm sure I looked the part.

"You're about a half-mile from Rockwood, Tennessee."

I smiled and paid for my food with a credit card I'm sure she thought was going to be denied.

Then I stepped outside and called Ness.

***

She cried, and asked if I was okay. Then she came and got me.

I squatted on the stoop in front of the mini-mart, drinking coffee, waiting, and wondering how I was going to tell her what had happened. I was angry and embarrassed. I felt grime, a dirtiness that went well past the sweat and soil that lined the wrinkles in my skin and made me feel sticky and oily. How was I supposed to talk about this? Who the hell would believe me?

As time passed, Ness's impending arrival began to feel like a time-bomb waiting to go off. Until then I was safe. No one had to know anything. But I owed her the truth, and I felt the countdown as a physical thing, every second passing with a nearly audible click. I stood and paced.

But I didn't leave.

She pulled into the mini-mart three hours after we spoke. She was hungry and I hadn't seen any sign of the Fergusons in the time I had waited. So we went to the waffle place, and I sat her down and I told her everything I could think of to tell her.

She took it in, stopping me at times to ask questions. Mostly, though, she was quiet.

"Do you believe me?" I asked when I was finished.

She put her fork down on a finished plate of eggs over-easy. "Well, it makes sense."

"Seriously?"

"I noticed the shovel was out of place when I got into the garage last night."

I laughed. It was probably the first time in our history together that her precise memory of where everything in the house was supposed to be actually brought us closer together.

She leaned in. "What are you going to tell everyone?"

"I don't know. Maybe I won't say anything."

She just looked at me.

"People will say I'm insane. There's a lot to lose here."

She was still silent. I felt embarrassed. Finally, she spoke. "I love you. Do what you think is right."

A sense of relief washed over me.

I reached out to touch her hand.

***

When we got home, I picked up the phone and called the CIA.

You have to start somewhere.

***

That was two months ago.

I know things now that I didn't know then. I know Tomas Ferguson dug up the three holes in his back yard, and filled in the dirt. I know they were renting, and that the real estate agent was surprised to find the place so thoroughly cleared out. It seems the Fergusons travel light.

I also know that both the CIA and the FBI are condescending assholes who think I'm a loon, and don't plan to do a damned thing. SETI is interested, but they're too unorganized to do much more than ask folks to point their telescopes toward the asteroid belt. My story just gets lost in the frightful buzz at the various extraterrestrial web sites, though they still send me email every day.

I now know there's a branch of psychoanalysis reserved completely for those of us who report alien encounters. One snide doctor actually said to me: "Did you know it runs in families? Maybe I should talk to your daughter."

I know people in Martinsville get quiet when I come around, or they make jokes about tightening their asteroid belt or give me any of several other inane shots I've heard since the media firestorm passed. If I hear "Preparation H will get rid of that pain in the asteroid" one more time, I may just bust a gut.

And I know I'm at a loss for what else to do. Who else is left? Drug lords? The Mob? Hamas? No thank you.

Finally, I know Ness and Mercy have had a hard time because of my story, but neither has made it a problem at home. Mercy in particular suffers because she gets it from teenagers who have yet to learn the fine art of buffering their disdain.

On the other hand, sales of my last book shot through the roof, and I've got a contract offer to write about my abduction if I want to do it. It may be all that's left to try.

Again, all these things I know.

What I don't know is where Tomas and Willie Ferguson are today. What neighborhood are they watching? What information are they sending their cohorts? What are those cohorts planning to do?

I think about these questions every day, and as with so many other things, it's what I don't know that scares me.

So, you might ask, why am I writing this? Why now?

It's like this:

Today I took Mercy and some of her friends to a mall in Indianapolis. I've taken to enjoying Indy because it's big enough I can go places without creating a stir. The girls paraded through the mall. I know the rules — it's uncool for a parent to actually be seen with a flock of teenage girls, so I trailed a distance behind. I didn't mind. It let me watch and absorb, which is what writers do best. The girls laughed and looked brilliant and young and lithe and glowing. I had just smiled to myself when a man coming the other direction turned to his wife and said: "Wish the damned spics would just go back to Mexico."

I can blame lack of sleep or PTSD or whatever — I had, after all, heard these things hundreds of times before. I am a white male. People speak freely with me in the room. But this time, before I could stop myself, I punched the man square in the jaw. He stepped into it and went down like sack of flour, gazing upward with wide, boggling eyes, and with blood gushing red from his lips. His wife screamed. People reacted. I stood over him, shaking and muttering something about never saying that again and what the hell did he think he was doing. I kicked him ineffectually. Then security pulled me away.

They let me go after a long discussion.

Mercy was, of course, completely embarrassed. Ness cried when we got home.

It's evening now. The sun is just setting.

I'm sitting on my back porch, looking at what used to be the Fergusons' yard. The piece of plastic skin is on the table before me, a glass of tea beside it. Across the yard, three depressions mark the spots where machines were once buried. The sky above grows darker, and the stars begin to shine.

My hand hurts from where I hit the man.

The thought of him makes me mad again, but this time the feeling is closer to home, close to the bone. What did I know of Tomas or Willie Ferguson? I lived next to them for half a year, and knew nothing. It never bothered me that I didn't know them — never crossed my mind that we should have them over for dinner or evening drinks. They lived in their house, as Kal and Della do in theirs, and as Halle does in hers, and we do in ours. During the day some of us emerge from these houses and drive our cars to work, waving sprightly to each other from behind our windshields. At night we come home, collect the mail, and retreat into our havens to watch television.

We are separate.

We are alone.

I think about government agencies that pretend to wield real power. I think about shrinks, and media personalities prowling for stories. I think about the man in the mall who would have accepted tall, white Tomas and Willie Ferguson on face value — as I, too, had done — yet threw vitriol at a teenage girl whose DNA came from Mexico.

Are we different, this man and I?

I reach out and touch the quicksilver material.

And I wonder if we truly deserve what is coming.

Ron's Afterword

It's probably true that I learn something from every story I write.

I recall a review of "Ellipses…" that was generally positive, but suggested the big reveal that the next-door neighbors were aliens did not come as much of a surprise simply because the story appeared in the pages of *Analog*. I'd guess the fact that the story doesn't contain any other elements of true science fiction until that moment didn't help.

Analog is about Science Fiction, after all.

It's got to be coming sometime.

Until that moment, I'd say the idea of a story being a communication between a reader and a writer was, for me, an intellectual thing. I knew it was there. I felt that connection when I read other people's work, after all. The idea that readers bring themselves into a story and, in that bringing, change the story in their own, individual ways, is a thing. The idea that expectations come with a brand is true, too. I knew those things intuitively, but this was the first time I could see it happening to me, the first time that I was aware that the brand of the venue that published a story affected the actual consumption of that story.

This was always obvious.

But the review made me pause.

I still think about that sometimes as I'm plinking along on another story. I try to imagine where people are as they read, and how they came about the work. In the end, I'm not sure I can always do anything about it, but it's there. And it does sometimes change the words I'm using.

So, yeah. I'd say "Ellipses…" taught me something.

Following Jules
ANALOG OCTOBER 2013

"Watch this," Jules said.

They stood on a tall tower in Jules' self-space. Toadstool-like houses with red polka-dotted roofs ringed the hillside below. She spread her arms, arched her back, then jumped headfirst into the open sky to plummet toward the electric green carpet a thousand feet below.

Jaime leaned over the crenellation, gripping its rough surface as if it was really there. The vertigo that fired her brain was definitely real, as was the adrenaline-laced anxiety that froze her heart. Halfway to the ground, Jules tucked and did a crisp one-eighty. She landed on her feet, but the meadow puckered like a trampoline and launched her skyward again. She flew upward, bringing a graceful knee slowly forward, lifting her arms, and raising her gaze. She reached her apex and turned a reverse somersault that was accompanied by a musical peal as she posed in mid-air like a gymnast sticking a landing.

"Ta-da!" she said with a smile.

"Freaky," Jaime replied. "How did you stop like that?"

"Adjusted the value of gravity at my shoe."

"Smart."

"Not smart," Jules' lips came up in a half-smile. "Creative."

She walked across open sky with an athletic sway, slim and beautiful in her two-toned purple-black leotard and white tank-top. Her cheeks glowed and her eyes, now slitted, blazed emerald green. Jamie had once told a friend that Jules lived as if every moment of her life was performance art. She thought about that a lot these days. The entire dive, for example, was more poem than event.

"Now you try it," Jules said.

Jaime looked down.

"I'm not so good with heights."

"Come on, girl. You can't get hurt."

"I can't help it."

"I'll do the think-code if you're worried about it. I'll make the drop shorter."

Before Jaime could reply, the ground rose up close enough she could smell the faint scent of wintergreen that had become Jules' OC trademark.

Jaime knew what was going to happen.

She was going to jump.

It would terrify her, but she would do it because this was Jules standing beside her. In fact, the mere idea she could refuse made her feel weak because she knew she wouldn't resist, no matter her terror. She would get mad, of course, she might even snap at Jules. But she would do it.

Jaime glanced down.

Her bare toes curled and desperation cleaved to her like a drunk undergrad at closing time. Why did Jules do this to her? She knew heights terrified her, yet here they were.

"Okay," she said.

She took a deep breath and jumped.

Her scream seemed to come from other worlds. Her arms flailed in spastic attempts to find balance and her body pitched and rolled, her feet kicking in all directions at once. She moved her arms to cover her head, creating new physics that wrenched her body around. She landed on her back. Pressure crushed wind from her lungs, her stomach pushed against her throat. She clenched her eyes shut as the ground flung her upward. Maybe she screamed again.

A moment later she was face-up, lying stationary, panting for breath.

Jules let out a joyful whoop and clapped her hands.

Jamie opened her eyes. It was sky all around. She saw Jules walking across the open span to give her a hug. Her cheeks flushed, and she felt dizzy. She wanted to get back to something that resembled firm ground. She wanted to breathe.

But mostly she wanted to savor the scant hint of wintergreen, and bask in the warmth of Jules' physical contact as she wrapped her arms around her.

**

As most large advances are, OC — Open Community — was inevitable in hindsight. At its root it was a simple hub that brought massively multi-player online games together as a single entity, connecting dwarves, dragons, rogues, and shamans with Victorian beats, gamblers, time cubes, and rocket jockeys.

But it was much more than just a link.

OC tech provided a smoother gaming experience by sharing user load and balancing information across millions of processors. It allowed developers to reach through the virtual membranes that separated each environment — hence allowing gamers to step from one world to the next as if it was all one interconnected universe. OC's eighty-five/fifteen licensing made it an obvious sell to business owners, as small companies quickly realized their share of the cash flow generated by the entire gamer population dwarfed 15% of their own direct revenue, and the big guys who lost out on margin, like SimJazz and Media Arc, easily made up for it in expanded volume, or with reduced hardware inventories and restructured tax planning.

Every respectable MMO opted in and everyone got rich.

Each OC member got his or her own 40 acres of self-space to build in any way they wanted, and could use any tools from any connected universe at any time. Soon the hub itself took on its own life.

The rest of the world absorbed OC like it did any other social discovery. One reviewer called it the internet's answer to the multiple world quantum theories. Late-night comics joked on the obsessive-compulsive behavior of the stereotypical OC player. Psychologists studied it, liberals lauded its Utopic sharing, conservatives predicted it would turn kids into a Matrix-like race of pod-creatures, and economists reveled in the opportunity to examine the complex bartering systems that sprung up between everything from trolls to spacefaring races.

Jaime admitted she was afraid of OC.

Unlike, say, Alpha Centauri or the Crab Nebula, OC was an actual presence in her life. Its complexity was overwhelming because she could touch it and feel it, its danger more tangible because it changed her life so much more intimately than the average solar flare ever had. She enjoyed OC, but it felt like playing with mercury.

***

After they left OC, Jaime and Jules went to Afino's for dinner. It was a small place tucked into a strip mall on Campus Road, deeper than it was wide, with monstrous rows of CFLs that bled light through glass panes that faced the parking lot. Jules liked Afino's because the owner kept a tabby cat around named Jingles, who mostly slept in the front window or prowled along the baseboards. Jaime liked it because they had a mango salad she adored, and because its lighting made her feel safe.

They sat at a table for two.

"I'm tired," Jaime said, slouching so her butt balanced on the edge of the seat. She stretched her neck, feeling the beginnings of a headache.

"They say OC's a great place to work out because your body reacts to what your mind perceives." Jules beamed, apparently not fatigued at all.

Jamie shrugged. She didn't think Jules would understand that most of her fatigue was from her fear of falling. "I'm just lagged, and I could stand a shower."

Jules' phone beeped with a text. She dug it out.

"Piss." Jules tossed the phone on the table.

"What's wrong?"

"That bitch Helderman just failed my ass. Now I've got to take the goddamned thing over again."

Jaime grinned wickedly. "You could always go grease the skids with her."

"Hey," Jules' eyes grew big. "I love an adventure, but the woman is a goddamned republican. Even I have my standards."

"Yeah, she's not really your type."

Jules gave a sigh, put her elbow on the table and rested her forehead on her hand.

"I swear my dad will kill me if I don't graduate."

"He'll just cut off your cash."

"I'd rather he kill me."

Jaime laughed.

"Seriously. I suck at everything. What the hell am I going to do with my life?"

"Bag groceries?"

Jules sat back, crossed her arms around her stomach, and glowered.

"Look," Jaime said, leaning forward. "School has never really been your thing. Pretty much everyone knows that, right?"

"Yeah. I just don't get it, you know? Even if you know all the answers they still expect homework, or someone like Helderman gives an essay question about Tolstoy and expects you to tell her back exactly what she thinks. It's not fucking fair."

Jaime thought about her reply.

This might be the opportunity. Here. Right now.

This might be the moment she could tell Jules how special she was — that she needed something different, something unique, a fresh start, a different place, that maybe when Jaime graduated this summer they should get up and go someplace together, someplace exotic and interesting like Singapore or Tahiti or ... wherever. They had been friends forever, but Jaime had never told her how she really felt.

The idea scared her. Jules had always been sexually aggressive, but Jaime had not. Jaime was cautious and wary of offering herself, even if the door had been opened that one, single time.

Perhaps, though, this was the moment.

An electric chirp announced someone stepping through Afino's doorway.

"Look at that," Jules said, looking up.

At first glance he might have been a freshman, but as he grew closer Jaime realized he was just slight. He had jet-black hair from a bottle and wore a sleeveless red t-shirt torn at the neck. His arms were long and thin, but wiry rather than emaciated. A wave of blue and green ink covered his shoulder like a shield, and his black jeans clung to thin legs. His movement was measured but sharp, a demeanor that reminded Jaime of a spider crab.

The boy ordered at the counter, then stood waiting.

"Hey?" Jules yelled.

"What are you doing?" Jaime whispered.

She noticed the vamp stamp as he turned toward them and Jules waved him over. Normal access to Open Community was achieved by a series of connections along the arms and legs and around the base of the hairline. These let the environment capture information through the user's nervous system, and pass it back via gentle electrical stimulus. The boy showed the traditional pinkness at the back of the neck and along the arms, but he also had four stronger welts, bright red marks at each temple and a tightly aligned pair toward the back of his neck. It was a direct IO system, said to sync so perfectly with the brain that a user couldn't tell they were having a virtual experience at all. The links were called a vamp stamp because they gave the appearance of having been bitten by a vampire.

The boy drew closer, followed by the odor of stale incense. He turned a chair backward and sat down between them, his awkward arms resting on the back.

"I'm Jules." Jules held out her hand. "This is Jamie."

He took it. "Reb."

"Short for Rebel?"

He shook his head no, and bangs fell into his eyes as he scanned Jules, lingering on the pinkness along the nape of her neck.

"Then what's it for?"

"Something else. You OC?" he asked.

"Of course. Can I look at your stamp?"

"Help yourself." He raised his chin.

Jules used one hand to turn his head away. He smiled as if he was enjoying himself, and Jaime was suddenly angry.

The connections were wires placed into the brain at each temple, with signal returns at the base of the neck. Delicate work, though not as dangerous as it might seem.

The guy behind the counter brought Reb half of a veggie wrap and a fruit cup of mostly grapes and oranges. He popped the top off and ate a grape.

"It's a lot of cash," Jaime asked. "Is it worth it?"

"Every penny."

The two exchanged smiles and Jules leaned closer.

"How does it feel?"

"It stung for a couple days."

"I mean how does it feel to be direct linked?"

"Oh. Absolutely delicious," he said, eating another grape. "Absolutely. Delicious. It changes everything. You may think anything is possible without it, but it's like ... it's like you've shed your skin and the one below it is some kind of electric clay or plasma or ... I don't know. Everything is so smooth.

Someone said it's the closest thing we can get to being a god." Reb paused, then shrugged. "I guess you just have to be there." He left his fork in the fruit cup and looked at Jules. "Sometimes I forget what's real until I get so hungry it hurts."

Jules put her hand on his arm. "Better eat, then."

He gave a sheepish grin.

"I can give you a side-car. It's not the same thing, but it'll give you a flavor of it."

Jules smiled.

It was an expression Jaime had seen a hundred times before. The game was afoot, party time, let's roll. Whichever. All Jaime knew for sure was that her moment was gone, and she wanted to disappear into the linoleum floor.

***

Two days later Jaime decided being a business major sucked.

She was sitting in their third-floor dorm room, chair propped back, one bare foot resting against the windowsill, a late April breeze carrying sounds of other students.

A computer slate sat on her lap.

"Explore the five traits of leadership."

She grumbled.

When she first came to Darver College she was interested in anthropology, but she didn't make it past Australopithecus before realizing she was bored. Being an English teacher lasted four weeks, though she finished the semester with solid grades. She had been a business major for over two years.

Now she needed to explore the five traits of leadership.

How bogus was that?

You could pick just about anything and call it a trait of leadership. Staffing? Teamwork? Goal Setting? Coaching? Individual development? Conflict Management? Communications? Media Relations? Strategic Thinking?

Business Planning? The list could go on and on, but the question presumed five, and only five, traits.

What was she doing here?

She was twenty-two years old and nearly ready to start her own life, yet the only thing that mattered to her right now was Jules.

She was surprised to find herself crying.

She remembered the first time she had seriously faced her interest in Jules.

It was their freshman year. They had gone to a club and Jules had jumped into the mosh. Jules was vibrant, rocking a glow only Jules could carry, and for whatever reason Jules chose to focus all that glow on her. Jaime felt like she was floating all night, like her skin might catch fire at any moment, and then in the darkened corner of the club Jules had kissed her and Jaime had kissed back. She had let go for once in her life, made a decision and kissed Jules with every part of her body, with every piece of the universe behind her, lips to lips, their warm breath damp, feeling the slow beat of Jules' exhale against the frenetic pound of the bass drum from the speaker system screaming above them.

The next morning she woke up in Jules' bed.

Jules was gone.

When they met for lunch Jules joked about it. "Now we've got a game we can play to turn on all the guys," she said. "Guys get off on girls who kiss."

Jaime didn't reply.

"Or girls for that matter," Jules added with one of her racy smiles. "Believe me."

And Jaime did believe her.

The words lesbian and gay were not new to her, but though others had so obviously blazed the trail before her the idea she might be gay still made her skittish. Eventually, that skittishness faded. It wasn't about liking women or not liking men. It was about Jules. It had always been about Jules.

The problem, of course, was that Jules and Reb were spending every hour they could wired into OC, dancing on waterfalls and diving into black holes or whatever the fuck they did. For his part, Reb was quaint. He actually seemed to think Jules liked him. But Jaime had seen it before. Jules would use him up — she would suck up everything interesting about him, and when she got bored she would be gone forever.

She did it to everyone — everyone except Jaime.

Jaime was the padded bumper that protected Jules' fall, the trampoline in her OC space. She didn't know why. She didn't understand that part of their relationship, nor did she like it. But it was true, it was real as OC and as hard to fathom as life on Mars.

She thought about that night, then tossed her slate onto her desk, realizing she wasn't going to get any work done. Low voices came through the open window. Breeze made her watering eyes burn cold.

***

By the time Jules got home it was dark outside. She fell into her bed, clearly exhausted.

"My entire body hurts," Jules said.

Jaime deliberately paused the video she was watching off the web. She stared at the posters and pictures Jules had plastered on her wall. Amelia Earhart and Emma Goldman were side-by-side. Gloria Steinem was toward the left, and Whoopi Goldberg toward the center. Brandi Carlile was in there, as was Ayn Rand, who Jules oddly thought of as apolitical. Amy Winehouse. Danica Patrick. Ellen peered out from behind Tara Dakides, who with her cascading blonde hair could have been Jules' double as she stood defiantly behind a pair of sunglasses. Somewhere toward the top of the collage, tucked between Gretchen Bleiler and Emma Frost, was a photo of Jaime — her senior photo, the one with her leaning against a fence post and smiling.

Jaime couldn't be mad at Jules for long, but she was still feeling hurt, and wasn't sure she trusted herself to speak.

"What?" Jules said.

"Are you going to get a vamp stamp?"

Jules let out a long sigh. "A stamp would be amazing," Jules finally said. "Maybe my granddad will give me some money for my birthday."

Jaime couldn't help but raise an eyebrow.

"You're not going to go all preachy on me, are you?"

"No," Jaime replied.

"Because it's really incredible, Jaime. It's ..."

"Delicious?"

"Yeah." Jules raised herself to one elbow. "It's some serious delicious. You really can do anything — make yourself a baboon with cats' ears, go boarding on Europa, or ride a proton beam and watch the explosions when they collide. You absolutely have to see it, Jaime. Reb showed me one last night. It's the best freaking fireworks you can imagine."

"You can do all that without a stamp."

"Yes, but that's like saying you're snowboarding when you're only cutting green slopes."

She lay back on her pillow.

"I can't wait to be in control of it myself."

Jaime looked at Jules sprawled over her bed and realized Jules had a plan.

"Poor Reb. Less than a week and he's already lost you."

"Ah, yes, I do tend to love 'em and leave 'em, but you may not want to cry for young Reb just yet."

"What do you mean?"

Jules rolled to sit up on the edge of her bed. "We're looking for Magicman."

"Get serious."

"I am serious."

Jaime raised another quizzical eyebrow.

Magicman was an urban legend among OCers, a ghost of a character who supposedly downloaded himself into OC's databanks, and now lived full-time in the digital.

"Reb thinks he exists, and he makes a good case. There was a kid in Illinois who died while attached to OC. They say he just starved to death, but Reb and I think he actually DLed."

Jaime laughed in spite of herself.

Classic Jules. A minute ago she was so tired she could barely stand, now she was sitting on the edge of her bed with her eyes sparkling.

"You know, Jules," Jaime spoke in soft, vacant tones. "I used to think you were oblivious. But that's not it."

"Huh?"

"You're just self-absorbed."

"Seriously, girl. What are you talking about?"

Jaime looked out into the darkness and spoke the one question she had never before let herself vocalize.

"Why don't you love me?"

She immediately wished she hadn't said it, but it was too late. The words lay there, exposed and open.

Jules sat still a moment, then stood up. Jaime thought she might leave, but instead she came to stand behind Jaime's chair. She put her hands on Jaime's shoulders and rubbed her neck.

Jaime groaned and rolled her head forward.

"Remember when we went to the party and you threw yourself into the pit?" she said.

"That was a great night," Jules replied.

"Remember what you said when I asked why you did it?"

"No. I'm sorry. I don't."

"You said you wanted to see if they would catch you."

"Good thing they did, eh?"

Jaime nodded, then laid her head back, feeling Jules' fingertips all the way down her spine. Music came from the room next door. Footsteps went down the hall.

"I'm sorry," Jaime said. "I shouldn't have asked that."

"Will you come to OC with me tomorrow?"

"Yes," Jaime replied, not knowing what else to say.

Jules leaned down to kiss the top of her head.

"Thank you."

***

Jaime skipped Econ next morning and they went to the dining hall for a quick breakfast.

They had eaten here together hundreds of times before, but today felt awkward. Jaime had laid herself bare last night, and she still wasn't sure what to make of Jules' non-reaction. But, she also felt a sense of comfort that she had asked the question.

With a full night's sleep behind her, Jules was glowing again. "We'll do the prep work at my place, if that's okay," she said. "Then we'll be off into wonderland. You'll see what I mean." She ate a banana by first ripping off stages in her fingers. She drank grapefruit juice. Jaime knew Jules didn't particularly like juice, but her body would need the energy, and it was a sacrifice she was willing to make.

They hooked in as soon as they arrived back at their room.

Reb was waiting in Jules' self-space.

He looked like a psychedelic mix of dope fiend and soldier, his blood-red overcoat square at the shoulders, his glasses translucent triangles mounted point-down and carrying neon-laced images of spiders.

"Hey," he said, giving Jules a *what's she doing here?* glance.

"Jaime wants to feel the stamp. You'll need to do the think-code for both of us."

"I'm not sure I can."

Jules laughed. "Want me to tell everyone you can't handle two women at the same time?"

"Three might degrade the experience."

"Then you'll focus on her, okay? I want Jaime to feel this."

Reb gave a shrug. "Okay."

He stood in place but looped a digital arm around Jaime to press his fingers against her neck. She felt a sharp pinch in her spine.

Snap. Her mind was on fire. *Snap.* An electric essence started at the cap of her head and fell like rain. Snap. Everything slowed down, and each movement, while still a series of digitized steps, passed in spans of time that had never existed before. *Snap.* Her vision grew smooth and deep, her sense of smell robust. The buzz of a hummingbird came from somewhere distant and she could immediately break it into its harmonics. She mapped each tone to the feather of its origination and realized she could shape the sound to different ranges with the flip of an imaginary equalizer.

Snap.

"See what I mean?"

Jules' voice came in warped waves that fell together like an audible jigsaw puzzle. She put her hand around Jaime's waist, and their digital atoms merged in ways impossible on the outside. It was an exquisite pain, so intimate that Jaime nearly climaxed. She was embarrassed and tried to pull back, but Jules held firm.

"It's all right," Jules whispered.

"Your brain is recalibrating," Reb explained, apparently oblivious to Jaime's full state. "It's getting digitized data in paths it's never gotten before. It'll settle down in a few minutes."

"I'm cool," she said with a tremble to her voice.

Reb gave a satisfied nod. "I think we'll be okay with three. That's *tres* fucking glorious, man. I am the goddamned man! Let's go, baby!"

"Give her another minute," Jules demanded.

Reb looked like he was going to argue, but Jules just raised a hand, and he held off.

"You okay?" Jules asked.

Jaime's stomach settled. Shadows stopped forming around movement.

"Yeah," she said. "I think I'm ready."

Reb didn't wait. Code flowed.

Suddenly they were flying over OC. Despite the height, Jaime was not afraid. She let her tongue slide between her lips as they flew over segments owned by millions of users. The air was coarse with the flavors of smoke and citrus and grass. They turned, breaking into thousands of pieces and reforming in fractaline patterns like flocks of birds that turned together with the beat of a wing — separating, coming together, flying as a whole like they had been born to it. Jaime laughed. She could not get the sensation of a smile out of her head. It was so real it hurt.

"Can we look for Magicman?" she said with wild abandon.

Jules' essence came to her then — Jules, pure Jules, her achingly beautiful soul pressed itself into Jaime's thoughts, and in this instant Jules opened to her completely for the first time in her entire life. Beneath bravado and beneath panache Jules was as afraid as Jaime, but hers was a different fear.

Jaime knew her parents split when Jules was five, and that her mother was an addict. But Jaime now saw how Jules' father struggled with two jobs, and used it to cover the fact that he was lost about what it took to raise a little girl. She saw what twelve apartments in eight years had done to Jules — spending a week at each grandparent's place each year, summers maybe at Uncle Carl's or with her mom's sister or at camps she didn't want to be at.

Jules had no place.

The act of change itself was probably the only constant she had in her life. She was good at it. It was something she could control. But it meant that she had grown up with no core, no sense of being home. And it meant she had no one she could trust.

Except for Jaime.

They merged then completely, each sharing, each knowing, and in that instant Jaime understood Jules was coming back to her again, this time for good.

It was the most absolutely delicious moment of her life.

***

They slept in the same bed that night, but Jaime felt distance the next morning. Jules was quiet, a distance that might have crushed Jaime if she had not been so elated to have finally won, and if she didn't realize now how much Jules needed her own space at times. Reb called twice and texted continuously, but Jules ignored him until the barrage trailed away. He left notes on the white board on the wall outside their room, but Jules kept to herself.

Jaime and Jules walked campus, holding hands and talking. They rented videos and they went to OC. It wasn't the same as when Reb had escorted them, of course, but Jules still seemed to enjoy it.

One night Jaime woke to see Jules was awake and sitting at the computer console studying for Helderman's final. The next weekend Jules decided to go to a tree gliding. Jaime watched her strap on a contraption that turned her into something resembling a giant paper airplane, and let her soar over an open field. Watching Jules under the brilliant afternoon sun, seeing her hair twist in the wind, and hearing her clear laughter ride the breeze, Jaime realized what was wrong.

And with clarity as stunning as the image of Jules flying, she knew what she needed to do.

***

They had dinner that evening in the Manor, an open-air food court south of the student center. It was a warm evening, so they sat at a picnic table outside. A distant PA played the ripping guitars of Shining Commandos, the smell of automobile exhaust mixed with the aroma of hot food.

"I want to give you something," Jaime said. She put her console on the table, tapped a few commands, and turned it toward Jules.

It was a banking transaction for a thousand dollars, the description read Vamp Stamp.

"I can't take your money."

"I want you to have it." Jaime sent the transfer check to Jules' account. "If you don't accept it, I'll just deposit it in your Darverbucks account."

Jules stared at the screen.

"It's important to me," Jaime said.

"I appreciate it. I just ..." Jules sat silently.

"What's wrong?"

"I don't need it."

"Come on, Jules. You're the poster child for people who need a vamp stamp."

"That's not what I mean."

Jaime clenched her teeth. "Okay, what do you mean?"

"I found Magicman."

"Come on, Jules. You know Magicman is not real. There's no way to load yourself into a computer."

"Yes there is. I've talked to him. He's already sent me his rig. It came in the mail today."

Jaime tried to take it in. She played a fingertip along the condensation around her drink cup. The words rig, mail, and today kept jumbling in her head.

"You knew you were going to do this when you had Reb think-code for me in OC, didn't you?"

She nodded. "I needed you to know. To really know what this is all about for me."

Jaime took a sip of her drink and tried to ignore the oppressive essence of betrayal.

"What do you want?"

"Come with me."

"I don't understand."

Jules took her hand. Her touch was firm and urgent.

"I want you to live with me in OC."

Jaime was stunned. "This is crazy. I mean, you are talking about killing yourself, right?"

"No. We'll still be alive — we'll just be in OC."

"But didn't this Magicman die?"

"Just his body."

"Oh, I see. Am I Romeo or Juliette?"

Jules' eyes turned downcast.

Jaime saw she had hurt Jules deeply and for a flashing instant she admitted it felt good to be on the side dishing it out. A wave of remorse replaced that quickly.

"They say it takes ten years to replace every atom we have. That means we die without even a single physical piece of what we were originally born with. My grandma's still breathing, but she's been in Neverland since I was twelve. That body is not her. She loved daisies and dandelions as long as they both were picked by her granddaughter. She ran a company and paid for my dad's school. She was fucking incredible. When she was here, I thought she was beautiful, but her body is probably sitting right this minute in a dingy hallway that smells like piss."

Jules paused for a breath.

"This body is not me, Jaime. That body is not you. This is not about suicide."

"I'm sorry," Jaime said. "Can we try this again?"

Jules nodded, sat back, and glanced away.

"You want me to follow you?"

"Yes. But there's only one rig, so we'll have to do it one at a time, and Magicman said the DL takes up major processor clock so it's best to wait awhile between transfers, otherwise the admins might be able to shut the second one down."

"Okay."

"And we don't want anyone to know where we've gone. So after I've DLed you'll need to remove the rig. After my process completes, you'll need to hook up and come, too."

The situation settled in Jaime's mind.

"I don't like the idea of seeing your body."

"You can do it, Jaime. You're stronger than you think."

"Who would do it for me?"

"Reb."

"I don't trust him."

"He lives for secret agent crap. His nickname is short for reborn because he thinks he's some kind of resistance fighter against the government. If I sell him just right, he'll think it's all so subversive that he'll keep it quiet forever."

For a moment Jaime actually thought about asking why Jules didn't ask Reb to DL if he was so into it, but that was just her anger rising. She wasn't in high school anymore. To ask this kind of question now would have merely been hurtful.

"I don't know, Jules. This is pretty extreme."

"It's not extreme if it's right. You feel it, don't you? You and me, forever."

"Let me think about it. This is going too fast."

"What's there to think about?"

Jules leaned over the table. Her blonde hair fell forward in a shroud. Her eyes were watery blue, her lips thin and soft.

"I want to do it tonight."

***

This was a bad idea. It was crazy. Astronomically idiotic. Every part of Jaime's being wanted to say no.

Yet, OC was Jules' element.

And underneath her terror, this idea of electronic elopement gave Jaime a feeling of tragic oneness with Jules. Did it matter where they went? Did it matter if they had no bodies if they could truly become one in OC?

***

The rig was a netting of interlaced components that lay together to form a high-tech skullcap. Each nexus was bound by a stud with an attached wire, each wire fed into a connector that attached to a box with three switches and a bank of LEDs. Jules had hooked the box to her computer via an extended USB port. Wearing it made Jules look like a character from an old Mad Max movie.

"When it's done," Jules said, "take it off and leave for a couple hours."

"How will I know it's worked?"

"Log into OC." Jules smiled. "I'll find you. It might take a while. Magicman said DL scattered him a bit and it took an hour or so in real time to find himself."

"Okay."

"All right, then," Jules said, arranging herself at the table. "Let's get this party started."

Jaime leaned over and kissed her, feeling the sensation of Jules' hand on the back of her neck.

"Goodbye," she said.

"Don't worry, girl," Jules replied. "I'll see you in a bit."

Jaime flipped the switches. Jules clenched her jaw and the hair along the side of her head rose with static electricity. Air seemed to slide from her lungs in a single, slow exhale. She slumped. Then silence.

That was it.

One moment Jules was breathing, the next she wasn't.

Jaime wanted to divert her eyes but couldn't help looking. It felt strange that the nearly imperceptible movement of a chest rising and falling could be missed so much. She pulled the first connection away. She could not help herself. A tear came to her eye and fell down her cheek. Then another. She cried harder as she stripped the rig, pulling strands of Jules' hair with each node.

What the hell have I done? Jaime thought as she finished disconnecting the rig. *What the hell have I done?*

When she was done Jules slumped peacefully in front of the computer console, her hair streaming toward the floor, her hands crossed over her belly.

She looked like she was sleeping.

Jaime waited for an LED to turn from red to green, as she had been instructed, then pulled the box from its connection. She left, trying not to glance behind as she closed the door.

***

They hadn't planned on the RA calling 911. They hadn't planned for the police cruisers with their flashing blues, or the ambulance, or the gurney wheeling out Jules' body covered in white. The cop who questioned her tried to be gentle, but Jaime was overwhelmed. All she could think of was the box hidden behind the bushes of McKinley Hall and the fact that she was going to be late for her meet-up with Reb.

They sat in the dorm lobby.

The cop was a big man with a radio that constantly crackled with remote voices and random blasts of static. The shiny parts of his uniform gleamed like spikes.

"Can you tell me anything about Jules?"

"Like what?"

"How was she the past few weeks?"

"You mean was she depressed?"

"Yes. That's the idea. What was her frame of mind?"

"I guess she was a little depressed at times. She was failing a class. She didn't have a job."

"Boyfriends?"

The question stung more than Jaime expected. "Jules was non-denominational."

Her response took him back a little, but it didn't change his fatherly drawl. "Was she having any relationship issues?"

"No."

"Maybe that was the problem?"

She shrugged.

"Drugs?"

"I don't think so."

"Don't lie to me. You know we'll run the tox report, right?"

"Jules didn't really need anything to get along."

He scribbled on his pad. "She didn't leave a note," he said.

Jamie shrugged again, fighting back tears.

"When was the last time you talked to her?"

"This afternoon. We went for lunch. She was happy." That wasn't a complete lie, anyway. A tear finally made it through her defenses and rolled down her cheek. Her head was beginning to pound.

The cop reached into a folder and pulled out a plastic bag. He put it on the coffee table and pushed it toward her. Inside was Jaime's photo, bent on the bottom, a crisp crease that split the corner into an isosceles triangle. She didn't remember it being bent at all previously.

"Did you give her this?"

Jaime looked at the kid staring back at her from the photo. It seemed so long ago. She raised her gaze. "Yes, I gave it to her. Why?"

"She had it in her pocket."

She furrowed her brow. "Really?"

"I'm sorry to tell you that. How long had you been roommates?"

She looked into the cop's brown eyes, then down at the picture with the creased corner. Why would Jules put that picture in her pocket today? What the hell did it mean? The questions made her stomach go queasy. Everything about this seemed wrong.

"Forever," she said. "We've been roommates forever."

The rest of the interrogation went by in a blur.

When he was finished, the cop thanked her and wished her well. He gave her the number of a helpline, and suggested she talk to a campus counselor.

The RA spoke to her then in hushed tones. The police would need the room to be locked down, but they could get her another for the night. Jules' father was jetting in from Massachusetts midday. Her sister was a sophomore at Princeton and was supposed to arrive in the morning. Did she know where Jules' mother was? Jaime said no. She found the never-ending string of information increasingly annoying.

She had only one thought now. Get into OC to check on Jules. It was all that mattered.

The cops wouldn't let her take her computer console until at least tomorrow, but the building admin lent her an old notebook and she tucked it under one arm and headed to the library. She took a pass behind McKinley Hall on the way. Reb wasn't there, which didn't surprise her at all, but she was glad to see the rig had not been disturbed. She would call him later. Right now all she wanted to do was find Jules. She entered the library, found a stall, and collected herself before logging into OC. It had been well over eight hours since the DL. Jules should be able to find her.

Jaime entered her own self-space but felt nothing. She opened up all her public communication flags and immediately got hit on by a dwarf wearing a blue basketball shirt. She went to DigiJaz, a virt-bar where Jules liked to dance, but didn't see anyone remotely like Jules.

Finally, she tried Jules' self-space.

It hadn't changed since the last time she had been there — a fact she found unnerving.

She floated through trees that grew snowboards and glazed goggles. A marshmallow stand sat in one twisting corridor. A koi pond teemed with catpoles, little amphibians who would grow to be cats, Jaime supposed. Music came from a living room — Silent Sixes, Jaime's favorite band. The band was hooked up and jamming, Pauline scatting into the phones, Uma McJaynes pounding shit out of the drums.

The band ignored her.

"Jules?" she called.

No response.

She stepped into the kitchen. It was an open area. Light from an unseen sun splayed warmly over a table and illuminated the centerpiece — Jaime's high school picture, zoomed to twice its original size. The corner was not bent, but instead was marked with a small icon.

She didn't leave a note.

Jaime sat down at the table and pressed the icon.

Hey, girl.

It was an image of Jules in the chair opposite her.

If you're getting this, I'm sorry. I didn't tell you everything. I know how bad that sounds, but if you knew things could go wrong you wouldn't have let me do this. And I needed it. You, of all people, know how true that is.

Here's the rest of the story.

Magicman said DL can result in three possible outcomes. Most of the time everything should go well, and you make it into OC just fine. But sometimes everything can get corrupted. If this happens you just disappear. The other possibility is that you can get stuck in what he called a load block — like a temporary folder that computers use to extract new programs.

If you're reading this, I am either dead or stuck in a silicon jail. Either way it's not good. Magicman thinks the block interface is unidirectional, so it all amounts to the same thing, I guess.

Sounds juicy, doesn't it?

The image paused to run her hand through her hair.

I want to tell you how beautiful you are — inside and out. You are the person I always wanted to be. Whatever you do with yourself, I want you to live. Step off ledges. Take risks. Feel it. Don't hold back. Don't fear. And every now and then, if you can manage it, think of me without hating me.

Because I love you.

With all my heart.

***

Jaime unplugged.

She went back to McKinley and dug up the rig. It was late. She went back to her temporary room and sat on the bunk, leaning against the barren wall with lights off, her legs crossed together, and the rig heavy and cold on her lap. The room was empty except for the bed and an old digital clock that blazed with blue numbers. There were no drapes.

She put her head back against the wall and cried.

She was so tired.

If Jules were dead, at least Jaime could concoct some version of a heaven or a Valhalla or whatever. But the idea of her being forever locked in a cell of computer code was horrific.

Sometime in the night, reality faded into a lucid dream where Jules was stranded on an ice floe, tied to a post and wrapped in a candy-striped straightjacket. Then she was remembering their first day on campus, Jules dressed in shorts and an orange t-shirt, looking out the window. "I feel like I can fly," she said. Jaime laughed. "Don't make me clean up that mess on our first day." Jules turned and smiled.

Jaime woke with a start.

The clock read 4:43 am.

Wind rustled past the window like a whisper. She was cold, so she pulled a sheet over her shoulders.

What the hell was she going to do?

She looked at the rig for a very long time. It was heavy in her hands. The studs at each nexus were hard and pointed. They reflected an otherworldly metallic sheen. Just the thought of putting the cap on her head made her want to vomit. She thought about Jules' family flying in. She imagined her own mother and father, and Cindy and Jake, her sister and brother.

Two impossibilities — she couldn't bring herself to DL, yet she couldn't live with leaving Jules in OC. She loved Jules. She knew this now more than she had ever known it. The idea of being without her forever was unbearable.

She put the rig down, stepped out of bed, and pulled the sheets around her as if they were a gown. She walked to the window and looked at the campus sprawling away from her. The sky to the east was growing perceptively lighter.

***

Jules' sister, Kara, arrived shortly before lunchtime.

Jaime had been waiting for her in the lobby.

Kara was taller than Jules and had long auburn hair that was straight and fell over one side of her face. She wore a knee-length skirt and a navy blouse buttoned to just under her throat. Her purse was looped over one shoulder — very prim as befitting her own image of a law student.

Jaime didn't particularly like Kara, never really had. She was the anti-Jules, a young woman who hid behind barriers of restraint and self-control that made conversation uncomfortable. And she was intellectually superior. Her dad couldn't afford Princeton any more than he could afford Darver, but Kara had a sharp, brilliant mind, and a bloodhound's persistence. She won a full ride from Downy, Barnes, and Clauster as a senior in high school. Her resume and her demeanor gave Kara a sense of elitism that made Jaime feel inadequate.

Kara's hug was perfunctory.

"How are you?" Jaime said.

Kara adjusted her bag's shoulder strap. "Trying to sort it all out."

"I understand. Would you like to sit?" She pointed to the chairs and coffee table where she had been waiting. "I can get you some coffee or a soft drink from the desk."

"It's been a long morning. Coffee would be great," Kara said as she sat in the same chair the cop had been in last night.

Jaime retrieved two cups from the desk.

"What happened?" Kara asked as Jaime returned.

"I wish I knew. We went to lunch," Jaime continued. "Then we came back to the room to study for finals. I went out for a walk, and when I came back the cops were here."

"You were close, weren't you?" Kara's question was said in a matter-of-fact tone that could have just as well been used to ask about a grocery list or a movie recommendation. "You were probably more of a sister than I was."

"I wouldn't say that." It came out inanely lame.

"I read the police reports this morning," Kara said. "I think they're expecting to find drugs."

"I don't think they're going to be happy then."

"Why not?"

"Jules drank a little, but she never used drugs."

Kara nodded. "You really were close, weren't you?"

Jaime felt a chill in Kara's gaze. It was an accusing gaze, a gaze that said she thought Jaime knew more than she was telling. The silence between them grew a bit too long.

"Never mind," Kara said. She settled back into the chair and pulled out her phone to check the time. "Do you know when Dad is supposed to get here? We've got a lot to do before the weekend is over."

"This evening," Jaime said. "Just before dinner."

Kara grimaced. She glanced at the papers Jaime had spread over the table. "Are those applications?"

Jaime suddenly felt a sudden sense of exposure. Her cheeks flushed. She gathered up the pages, and straightened them, wishing she had put them away earlier. "Yes," she said. "I'm thinking of changing my major."

"Aren't you close to graduating?"

"Yeah. But I don't think business is my thing." She shoved the pages into a big brown envelope.

"Really? I always thought it fit you."

"I'm not that interested in it anymore."

Kara blew on her coffee before sipping, then nodded toward the envelope. "So what are you going to do now?"

Jaime felt the coarseness of the envelope's surface. She shrugged in a way she hoped came off as nonchalant, but felt Kara's gaze as if they were bright lights filling her eyes. She put the application into the slot between the couch's cushion and its arm. Its edge grazed the inside of her arm as she sat back and regarded Kara.

She felt protective now, as if the application itself held a piece of Jules inside it. It made her feel good.

She couldn't DL, not like this. She didn't know anything about OC, and if no one — not even Magicman — could tell Jules how to get out of load-block purgatory, she needed to learn something more about the technology behind OC before doing something that would most likely go terribly wrong.

"I'm thinking of something in technology."

"Interesting," Kara replied. "It's pretty late in the game for that kind of a leap."

Jaime looked at Kara and smiled, feeling more certain about her decision as each moment passed. The road before her seemed long and very lonely, but in the end there were only two things that mattered to her now: she loved Jules, and Jules loved her.

She ran a finger over the corner of the envelope that stuck up beside her.

"Yes," she said. "It's a big leap. But sometimes you have to jump anyway."

Ron's Afterword

I will occasionally use music and songs as devices to jump into stories. I call one of my short stories, for example, (which I titled "Tumbling Dice" in homage) a "retelling" of the Rolling Stones' *Exile on Main Street* album, though one would never tell it from the story. Another uses Patti Smith's "Dancing Barefoot," but since there are no story similarities, you would never know unless I told you. Parts of my fantasy series, *Glamour of the God-Touched Mage,* were written under the influence of Pink's pop music. As strange as that may seem.

My method for using music as a jumping place is mostly in the creation of a tone. Occasionally I'll pick a single word from a song to use in a place, and that word will spin me off into a new and unexpected direction, but, on the whole, when I'm using music as a leaping point, I'm using the sense of feeling I get from it as a guidepost.

"Following Jules" was written under the influence of "Angels of Search and Rescue," which is a song released by Perpetual Dream Theory, a small indie band that I stumbled upon by some random accident and that, as far as I can tell, no longer exists. I loved how it made me feel. I loved the idea of lost people in need of rescue. At the same time, I was doing a lot of thinking about virtual reality and the expansion of computing and gaming into the metaverse. It's a scary thing for some folks, isn't it? The idea of a reality that isn't ours.

Or is it?

Anyway, Jules came about as I was thinking of the main character of that song. I also used a moment where the characters physically jump into the void as an entry into the story because I felt like it was evocative. What came out was a big and maybe sprawling mess, but one I thought had something to say about what it means to love and to be loved. Lois Tilton reviewed it in *Locus* magazine and had this to say: *"This is a love story and a story of character. It's all very well to say that Jules doesn't really deserve Jaime's love, but love doesn't care whether it's deserved. The question is what Jaime needs to do, given how she loves."*

I like that.

Stealing the Sun
ANALOG OCTOBER 1999

Alpha Centauri A was chosen for a few very simple reasons. First, it was close, a mere 4.3 light years from Earth. Second, it was a G2-type star, similar enough to the sun that data taken directly from Sol could be used in software models without requiring complex conversions.

But the most important factor was greed.

Each star in the Centauri system had adequate fusion material to support the new propulsion systems, but Centauri A was the largest of the three, with a mass ten times that of Proxima and 20 percent greater than Centauri B. The supply of resources in A would last that much longer.

And in the end, that was the factor that doomed the star to an accelerated death.

***

Lieutenant Commander Torrance Black stood on the gunmetal runway that circled *Everguard*'s pod engineering assembly area. The rail was cold against his grip and seemed to adhere to his palms. Machinery ozone seeped through the open grate of the floor and hung around him like an acrid memory, unchangeable but vaguely distant.

Everything appeared to be on plan.

Each tube bay stood open, the collection forming a perfectly spaced row of a dozen chambers, their three-meter-diameter spans empty, pristinely round, and gleaming with stainless steel beauty.

The wormhole pods that went into these tubes were the size of G-class riders — fifty meters tip to tip but rounded in cross-section to fit into the circular tubes. Their surfaces were coated with rugged brown thermal material that made them appear starkly utilitarian in the brightly lit assembly area. Each end was capped with conical black boots of heat-treated alloy, and banded with a titanium-steel composite fashioned in the zero-g environment of Armstrong station.

His staff wore their fresh whites today. Their voices echoed with professional bearing in the open expanse. A computer reported the status of an automated routine that controlled much of the launch sequence.

"I want these tubes loaded by 1800 hours, folks," he barked at them with what, even he realized, was a little too much vinegar.

"We'll make it, LC," Malloy replied with a quick salute.

Torrance returned the gesture half-heartedly, then stepped into his glass-enclosed office. He settled into his chair, sighed, and stared through the computer's holographic image of the wormhole pod's internal guts.

LC. The title echoed in his mind like silence after an angry scream. Lieutenant Commander.

That was the thing about rank in the military.

Everyone understood what a rank meant. Rank labeled a man, and it stayed with him. It would not be long before the promotion list was made public, not long before everyone knew where Torrance stood.

He would change the world today. As chief launch engineer, he would release a dozen wormhole pods that would burrow into Centauri A. Their external shells would burn rapidly inside the star's core, and if at least nine of the twelve systems made it to the target point, they would rend space and create the far end of a wormhole. Raw hydrogen and helium would flow to the other side where fellow servicemen would latch these extradimensional warps to the back end of starships.

And then the universe would be open for the first time.

FTL. Faster-than-light travel. Sirius for breakfast, the Aldebaran double star for dinner.

He supposed he should feel something appropriate.

But Kip Levitt, commanding officer of the ship's Propulsion Center, and a man Torrance had gone to school with so many years ago, had been promoted to full commander today.

Torrance had not.

And it didn't take a lifer to know that when a man in the chain of command is passed over for promotion, his career, for all effective purposes, is over.

***

The comm light flashed green on Torrance's desktop.

"Messages, please," he said.

The image of one of his ensigns filled the desk's primary view screen. "All tubes loaded, and the power system is charged, sir. Final prognostics are running now."

"Thank you," Torrance replied, "I'll be there in a minute. We're on hold until the admiral arrives."

"Aye, sir, I'll tell Lieutenant Malloy."

The display returned to software circuitry Torrance had been working with prior to the message. He pressed a control pad and accessed data from the propulsion system. Green numbers read three hundred plus terra electron volts. A collider ringed the ship at a radius of fifty-three-kilometers. Outside the observation panel, Centauri A's light made it a gleaming sliver of silver against the black velvet sky.

Torrance grimaced, thinking about the particles inside the ring with something akin to jealousy.

They were lucky, he thought.

Their fate was revealed on a time scale of picoseconds.

Torrance sighed.

Every member of the pod crew, including Torrance himself, filled other jobs during the flight and would be reassigned back to them during the trip home. For example, Lieutenant Karl Malloy, his chief operations officer, was a nav analyst second class, a job that amounted to gathering data for shipboard navigation controllers. When he wasn't in charge of probes, Torrance was the chief service engineer, responsible for resolving problems with anything from fried communications systems to stopped-up toilets.

Not exactly glamorous.

But then he supposed that could be said about his entire career. He had never been one to seek out the limelight — like Kip Levitt. He hadn't been a football hero at the Academy or a leading officer candidate. He didn't grab control in survival school in times of emergency. Instead, Torrance faced difficult times by immersing himself in work, filling his thoughts with code so that his brain didn't have time to spin out of control over something it could not change. Hell, the entire *Everguard* mission was just another case of burying his head in the sand.

He rose from his upholstered chair and stepped around his curved desk to walk into the main assembly area. At the same moment, the entry doors dilated, and Admiral Hatch entered with a full escort of petty officers and assistants, including Torrance's CO, Captain Alexandir Romanov.

"Admiral on the floor," Torrance shouted briskly and presented a stiff-backed salute.

"As you were," the admiral replied.

The admiral was an older man with brown hair that showed gray at the razor line of his nonexistent sideburns. His green eyes sparkled, and he walked with an efficient stride that spoke of attention to detail and purpose of mind. "What is our status, Lieutenant Commander?"

"Green for launch, sir."

"That's good. Your men are a credit to the service, Torrance."

"Thank you, sir," Torrance replied, glancing toward Captain Romanov.

Romanov smiled. "Indeed you are."

The captain's presence sizzled against Torrance's mind. *Indeed you are.* What bullshit. Without doubt it had been Romanov, a rigid, by-the-book-at-all-costs type of man, who allowed the promotion billet to pass Torrance by.

The staff worked in the area below them, checking status displays and ensuring every firing assembly, safety release, and navigation system was operational. They closed the hatches of each tube, leaving behind a dozen anodized black discs evenly spaced along the curved wall like rounds in an old Remington Colt.

Power surged in the launch system. Twelve external launch doors dilated open with the recognizable groan of hydraulic pressure.

"Ten seconds to engage," a recorded voice echoed the red readout that hung on the wall.

Torrance's spine tingled. He thought about his mother and father, and he wondered how they were. With the time it took message traffic to travel from Earth to *Everguard*, it was possible they were no longer even alive. He had never really thought of that before.

The digital readout said seven. The power coils whined as they sucked energy from the collider.

The image of Cal McKinley, a high-school friend, came over him. His years at the Academy, his first posting under Captain Jao. Torrance had worked through the ranks, receiving solid commendations at every posting. But at LC there were only so many positions above him.

And Romanov was by-the-book.

The readout read five.

Now Torrance's entire life was wrapped up in twelve wormhole pods.

Three.

The crew monitored the launch process. Software controllers ran on optical processors.

For the first time in a long while, he thought of Adrienne.

Everguard traveled at nearly a sixth the speed of light, translating into a twelve-local-year round-trip flight.

Two.

He would be forty-one when the mission was complete. The effects of time dilation would have aged the rest of the world three years beyond that. His investments would likely have doubled twice — not that there was much left after the divorce, but it should be enough to live on for a while.

One.

At least that was something.

"Launch initiated, sir."

Silence echoed where there should have been thunder. The compartment held its breath.

"What's wrong?" the admiral asked.

"I have no idea, sir," Torrance replied, his heart growing cold. "But the pods are not away."

***

"We're not getting anywhere, sir," the technician said.
"And your point would be?" Torrance snapped back.

The air was stale with day-old sweat. The staff was tired and defeated. Their mission-day whites hung from their bodies like whipped flags in dead wind. Displays of the launch system's microcircuitry and software execution paths flickered against glass boards.

It was 0300 and still they had no answers.

"I'm sorry," he said, rubbing cheeks that were plastic with fatigue. "I'm just like you guys, though — really frustrated, and even a little angry. Romanov wants a personal report at 0600, so I'll admit I'm anxious to get to the root of this. I apologize for snapping, all right?"

All around, the staff nodded.

"Maybe Romanov would like to take a ride in the tube to check it out personally," Malloy said with a grin, his eyebrow raised in mock anticipation. "We could probably arrange an inspection."

The collection of men and women chuckled, and the room loosened noticeably. Lieutenant Malloy had a knack for saying the right thing at the right time. The image of Romanov as an icon for the upper command structure, drifting out into space from a derelict launch tube, made everyone smile.

Torrance took a deep breath. "Maybe the answer isn't here."

"What do you mean, LC?"

"We've been over everything three times. If the problem were in the on-board systems, I know we'd have found it by now. Maybe it's something outside."

"Like what?"

Torrance scratched his cheek, fingering overnight stubble. "I don't know. How about we run the full spectrum of sensor scans again, okay?"

"Did that when we got here, sir," Malloy replied.

"I know," Torrance said. "But maybe we missed something."

Malloy nodded. "Okay, LC. We'll do it."

The crew stood to get to work.

"Finish the scan," Torrance said, with a grin. "Then I order you all to turn in for the night."

***

Scientists studied the Centauri system for decades prior to *Everguard*'s launch. They listened for signals and imaged it with deep-space telescopes. They scanned with radio interferometers looking for telltale wobble.

It was Mars station that finally discovered three planets orbiting A and two that orbited B. Only the second planet from Centauri A, however, was inside the zone where liquid water — and thereby intelligent life — was possible.

Scientists quickly dubbed the planet Eden, but closer study soon determined it to be anything but.

Its atmosphere was a horrific mixture of methane, carbon dioxide, and sulfuric acid that had created a runaway greenhouse effect similar to that of Venus. In addition, models suggested that extreme tidal forces of the Centari tri-star system would heat the planet's core and make for a volcanic world with a stormy weather pattern that continually raged across the surface.

The search for intelligent life, they said, would have to dig deeper into the universe.

***

The good news was that it wasn't his fault.

It was 0515. Torrance was early, but he knew his CO would be out of bed.

Trying to relax, he rang his CO's bell.

"Romanov here." The captain's voice was alert and responsive through the intercom.

"Lieutenant Commander Black, sir."

The door buzzed softly, then dilated open.

The ventilation system blew a cool breeze that made the back of Torrance's neck crawl. The room was quiet, decorated with a row of flat-panel images of starships and other vehicles. Romanov was fourth-generation military, and his compartment showed it. The far wall, though, carried a holo of a waterfall from the backlands of Maui. A glass table with three chairs sat in the corner of the room.

The captain rose from his meditation pad, dressed in a loose robe of red terry cloth. A thin film of sweat glistened from the curve of his collarbone.

"Good morning, Captain," Torrance said.

"I think it is acceptable to be informal before 0600, Torrance," Romanov said with only a trace of his Russian heritage in his accent. He gestured toward the table. "You look as if you've had a very long night. Have a seat and tell me what you've found."

Torrance sat down, not certain how to start. The captain sat across from him.

"We have a problem."

"Yes?"

"When *Everguard* opened the launch doors we encountered an electromagnetic disturbance."

"I see no problem, then. Just shield what we need to shield and let's get on with it."

"It's not that simple."

"Why not? We've got inventory."

"Yes, we do," Torrance admitted. "But the disturbance is coming from outside."

"Outside of what?"

"Outside of *Everguard,* sir. It's coming from the star's second planet."

Romanov thought.

"Why didn't it show up in our scan?"

"I checked the logs. It was there, but the configuration of the planets and the star cut the amplitude of what we received, and we overlooked it." Torrance didn't need to add that the *we* who just overlooked it did not include either Torrance Black or Alexandir Romanov.

"I see." The captain clasped his hands together and leaned against the table. His gaze bore into Torrance. "So, you're thinking that a stray burst of EMI says there may be life on Eden?"

"I don't see how we can read it any other way."

"Despite the fact that all our examinations confirm the planet's atmosphere is toxic?"

"Only a life-form could produce this EMI."

"The planet is a perpetual storm," Romanov said. "It is certainly possible that such a place could generate high-energy disturbances, is it not?"

"What we've received has been tight, Captain, not random white noise."

"Have you run our translator programs?"

"Yes."

"And?"

"Nothing yet, sir. But just because we don't recognize a pattern doesn't mean one can't exist. Our linguistic code should be reviewed before we go any further."

The ventilation system wheezed like the collected mumble of distant voices.

"Lieutenant Commander." The captain's voice became firm, and Torrance realized the discussion had just become formal. "We have a mission to accomplish. What you've found is not enough to warrant a jump to the conclusion of intelligent life when everything else we know to be true discounts that."

Torrance froze. He had expected Romanov to point the finger of blame to the External Sensor Command and postpone the mission. But now the captain seemed more determined than ever to push forward.

"But what if I'm right, Captain?"

"I don't think that is the case."

"But, sir, if this is intelligent life, draining their star will leave them without energy. Whatever civilization exists here will die."

"I understand, Torrance," the captain said, his eyes blazing like dark lasers. "But even a simple trip planetside could cost us a year both ways. And who knows what we would find? Probably nothing but static-generating clouds. Do you want to hold back our understanding of the entire universe because we piddled around looking for thunderstorms in Eden?"

Torrance did not reply.

"You're a good man, lieutenant Commander," Romanov continued. "You've always been a part of the team. You're a hard worker. When the going gets tough you stick your nose into the guts of our problems and figure out how to make things work. It's a trait I most admire in you. I know I can rely on you to do what's right for us in the big picture."

Suddenly, Torrance understood.

This was about position. It was about expectations and power. If they diverted for a false call, the careers of every officer aboard would hang in tenuous balance. Torrance's stomach burned, reminding him that the last thing he had eaten was the synthesized roast beef sandwich he had for lunch yesterday.

"Thank you, sir," Torrance said, more because it seemed he should than because he felt anything.

"I do understand your concerns," the captain said. "I'll take your report to the admiral for his confirmation of my order. But our mission here is clear. I have a duty to the people of our solar system, as do you.

"Those tubes need to be shielded and another launch profile prepared as soon as possible."

"I understand," Torrance said, standing.

He understood, yes. But a cold stone formed in his stomach. The captain had just supported potential genocide of what might be an intelligent species of creatures in the name of human longevity, and he had done so with barely a second thought.

"Thank you for your work, Lieutenant Commander," Romanov said.

Torrance sighed, giving into the weight of the waves crashing around him. "The staff had a late night, sir. I've ordered them to their beds. But I think we can be ready to launch in roughly twenty-four hours," he replied, saluting.

"Very good. Looks like you could use some sleep yourself."

"Yes, sir."

Torrance turned and strode out of the captain's office, his temples suddenly throbbing with a massive headache.

***

Torrance and Adrienne met right after he had entered the Academy. At quiet times he still thought about their wedding day, the sugary whiteness of their cake, Adrienne shoving an overly large bite into his mouth. He remembered buying their first house.

They had wanted children — Adrienne pushing for three, Torrance thinking more like ten.

But children never came.

A series of trips to fertility doctors eventually found he was the problem.

There were solutions, of course. Adoption, or donor transplants. Gene therapy. But at the time, Torrance was adamant. He couldn't raise someone else's children. Torrance didn't care that everyone else in the world was doing it. It wasn't right, and no gene therapy in the world could change the fact that every time he looked into the child's eyes he would see his own failure.

He had been scared and embarrassed.

And like usual, he had ignored the problem, letting it fester until it grew black and malignant.

They split a couple of months before the *Everguard* opportunity arose. Without Adrienne in his life, he found he needed something to focus on, something to throw himself into to take the pain away. All he had at hand was the military, with its structure and its rules that dictated what to do when and how to do it. He was suited to this environment, he realized. He felt comfortable with the service, understood how it was supposed to work.

The idea of twelve years aboard the *Everguard* had seemed so perfect.

***

The staff wore their workday blues this time.

They placed shielding around the most sensitive of the firing system's components. Torrance stared into the blackness of space. In less than two hours he would give an order that would expand his world, arguably saving it when looked at over millennia, but might doom another. The thought bubbled thickly in his gut.

He never asked for this.

His career was likely over. He would return to his own world tired and used. A forty-one-year-old man with no family, no future, and no dignity.

It was the last that twisted in his gut with an edge like a serrated hunting knife.

Deep down, Torrance knew his analysis was right. The signal was strong and cohesive. It was a message, but in a language their translator code had been unable to crack. There was life on that planet, and no argument the captain or anyone else aboard this ship could put forward would convince Torrance otherwise.

His uniform collar seemed tight against his neck.

The decision to launch the pods made him sick — made him feel exposed and dirty. He had twelve buttons to push. He was one commander. Twelve wormhole pods. One sun. One people with unknown technology.

Unknown technology, he thought. But technology at least advanced enough to release emissions that interfered with *Everguard*'s systems. Torrance's heart beat with the sudden change of pattern that let him know he was on to something. An idea dawned, a thought that gnawed at him like a rodent trying to claw out of his belly.

One technology.

Energy tickled his spine. It could work, he realized. Competitive reengineering had fueled human progress for centuries. It was a huge personal risk, though, with what was left of his career at stake.

He gazed out the observation panel.

The collider glimmered against black velvet.

Protons and neutrons raced inside the ring, scattering themselves into the netherworld of quarks and leptons — universes that lived and died in fractions of seconds. A collector gathered each of these particles, separating them and funneling each into channels where supercooled electromagnets ensured they would find their antimatter counterparts.

The resulting meeting of matter and antimatter pushed energy into the ship's propulsion unit. Soon a small fraction of that power would be funneled off to feed the launch tubes.

Torrance closed his eyes, listening to the ship. It was a sound he loved, a gentle hiss, soft and warm, reminding him of the wind that had blown past his open window when he was a teenager in Wisconsin.

That was a long time ago.

Lives, like military careers, can be made in the span of a single collision of a neutron and a proton. And they can be broken in similar time. Or they can merely fade away, decaying like radioactive waste with a half-life of a human being.

It was time, Torrance realized, feeling truly comfortable for the first time since he could remember.

He knew what he had to do.

***

"Fifteen seconds until launch," the mission controller said.

Again the admiral stood at Torrance's side. The power coil moaned. Switches clicked and firing systems armed.

The countdown clock read ten.

Twelve probes stood ready to forge the link that would give the human race the ability to explore millions of stars.

Five.

Torrance pursed his lips, feeling oddly proud. He had done his best, and that was all that any God — or any commander, for that matter — had the right to ask of any man. Perhaps it wouldn't be enough. But perhaps it would. And that was sometimes the most that any man could ask of himself.

Two.

One.

"Launch sequence is initiated," the controller replied.

The pods thrust against *Everguard*'s hull like the strikes of twelve sledgehammers. A dozen flaming arrows sliced through black space in formations of four.

One group fell toward the star, then another.

And then the last.

A single element of the last, however, edged off course, twisting slightly.

Adrenaline leapt through Torrance's body with the pod's initial lurch, and he stifled a proud smile. His calculations had been rapidly done, and the reprogramming had been equally hasty, but he knew this code like the back of his hand. If he got it right, the pod would land somewhere on the second planet.

With luck, whoever was there would look at it, would examine its circuitry and its propulsion system. With their new knowledge they might learn how to engineer spacefaring vessels themselves.

And they might find a way to save themselves.

The pod turned, rolling off the original flight plan and heading away from the sun.

"What's wrong?" the admiral said.

"I'm not certain, sir," Torrance replied before Captain Romanov could. "But I'll run a full investigation. The good news is that we have eleven birds on course and heading for home. We only need nine to be successful."

Romanov stared at Torrance, seeming to note the grin that rode his face. But he did not say anything.

***

Of the remaining pods, one lost power and drifted slowly toward the star, pulled to a fiery death by Centauri A's gravity well. The rest stayed on course, and pierced the star's surface. Thermal shielding held back the heat for the milliseconds each electronic package needed.

The wormhole actuators engaged.

Energy, hydrogen fusing to helium, began to flow.

***

Captain Romanov sat at his glass table, waiting patiently as Torrance entered. A cup of coffee and scraps of the captain's dinner sat on the table.

"You wanted to see me, sir?"

Romanov gestured toward an empty chair, and Torrance sat.

"That was a gutsy move, Torrance."

"I beg your pardon?"

"I've examined the preflight records. The last probe's navigation software was altered."

Torrance considered denying it but could see firmness in his CO's eyes. "They deserved a fighting chance, sir."

The captain nodded. "Deliberately altering a mission profile without authorization is a trick that can get a man court-martialed."

Silence reigned for several heartbeats.

"We're stealing their sun, sir," Torrance finally said. "I figure they've got maybe ten thousand years before their planet gets too cold to support life. If they're of advanced technology, they'll be able to study the pod and maybe save themselves."

"And if they're not?"

Torrance stared into a wall scene of the Ural Mountains and waited for the captain's other shoe to drop. He wondered if it would be court-martial, or merely some form of censure. Certainly he would lose at least one rank.

"You don't have a family, do you?" Romanov said.

"My parents live in Wisconsin."

"I mean children."

Torrance furrowed his brow. "No, sir. No children."

Romanov gave an indecipherable grunt and absentmindedly fingered his coffee cup. "I'm sorry you were passed over for promotion, Torrance. You're a good man. But we have only so many billets."

"Thank you, sir."

"You've always worked hard. It is a long flight back home. A lot of good things can happen to a man who works hard for six years."

Torrance stared at his CO, who sat back in his chair and regarded him openly. Alexandir Romanov's brown eyes told him everything Torrance needed to know. Romanov had made a snap decision. But he had understood its importance, and he had looked in the mirror since that moment knowing the extinction of a race might go against him in the end.

Now the future of that unknown species rested in a wormhole pod that was speeding off into space.

"I am thinking," the captain said, "that the report I give the admiral should describe a technical problem with the guidance software of the twelfth pod."

Torrance smiled.

"That could be done, sir."

The captain nodded. "Then make it happen," he said.

***

Lieutenant Commander Torrance Black walked briskly into his office. He needed to prepare a report, and he needed to think about his life, to plan.

He had six years aboard *Everguard*, and if any man could get back on the promotion path, it was going to be him.

And if he didn't, well...

There were options.

Ron's Afterword

If you follow me much at all, you might know that I wrote this story as my "24 hour" piece while at the Writers of Future. I will always love it for the moment with Algis Budrys that it gave me. He had gotten slightly sick on the evening he was reading the stories for comment, and had to pass when his turn came. He promised me, though, that he would read it that night and offered to meet for breakfast the next morning to talk about it.

Of course, I accepted.

Who wouldn't?

I mean, when a legend says "Let's meet for breakfast," you go to breakfast.

So that next morning, over eggs and bagels or whatever, we got to his critique. Which consisted simply of him putting the manuscript on the table between us, and then using one hand to push it across toward me.

"Pretty good," he said. "Send it off."

We then proceeded to discuss what it meant to have a lifetime career working in the world of science fiction.

Which is something else he understood as well as anyone in the business.

The epilog to this story is that Dr. Schmidt, of course, bought it for *Analog* first time out of the gate. His letter of acceptance included a question: "What comes next?"

The answer to that question is next up.

The Taranth Stone
ANALOG OCTOBER 2000

An orange-white umbrella of fire bent from the pod's surface. Brown smoke curled in its wake. The craft was designed to withstand Alpha Centauri A's six-million-degree corona, though, and it survived to glide through the dense clouds of sulfuric acid and corrosive oxides in the upper atmosphere of a planet those from Earth called Eden.

If it were a manned craft, the pilot would have been surprised to find the lowest layer of the planet's atmosphere rich with oxygen. But it was only a programmed machine from a spacecraft that had recently visited the tri-star system.

Pressures as strong as deep ocean scrubbed speed. The pod nosed downward as it drew close to the surface.

Its velocity was forty kilometers per hour at impact.

The ground shook. Rocks and dust flew. The pod crumpled and rolled, flipping end over end like an errant rock tossed down a hill, eventually coming to rest between a pair of basaltic boulders.

***

The door opened and the chime rang. A delivery runner's engine sputtered as it labored past.

The man who entered Baraq's shop wore the orange robe and obsidian jewelry of the Quadarti Council. His skin was leathered brown and smelled of *kadea* oil. His primaries were yellow orbs of iridescence that blinked in the shop's dimness, and his central was a crystal blue orb high on his forehead that marked him as from the northern regions. He stepped through an aisle, gliding past a row of hand tools. A mobile of changa gliders spun lazily near his head.

Baraq's three hearts beat rapidly, chilling his own leathery skin. A hand-tall stack of accounts to be paid sat in a sloppy pile on his counter, and the ledger he was filling was only halfway complete. *Wonderful,* he thought morosely as he looked at the Quadarti. *I needed something else today.*

He glanced to where his weapon lay waiting. It was a recent-model Tegra he acquired in trade for diverting a shipment of root, a good gun with lots of stoppage but less than accurate at longer ranges. Crissandr despised the weapon, of course, and hated that he kept it loaded and in such easy reach. "No one will touch a Waganat," she explained. But desperation leads to a certain lack of caution, and a family name is good for only so much.

There was something else about the gun, too, something he would never tell Crissandr. The gun made him feel independent, his own man, separate from and unreliant upon his family.

The Quadarti guard approached the counter, surrounded by the billowing spiced odor of sulfur and kha. He pulled his upper lip back in a smile that showed yellow teeth matching his now slim irises.

"You will come," the man said.
"Good day to you, too, my friend."
"You will come."
"I'm busy," he said, pointing to his paperwork.
"Paper can be shuffled any time."
"I cannot leave. Who will run my business?"
The guard gazed around the empty shop. "Your aisles overflow with customers. Maybe you should purchase a larger building."

Baraq shrugged. "It is a slow moment."

The guard put four-fingered fists on the counter and leaned forward. His jewelry glinted. The heavy ridge above his primaries drew together, bulging like a distended rock worm.

"You come."

A hackle clawed its way up Baraq's spine. Despite being far down the line of succession, and nearly invisible to his family's power structure, he was still a Waganat. He could send the guard away. But the council would make things difficult, and it was best not to trifle with them if it could be avoided.

"Just a moment," Baraq said.

He went to the back of the store and engaged a series of switches. Metal bars fell across windows. Levers clanged into place. He had installed the device during the last Convergence, when the heat light of Eldoro and Katon filled the sky together in the daytime. He remembered the timing because the clouds had thinned then, and the temperature had dropped so far that water actually formed on the ground in the mornings.

"I'm ready," he said.

The Quadarti guard nodded, then led him away.

***

The council chamber was a tall, rounded room that smelled of influence and was ringed with columns of gray-veined basalt that rose to an open-air ceiling. It was midday of Katon Leading, and the smaller of the two heats was a hazy blot glaring through the domed opening. Eldoro had risen, but was too low to be seen in the chamber. The floor was flat rock inlaid with a spiral of shining obsidian from the foothills of Holy Esgarat.

Baraq had expected to see the council in session.

Instead, only Councilor Hateri greeted him, his ceremonial robes wrapped about him as if they were armor. His hairless skull was nearly perfect in its roundness, dimpled only at the back of his parietal temple. His primaries were pinpoints of darkest brown, and his ear flaps drooped slightly at their ends.

Baraq kept a disdainful grace to his stride despite his hearts' pounding. "What do you want?" he said.

"Good day to you, too," Hateri replied dryly.

"You are the last councilor I would expect to arrange a personal meeting with a Waganat."

"Come, Baraq. Let's not get mired in trivial arguments."

Hateri was a proponent of Quadarti regulation. Every session saw him propose new constraints on trade, and new taxes on materials.

"Open trade may be a triviality to you, but it is life to me."

The councilor's face betrayed no emotion. "I'm sure the Waganats would get along under any laws set forth."

"What does my family have to do with this?" he said with more anger than he meant to reveal.

"Nothing, Baraq. Absolutely nothing."

"Well then, what am I here for?"

Hateri motioned with one arm. "Follow me, please."

Without waiting, the councilor stepped into a long hallway. Baraq followed in uncertain silence. The guard's sandaled footsteps rustled behind. After several corridors, a lift ride to lower levels, and more corridors they came to a set of double doors that led to a small room filled with cabinets, a long table, and several chairs. A row of brown smocks hung from hooks on the wall.

Hateri motioned Baraq forward.

The guard remained behind as Baraq entered.

"Grab a covering," Hateri said, pulling one over his robes, and putting a key to another door.

Baraq felt like a child as he did as he was told. That was his lot in life. Do as you are told. Follow in the lines. He was well past half-age, well past the time when he might do something new, past the time where people expected brilliance.

When he was ready, Hateri pushed the last door open.

A dry, camphorous odor came from all directions. The lab was almost as large as the council's chamber. But where the council's home was garnished and ancient, this room was an austere grid of tables, machinery, and test panels with rows of glass bulbs glowing xenon colors. Diagrams and sketches were gummed to the walls. But the item that drew his attention sat on a long row of eight tables lashed together. The thing was huge and brown, long and rounded, easily eight to ten times as long as Baraq was tall.

He stepped forward.

Its shell was pebbled like a stone lizard's skin, broken and torn apart in places. Fine igneous dust covered much of the body. Inside were boxes with green and white and black wire protruding from them.

"What is it?"

Hateri's grin was bright as Eldoro at midday. "Can you not guess?"

Its shape was sleek and bulletlike, its nose smashed, its tail open and blackened. Baraq's hearts pounded. He tenderly ran a webbed finger along the thing's surface.

"The Taranth stone?" Baraq said.

Hateri nodded, obviously enjoying Baraq's expression of incredulity.

Maybe thirty years ago, a searing ball of flame was said to have scorched the nighttime sky over Esgarat. The council had sent a party to search for it, as had the Waganat family. But thirty years ago, their machines were unreliable and almost incapable of making the trip. By the time they arrived, the mountain's volcanic landscape had shifted to cover whatever secrets the site may have provided.

That didn't stop rumors from building, though.

Esgarat, the tallest mountain peak on the continent, was thought to be the place their species first emerged from the caves to walk the surface. It was no surprise that the holy light landed there, priests proclaimed. It was only fitting that the Gods would send fire to the place of all Quadar's origin. Some churches said the light brought Eldoro's power and had the ability to strike down enemies with rays of death. Scholars debunked those claims and suggested the ball of flame was more likely just a trick of the clouds, reflecting distant firelight in a spectacular fashion.

Amid the heated spiritual battles was another intriguing story, one that said a villager named Taranth had found the remains of a great stone and hauled it to a place of safekeeping.

"How did it come to be here?"

"The truth?" Hateri said.

Baraq gazed at him, his central expressing impatience.

"We've had it here since the first expedition."

Baraq's central whipped directly to the councilor. "You've had it here all along?"

"We wanted to study it."

"Likely story."

"But true, nonetheless."

"Whatever you say." Baraq fought a flickering anger. Bureaucracy delays progress, and this was among the more egregious examples. "The end result is still withholding the existence of the stone from the public."

"It's not a worse deal than your family would have given."

In that, Baraq had to admit the councilor was right. His family developed technology and sold it to the highest bidder. It was an ugly field, one that made him uncomfortable every time decisions were made that tied progress to financial rewards. The family was really no better than the council, withholding beneficial inventions until the price was right.

"Why am I here?" Baraq answered.

"Why do you think you're here?"

Baraq thought for a moment. The room hummed with the heavy sound of a floor fan. The lab was empty, he realized. No one was working.

"The thing is obviously a device of some sort."

"True," Hateri replied patiently.

"So, somebody had to make it."

"Again, quite astute."

"You haven't been able to figure out how it works," Baraq said, the truth dawning.

Hateri smiled. "We've made progress, of course. Instructor Geldour-enet and his assistant have learned much about its aerodynamics. The university is working with an advanced heat-bearing composite based on the outer shell's chemistry, and we've got a student developing approaches to power generation based on the system's configuration."

Baraq focused his central on the councilor. "What kind of power systems is he creating?"

"I'm just a politician, Baraq. You'll have to ask someone who understands all that."

"So, what's the problem?"

Hateri sighed hollowly. "The problem is us, Baraq. The council can no longer agree what to do. Jie-Kandor of the Soundt will not accept less than debating where we send each subsystem for study, then he bogs us down with reasons why his sector should do all the examinations. Obala e'Lan of Esgarat thinks that, as the device came from her region, her scientists should be allowed to discover how the device works. The aligned churches want merely to bury it — although the Prime Dias of

Eldoro sees it as proof that the creator exists outside the sky, and is petitioning to use it as an icon for his services."

"And all the while the system sits waiting."

Hateri nodded. "And just as important — every day we lose in determining how it works leaves the people who made this that much further ahead of us."

Baraq gazed at the councilor, sensing something deeper to his comment. "You're afraid of them, aren't you?"

"The council has searched everywhere, Baraq. We thought we knew everything about the world. We thought we had discovered all there is to discover. Now we find a device of mysterious power developed by someone we cannot find. Wouldn't you be afraid?"

"What do you want me to do about it?" Baraq said.

Hateri's pupils gleamed blackly in the room's light. "I can arrange to ship pieces of the device to you. I would expect you to use whatever contacts you think are best for whatever study you undertake. I want you to discover what you can."

The device lay on the table before him. Baraq could almost hear it whisper, luring him, seducing him like rock fates tempting Drath in tales his mother had once told him. Reason spoke inside him, though. The Waganats did not develop technology for any but themselves. It was more than a policy. It was an oath that ran in his family's veins as surely as did their blood. If he took this job, it would cause a rift.

"My family—"

"Your family is there, and I expect you will use your connections wisely. But given what I've said of the politics regarding the device, you see why they cannot participate."

"No, I don't."

"Your family would attempt to control its results and would hold its benefits ransom."

1100 DIGITAL STORIES IN AN ANALOG WORLD

Baraq was taken back. "Why me, then?" he asked.

"You're a good quadarti, Baraq. You care about our people and you respect technology. In that sense you are better than the rest of your family, you know?" Hateri's expression grew serious. "Look at this device. You see what it means, don't you? You see how much we can gain from it."

Baraq never cared for politics. What he loved, what kept him rising from his pallet every morning to work in his grungy little shop, was understanding how things worked. Now Hateri was offering an opportunity to study what was quite possibly the technological discovery of their species' history.

The image of his father flashed into Baraq's mind. He shouldn't do this. But he thought of returning to his shop to face the pile of bills. The Taranth stone lay before him, making his hearts pump blood chilled with acid energy.

"I'm sure we can work something out." The words slipped from his tongue before he realized he had thought them.

***

Hateri left him with the Taranth stone for the rest of the day. Baraq poked and prodded and studied diagrams. He devoured the layout, elegant in its own fashion, trying to understand the minds of the people who did this. The way the wiring ran and looped described them as efficient but generous. The way the system's weight appeared unevenly distributed judged them perhaps a bit hasty in their action. The sharp flavor of knowledge oozed from every component, a taste full of intrigue and fear and flat-out envy.

He considered keeping the study to himself. He wanted to do it, of course. But it was obvious the technology was beyond his capabilities. Hateri had chosen him more for his contacts than his skill — a fact Baraq found he could suddenly live with. The people he chose to work on this would have to be the best in their fields, and they would have to operate under the guideline of silence until the entire effort was finished.

By the end of the day, he knew what he was going to do.

One of the more interesting pieces of technology he could see was a series of smooth-walled chambers connected by necked orifices. The assembly filled the rear of the device. This, Baraq would give to Kaatla Regonar. Kaatla understood engines, and he was pioneering a flying craft of his own, and more important, Kaatla knew how to be silent when the time came.

A box filled with metallic etchings and red, black, and blue wafers would go to Estaut, a friend from his university days who had designed electronic circuits almost from the day he was born.

And finally, Baraq would provide the last item, a package that had been bolted onto a sliding bay door in the Taranth stone's underbelly, to Louratna. Its cylindrical system was made of a white material he had never seen. Inside were more of what he took to be electronics, and a collection of hourglass-shaped components linked like wheel spokes. A cracked light bulb sat in the center, and a twisted ring of tarnished metal wrapped around the wheel's circumference giving the hourglass components bare clearance.

If anyone could figure out what this was, it would be Louratna, an old woman who had taught him more than he could ever truly understand.

***

Eldoro's heat was a red blot on the horizon when Baraq finally went home. The clouds had broken on the dark side of the sky.

Until a year ago, the clouds had been a constant, never changing blanket — light tan and gray in the heated hours and an inky brown in the darkness. The heats of Eldoro and Katon were thought to be just that, massive blobs of energy that floated through the clouds like fish swim in the underground sea. But that changed when the clouds parted.

The first rending was cataclysmic, bringing life to a halt for days as people cowered in their homes. That it occurred in tandem with the melting water from the sky — drops laced with acid that slowly burned through houses, destroyed plants, and ate away flesh with agonizing pain — made the hysteria worse. Tiny Eterdane had been discovered then, a new heat too tiny to burn through clouds but far larger than the other points of light revealed by the parted clouds. And Eldoro and Katon were revealed for their true nature, massive balls of flame behind the curtain of clouds.

Now Eterdane gleamed in the blackness amid hundreds or, if philosophers were right, thousands of other glimmering points. Everything was changing now. Some philosophers were suggesting that perhaps Quadar was the object that moved, not the heats themselves. One thought in particular was that both Quadar and Katon circled Eldoro, giving rise to Eldoro's smooth path in relation to their home, and the more erratic movement of his sister. It was dangerous to put too much weight behind a philosopher's opinions, though. They tended to extrapolate answers from outside of the known, sometimes making claims as wildly unsupported as those of the church. As such, mainstream scientists viewed them with dubious eyes.

Still, Eterdane's appearances drew crowds, and as usual, a gathering stood on a slope of basaltic rock, staring at her with slack-jawed wonder.

"It is a new day, I say. A Holy day," a woman in white robes said from a hastily constructed podium. "Three heats for three hearts. Come with us as Eterdane grows to her rightful place and takes her seat with Eldoro. Be blessed in the growing warmth of our Goddess as she replaces Katon."

Rubbish, Baraq thought, scowling.

He had no place for such misguided hash. That there were three heats had nothing to do with the fact that they had three hearts. The world was hot, and a Quadar's blood was used both to pass oxygen to the body as well as to cool it. Each heart absorbed heat and returned it to the atmosphere via plates on the Quadar's shoulder blades. Everyone knew that. If a single heart failed, the Quadar was more likely to die of heat exposure than of a lack of oxygen.

Still people gathered around the priestess, nodding at her distortions.

These were strange times.

Things were changing, and he understood people trying to grow comfortable with what it all meant. But he couldn't help being upset at opportunism that sprang up so readily. He had heard everything from religious portents like this woman's preaching, to raw environmentalists who screamed of global cooling and oceans of burning acid. Philosophers extrapolated the existence of other worlds and talked of travel to them. Beleaguered scientists, of course, were just trying to figure everything out.

Baraq's money had always been on the scientists.

He glanced at Eterdane. They knew precious little about her. It was a small heat, unable to be observed except during brief moments when the clouds parted in just the right way. But they had been able to ascertain that Eterdane's movement was erratic and similar to Katon's, not circular about Quadar as Eldoro's was. And, the priestess's ranting prophecies notwithstanding, Eterdane seemed to neither grow nor fade.

Baraq was too tired to think about it right now, though. But despite his fatigue, he couldn't stop his mind from filling with images of the device hidden in the council's network of buildings, running with memories of wires and boxes and materials that he had never before seen. For the first time in a very long time, Baraq realized he was humming.

He went straight to the kitchen.

"I'm glad you made it home," Crissandr said. She was seated at their table, reading.

He smiled. "Me, too."

No matter what happened throughout his day, a single word or sometimes merely a glance from Crissandr made things better. She wore a red *haldi*, a robelike dress that clasped at the side. Her central was flecked with green, and her head and face were rounded and perfectly formed, her lips full and graceful in the manner of females.

"There's *havra* and *jaran* in the box."

He pulled his dinner from the retainer. "How long ago did you eat?"

"A while. I was hungry. I'm sorry I didn't wait."

"I'm glad you didn't."

"Working on something important? Or did you just get caught up and lose time?"

He chewed his food, savoring the coarse taste of the *havra*. There was something about Crissandr tonight. Her face crinkled with an anxiety he could spot from paces away.

"What is it?" he asked.

Crissandr put her book down and took one of his hands. Her eyes softened and her irises dilated.

"We're going to have a child, Baraq."

Hara ran toward him, then, her tiny arms outstretched. She jumped, and he caught her, swinging her in the air as she giggled. She had been only six.

"You saw her just then, didn't you?"

Baraq drew a sharp breath. "Yes." He didn't tell her that his next thought was of the family — his father parading over his child's *jahalarat*, overseeing the process of bringing another Waganat into his clutches, looking at the child like the prospective laborer it would certainly be, like another of so many slaves.

"I think it's all right, don't you?"

He closed his eyes, surprised at the crispness of his memories. He could still feel his daughter's tiny body against his chest. She had been dead for over three years. "Not a day goes by that I don't think of her."

"Me, too," Crissandr said, her voice wavering between anxiety and guilt, her central clouding.

When he was younger, he would never have understood the power he had at this moment, the ability to crush his mate with a single word or to raise her up with a mere glance. The muscle over her brow was tight, and her lips were now drawn and bloodless. But hope flooded her primaries, and she held her body upright and forward, bold and proud like a warrior marching.

He nodded and smiled warmly. He kissed her lips, tasting her fear as it slipped away.

"It's better than all right."

Inside, though, his stomach twisted and he felt the clutches of his family name, saw images of Hara, and oddly — so oddly — smelled the arid chill of skies littered with blue-white pinpoints glimmering.

***

The year moved through Divergence — when Eldoro and Katon ruled opposite sides of morning and night — to the Time of Eldoro Leading, when the heat of that God rose early to be chased through the day by his smaller sister.

Crissandr began to show signs of their child.

They did the sacrifices, sixteen bows to the greater heat and eight to the lesser, to ask aid in preparing their home for the child's arrival. They attended a family outing, Baraq cringing when the topic of the *jahalarat* was brought up.

Part of his discomfort was the Taranth stone, of course. He studied it at night when he could slip away, deciding that the next piece of technology he looked at would be a device that appeared to shoot light into another box of electronics. He wanted to talk to someone about it. He wanted to share the wonder of his findings. But his first three experiments were not complete, and he didn't want to stretch himself too thin.

So he waited.

***

He was repairing a wall in his shop when he learned Kaatla Regonar had crashed and died in one of his flying machines.

Kaatla had briefed Baraq on his progress the week before. The system, he said, was designed to push the Taranth stone through the air at great speed. The basic dynamics of the process was similar to, but different from, those that propelled a bullet from a gun: fuel burned in a small compartment exhausted through a nozzle, resulting in a force in the opposite direction. Still, the equations that governed the process remained a mystery, as did anything about what kind of fuel the device used. Kaatla had sent a sample of the inner compartment to a lab for analysis, but had not heard back at the time of their meeting. In the meantime, he was experimenting with his own shaped chambers.

Kaatla's death was a setback, for certain, but Baraq thought nothing strange about it at the time. Kaatla was a risk taker, a trait that made him the inventor he was. He had been working on his flying machine for years, and people had been predicting a broken neck for him for just as long.

But three weeks later, Estaut's mate found Estaut floating in an underground pool.

He, too, had just briefed Baraq, reporting that the wafers seemed analogous to the Quadars' own component-driven electronics, and that microscopic examinations of each component revealed a vast collection of circuitry. He had been able to excite small pieces of the device, but had no way to probe the wafers themselves and did not understand how such a component might be built. The next step would be running studies of the silicon-based material to see if something could be learned from it.

But Estaut was dead the next day.

A cold shiver came over Baraq.

He went to the room where he had heard from both of the now dead scientists. A round table sat in the room's center. He stepped quietly about, looking under the table and chairs, and lifting decorations from the wall. He found what he was looking for behind a rendition of the legend of Eldoro chasing Katon from the sky with bolts of blue lightning.

A wave talker was embedded in the middle of the lower frame rail, placed there so as to avoid throwing the image out of balance. Wires led to thick battery packs in each corner.

Ironic, he thought. The rendition had been one of his personal favorites. Now it was forever ruined.

Two quadars were dead because of him.
And he knew exactly who had done it.

***

"You killed them," Baraq said, controlling his anger.

His father folded his hands over his belly. His face was rounded and jowly, his skin hanging from his cheekbones like molten slides of flesh.

"Why do you say that?"

"Because they both died shortly after briefing me, and because of the talker you have in my office. No one else has wave talkers, Father. I'm sure you understand that."

Some years ago, Jarka'el Waganat, Baraq's cousin a few times removed, had developed a machine that sent and received encoded waves of energy that could be descrambled with an appropriate receiver. It was a monstrous machine that created waves of incredible power. He demonstrated the device by sending a message asking his spouse to make *havra* stew for dinner. The family's fortune had been made through negotiations, and they didn't need schooling to recognize power in the ability to speak rapidly via invisible waves.

In a discussion that raged for weeks, the family decided to keep the wave talker for themselves rather than sell it. They improved it over time, learning to boost power and focus the waves and learning to use higher frequencies where waves could be made to carry voice more readily than the irregular, spark-generated waves of Jarka'el's first machine. They doled out systems when it suited them, using wave talking as bargaining levers for critical contracts and other business advantages.

"You should have known better than to develop technology for the council, Baraq," his father finally replied.

"It was work."

"You should have come to me."

Baraq remained silent.

"We've had this discussion before, Baraq. You have your business because of the family. You have your life, your wealth, and your home because of the family. Don't choose this time to forget that."

I'm drowning, Baraq thought. *As certainly as Estaut did in the caves, I'm drowning.* He was far removed from any real power, but there was nowhere to swim away from the family. He considered, for a moment, telling his father off. He thought of exposing him, going to the public with the existence of this glorious device.

"You will tell Hateri that you can find nothing of worth."

Baraq's stomach dropped. "You know who funds me."

His father gave a nonchalant shrug. "Hateri will be discredited shortly."

"What do you mean?"

"You think the rest of the council doesn't know he's broken from their ranks?"

"You told them?"

"That's what partners do."

The sentence settled fully.

"Does that surprise you?" his father said.

"No. Not really." Baraq's insides tried to rise up and clog his throat. A fire burned over his skin. For much of the past year he had felt alive. He was studying the Taranth stone, doing something important. And for once he was working on his own. At least, he thought he had been. Now he realized once again that he was no more than a sandworm. Useless. Meaningless. Removed from the structure of his family, unable to affect its decisions, unable to break from their clutches, and too weak to buck them.

"How big of a cut do they get in return for laws that keep others at bay?"

His father laughed with a smile full of yellow teeth. "You have grown into a good businessman, Baraq."

"How big?"

"Big enough."

Baraq considered recent events. How much did his father know of Louratna? She did not travel from her home and would not visit his office, so their discussions had been away from the prying wave talker.

"So, two quadars are dead, and you will discredit Hateri."

"Yes."

"What about me?"

"What about you?" His father's eyes were level and unwavering now, their challenge firmly placed. If Baraq let this go, he would live. He could continue to run his shop, continue to go home each day and sleep each night. But the family would protect itself. Wave recorders. Spies. Inspections. He would never know from one moment to the next when someone was watching him. And if he did not let this go, Baraq saw the result in his father's eyes.

The Waganats were not above disposing of their own if need be.

"What will happen to the Taranth stone?"

His father smiled. "Do not fear, Baraq. We will continue the investigation and will bring any useful discoveries to market, just as we always have."

"I understand, Father." And he understood something else, too. His father, he realized, did not know of Louratna's work.

***

Crissandr's belly swelled as the days passed.

Baraq worked in his shop, selling automatic door openers and machines that served food. Each transaction sent money to the family and a slice to the council. With every good sold, Waganat control fueled more Waganat control.

He wanted to contact Louratna. Every day he told himself that he would try, but someone from the family was constantly loitering around his shop, and he told himself that he could not risk causing Louratna a similar fate as Kaatla and Estaut. The truth, though, was that he was more afraid for himself than for Louratna.

Days passed. Katon caught slowly up to her brother, bringing in Convergence, the time when their heats were as close as they would get throughout the year. He walked home under night skies that were cold and occasionally cloudless, and with hearts that were equally empty.

It was on such a night that a dark form stopped Baraq.

"Come with me," it whispered with feminine softness. She grabbed his arm and pulled him along.

Baraq's hearts pounded. "Why? What's going on?"

"No time," the intruder replied fervently. "Come now."

Baraq soon found himself in the small candle-lit cellar of a shop.

"Louratna," he said.

She sat behind a simple table, wearing a headdress of twined *kava* that rested on her knobby head in several places. She looked at him, complete with her unshakable demeanor, as if they were merely sitting together in the middle of the bazaar and not as if he had just been essentially kidnapped.

The device he had given her sat on the table before her.

"Good evening," she replied in the throaty accent of the southern continent.

"I'm sorry I haven't contacted you," he explained rapidly. "But, there have been... complications."

"Complexities are bound to arise."

"What do you mean?"

"What did you suspect when you gave this to me?"
Baraq smiled.

His father would never have brought someone like Louratna into this study. Nor would Hateri have.

Louratna was a mathematician. She had studied in the university under Hunta Askalin, the quadar who had developed an understanding of numbers in an imaginary plane. But she was a philosopher, also, something she had proven to him during long discussions they had held when he was in school, discussions that ranged in topic from simple calculus to Devinian logic and all points in between. Yes, she was subject to the occasional stereotypical bout of a philosopher's overly optimistic enthusiasm for theories other scientists saw as being merely thought experiments. But Baraq had grown to appreciate her wisdom and her reason. It was this combination that had led Baraq to give her the strange mechanism he had found embedded in the heart of the device.

"I wasn't sure what to suspect."

"But you did suspect?"

Baraq nodded.

Louratna pursed her lips, then leveled her gaze. "I think the device rends space."

"Pardon me?"

"I said, I think the box tears a hole in space, connects one place with another."

Baraq laughed, feeling suddenly a bit foolish. Louratna's silent stare made him immediately uncomfortable.

"Why do you say that?" Baraq finally said.

"Dimensional breaks have been mathematically understood for many years."

"No one believes they can exist in the real world, though."

"Experimentalists are often limited by a lack of imagination."

Baraq let the words soak in. "All right. But how do you get there from this?" He waved his hand at the box of wire and hardware.

"I will walk you through it in detail when we have more time. But I'm convinced the system amplifies and funnels energy through its spokes. If enough energy is focused at a single point in space, singularities result."

"Singularities?"

"Holes. Holes in the fabric of the world."

Baraq shook his head. "Of what use is a singularity?"

"A good question," Louratna replied. "But there's another one that comes first."

Baraq hesitated, not wanting to appear stupid. "How much energy would it need?"

"More than we could harness — a great deal more. But that's not the question I had in mind."

"Where would the energy come from?"

"That is the right question." Louratna waited.

"Maybe one of the other systems on the Taranth stone is an energy generator."

"No, Baraq. There's nothing on the craft capable of generating that kind of energy on demand."

"Then I am at a loss," he admitted.

"What is our greatest source of energy? Think about what is happening to our world."

The answer brought him a cold chill, a touch of wrongness, something evil and dire and worrisome at a level that suddenly seemed so large as to be impossible to grasp.

"Eldoro," he said. "The energy source is Eldoro."

Louratna nodded. "Do you now know the answer to your first question?"

"Which was?"

"Why would someone want to open a singularity inside Eldoro?"

"To use it as a source," he said, falling back in his chair and feeling totally overwhelmed. "To take its energy."

Louratna nodded.

Suddenly, it all made sense — the clouds thinning, the melting rain of acid, temperatures dropping so slowly as to be unnoticeable unless looked at over a span of time. Eldoro was dying, its heat being siphoned slowly away. And as Eldoro diminished, their home was changing.

It all made terrible, terrible sense.

***

Baraq's hearts ached as he walked home. The night was crisp. Fresh dew sparkled with a glimmer that he once thought beautiful. He scanned the buildings along the path. People slept in each. People ate, and they joked with their families, and they struggled with making their bills. In between they made more families, and they read books. In the distance, the peaks of the Karash Mountains glimmered with the light of tiny Eterdane.

His stomach churned.

Louratna had talked further — about a great, vast universe, about alien creatures with intelligence and vigor. About Quadar, their world that was dying with no way to save itself, and about other worlds — worlds filled with people with technologies that those here on Quadar could barely imagine.

"You've got to convince your family to work on something that will break the singularity, Baraq," she had said.

Baraq had no reply.

If Louratna was right, the temperature would continue to drop. The clouds would dissipate, and the rain would fall. It may take hundreds of years, maybe thousands, but eventually Eldoro would be spent. But before that happened, the environment of their world would be a far different place, and the people known as Quadarti would almost certainly be long dead.

If Louratna was right, every scientist on his world should be working to find a way staunch the flow of Eldoro's energy through this singularity.

Councilor Hateri, he realized, had been right, too. Another mysterious race of people had made the Taranth stone. But the council would never find them because they were looking in the wrong place.

He stepped into his house.

"Baraq?" Crissandr's voice came from the bed chamber.

"I'm home."

As he shrugged off his coat, grimacing at what the night's chill might mean, a sense of total defeat nearly overwhelmed him. He was getting old. Old and tired. His world was dying. And he was powerless to change anything.

"Are you hungry?" she said from the dark doorway. She leaned against the wall, disheveled from sleep, her rounded belly bulging. "I put dinner in the box for you."

He walked to her and put his arms around her waist, resting his chin on her shoulder. Her smell engulfed him, and the sweet heat of her pregnant body radiated through his chest. For a moment, he saw Hara again and felt the hollow nothingness that she left inside him.

"What's wrong?" she asked after several moments.

He hesitated.

"It's nothing," he finally said.

"Don't do that, Baraq. Something is wrong, and I want to know what it is."

Baraq looked at Crissandr, then. She was his life partner, and they had been through so much. She deserved to know. He slowly walked around the room, lifting pictures and examining likely positions for wave talkers. There were none. Not really surprising, he thought. Waganats were not known for bringing their business home with them, and it wasn't hard to believe his father wouldn't conceive of him talking to his *kalla* about such delicate matters. Besides, his office was unoccupied long enough to ensure the wave talkers could be placed and wired, but no one could guarantee an uninterrupted time span that would be enough to wire his home.

He told her everything as he ate.

He told her about Hateri's request, about the death of two scientists, and about wave talkers and his family and his father. He was surprised how easily the last came, pouring like falls in underground pools, cascading, growing in power as he went, frothing and foaming with pent-up anger.

He explained what Louratna had suggested this evening.

"Your father will never work on the singularity," Crissandr said.

"Never," Baraq agreed. "There's no profit in it. He'll say that Louratna's viewpoint is merely the rantings of a mad philosopher." He couldn't bring himself to voice his concern that his father was just as likely to kill him if he found Baraq was working on such a device.

He sat back heavily in his chair. Beyond all this, another truth gnawed at him. "There is something else, though."

"Yes?"

"The council has had thirty years to work on it, admittedly with poor resources, but thirty years. I've had three of the most experienced people I know working on it for almost an entire year."

"You're worried that we won't be able to learn anything from it?"

"What have we gotten so far? A few theories and something we know is an electrical system, but wouldn't know how to build if Eldoro himself was to appear before us."

"That's a problem," Crissandr said. "But I think you need to face them one at a time."

Baraq said nothing for a long time.

He still had no idea of exactly what he should do, but he felt better. That evening, as he slipped into an unsettled sleep, he draped his arm across the swelling form of Crissandr's belly and held her close.

***

It was his idea. But it was Crissandr who finally convinced him he should do it.

It was grasping at straws — a million-to-one against. And if his father found out, he would certainly kill him. But it was all Baraq could think of that made any sense at all. When he posed the effort to Louratna, she had her people shake him free of his family watch as they had done the night of their conversation.

He stole the generator that had been stored in one of his family's warehouses since the earliest days of the wave talker's development. It was, in fact, the machine Jarka'el Waganat had first used to create waves all those years ago. He selected it specifically because it was so old no one would miss it, because it had been modified to push waves of great power, and also because it worked in the lowest frequencies, spectrums his family no longer monitored. The transmitter tower was built from parts he bought by depleting his accounts.

Louratna's men loaded the material onto a cart and drove them into the vastness of the Castanda desert where the wind was known to be devastating, but where there was also no one to interfere with their work. Two days later, the power system hummed and the wave talker burst into life with electric screeches that set his teeth to rattling. He stayed an additional day, making sure the system was operating, making sure the message was being sent.

We are here. Help us.

It was a simple message, sent in ragged bursts across an arching sweep of space. Louratna ensured there would always be at least two people staffing the transmitter, and that the message would be continually sent.

So Baraq traveled back to his home, back to Crissandr.

The night was clear and cold when he arrived. Crissandr smiled from their bed. One of Louratna's nurses handed him a bundle of brown cloth that swaddled a child.

He took Brada — his newborn son — Into his arms, felt his tiny grip, and listened to his small voice. In a moment's inspiration, Baraq carried his son out into the night and looked into a sky that was vast and clear and sprinkled with glimmering points of light.

There was nothing there, though. Nothing moving that he could see. For maybe the first time in his life, Baraq realized he wasn't sure of anything anymore. He wasn't certain of what he was doing, didn't know how to deal with his family. But mostly, he realized that it didn't matter.

He was who he was.

He had done what he could.

Maybe there wasn't anyone out there. Maybe there was.

Maybe people from other worlds would save them.

Maybe, instead, they would be monsters and arrive only to devour All of the Esgaroth.

Peering into the night, he thought he saw a movement.

Or maybe it was just a trick of his eyes.

RON COLLINS

Holding his son in his arms, and imagining waves that raced through the open sky, he prayed, wondering and wishing.

And hoping.

Ron's Afterword

"The Taranth Stone" was my first full jump into developing a completely different species living in a completely different world. It was a lot of fun. I mean, a lot.

By the end, I could feel the place. Esgaroth was a harsh place. A gritty world filled with a people who are survivors at heart, and are built in family units that are as much functional as they are personal.

I loved them all.

Until then, I hadn't thought a lot about what it meant to build worlds. At that point, I looked at the concept more like I looked at creating a place for the Dungeons and Dragons world that I moderated back in my time in college. For those campaigns I would spend hours putting every element of society in place, and really, I didn't want to do that for a short story. So I didn't. Imagine my surprise when I found out you can world-build in parts, just like you can tell stories in parts.

From the moment I wrote "The Taranth Stone" to the moment I finished book nine (and final) of *Stealing the Sun*, the series that sprang from it, I was constantly discovering new things about the quadars and their world. Oddly, things still fell together well enough that several reviews have complimented the series for the robustness of the world(s) that they, and the multiple humans in the series, inhabit.

Good to know, right?

Parchment in Glass
ANALOG MARCH 2002

Radio waves rose from the surface of a planet in the Alpha Centauri system, cutting through an atmosphere of oxygen and acid to break into the vacuum of space. Four years later the signals reached Martian highlands and fell upon a collection of listening dishes at Kochi Observatory.

At local noon, a program packaged the data and sent it on tight-beam laser to a satellite in near-earth orbit.

***

"I'm too old for this," Torrance thought as he checked his sideburns' trim. Lines and dry patches marred pebbled skin. His crew cut was graying to white. Extending a man's telomeres may double his life but signs of age remained as obvious as rings on a tree stump.

Even his eyes were worn and faded.

It was just past five in the morning. Torrance was in the Kedra Hotel, a high rise that overlooked the western shore of the Potomac River in Crystal City, Virginia. Willim Pinot — the United Governments Intelligence Officer — expected him at 0700. He still hadn't had breakfast.

He sighed ran a brush over his scalp.

The UGIO had been vague about the agenda, and no matter how often Torrance played the game, politics always left him uneasy.

He stepped back and yanked his blue dress jacket to the side. His buttons were aligned, his shoulders square. He was seventy-one — no longer the slender kid from *Everguard* — but he still presented the uniform with a bit of dignity. If he ever did decide to do something rash like retire, he would miss the uniform as much as anything else. He strapped his personal comm system over his forearm, punched up his temperature and blood sugar, and glanced at the time.

That was when he first noticed the red icon flashing.

***

The process ran every night.

It started at a Very Large Array spread over the three hundred square kilometers of Martian surface that comprised Kochi Observatory. Each day Kochi compressed data and transmitted it to a receiver in Earth orbit, which then split the signal and forwarded it to several destinations — one being a computer in an office just north of Milwaukee, Wisconsin. There, Torrance's program stored Kochi's data in overlapping fifteen-minute segments and compared these fresh radio emissions to stored files of noise *Everguard* had recorded during its last mission.

To Torrance the *Everguard* files were important. They were hand-inked parchment in green bottles floating on the currents of the most massive sea known to man, words sent from unknown people who lived on Alpha Centauri A's second planet. No one else shared his opinion, of course. Eden — his compatriots pointed out — was a poisonous place where life could not exist, a fact proven by every remote study ever undertaken.

He was, of course, shackled by his reluctance to release the *Everguard* noise data. If it became known that the mission had launched wormhole pods despite the possibility that life might exist on the planet, the entire command structure would be exposed to executive review. Torrance was loyal. His commanders were good people. They made a decision that opened the galaxy to the human race. He may, in fact, have made the same decision if he had been in their shoes.

Still...

Too much of his life was tied up in these files. He had commanded shipboard systems and weaponry aboard *Orion*, served as the mission officer for Ceta, the first colony in the Cassiopea Eta system, and advised the five Delta Pavonis colonies. Yet, he always returned to the files. They consumed his soul. Letting the issue of life on Eden drop within the scientific community did not mean Torrance had to give up. So he gathered data from Kochi, and he wrote a program—a simple routine, really, a correlation algorithm that looked for similarities between the Everguard files and Kochi's radio signals.

Now the icon was flashing on his personal comm system.

***

Bypassing breakfast, Torrance accessed his home unit. The screen changed to a familiar interface panel. He pulled reports and examined Kochi extracts. Data filled the screen. Automatic sorting routines charted key graphs. The passage of time faded to a blur. An hour later Torrance sat on the edge of his bed, deliriously dizzy.

The correlation was solid — full-spectrum frequency matches in nearly every frame.

The world was suddenly small but expansive, understood but unfathomable. It would take weeks of hard work to make the data presentable, but Torrance understood a truth massive like a block of granite — a truth that had eluded human beings since time itself.

Life existed outside the solar system.

His heart burst. He wanted to cry, wanted to hug someone, wanted to run into the streets and shake people by the shoulders or kiss them on the cheeks or just hold them tightly and howl at the sky like the crazy old men on Arazorn.

He wanted ... well. Mostly he just wanted to tell someone.

But the room was empty and quiet.

The heating system kicked on. The bed sat unmade, sheets wadded and rumpled at the foot. He rubbed his eyes and closed his system. His lips were dry and parched. He glanced at his watch. Forty-five minutes to get to Pinot's office.

He picked up his hat from the dresser and checked the mirror. Crisp. He smiled and gave himself a salute.

Politics be damned, there wasn't a thing in the world Willim Pinot could tell him today that would get him down.

***

He took the underground walkway to the monorail transfer and got off at Arlington.

The bioscanner allowed him to take the purple line from there.

This was Wilson Cross — a shelter dug deep under the eastern foothills of the Appalachian Mountains, a place where every door warranted a security code and every wall was made of reinforced concrete lined with radiation-hardened composites. His lighthearted mood gave the process of navigating checkpoints a feeling more like playing secret agent than its usual baggage of paranoid scrutiny.

Everything seemed so real — the smell of his escort's boot polish, the echoes of footsteps in the underground hallway, the dryness of cool air, the escort's name spelled in clean white letters on a black badge: Davies. The corridors were tight and brightly lit, the walls painted standard-issue beige. Image projectors at regular intervals gave the area a professional flare. Even the metallic clangs of tri-level stainless-steel security doors could not dampen his spirits.

They came to a doorway. A crimson laser flashed his optic nerve. The door slid open.

"Good morning, sir," Torrance said as he stepped forward.

The door closed.

"Good morning, Captain," Pinot answered in a graveled voice, motioning to a padded blue chair without looking up from his desktop screen. "Have a seat."

Willim Pinot was arguably the most powerful man in the solar system. He had Asia somewhere in the distant recesses of his ancestry. Black eyes sat hard and firm above rounded cheekbones like a pair of polished marbles, his nose upturned and flattened. A scraggly, gray-laced goatee grew in a sprawl around his lips. His shirt was white and open one button at the collar. It was early, yet already rings of sweat darkened the area under his armpits.

Torrance sat while Pinot marked something on his screen.

Pinot's dress coat hung from a rack in the far corner. Paperwork cluttered his desktop. The leather chair squealed as the UGIO put his stylus down, sat forward, and clasped his hands together.

"Can Tailor get you coffee?"

"That would be good, thank you."

Pinot spoke to the computer. "Coffee, please. Sugar." He paused and looked at Torrance. "Cream?"

Torrance shook his head.

"No cream."

Pinot smiled. "I suppose you wonder why you are here."

"The question has crossed my mind."

"I need you to kill a man."

"Sir?"

"You heard me."

"But ..." Torrance squirmed in his chair. "I'm not an assassin."

"Correct." Pinot nodded matter-of-factly. "You are a scientist — an engineer, actually, but close enough for government work, eh?"

Torrance frowned.

"I am in the unique spot, you see, of needing someone who is both a scientist and an assassin. Since there is no time to train an assassin to be a scientist, I think it wiser to go the opposite direction. Don't you agree?"

"I ... guess so," Torrance heard himself say.

The door opened and Tailor, Pinot's administrative assistant, entered with a coffee service.

An edgy Colombian aroma filled the room. The sound of liquid flowing over china was ritualistic in the silence. Pinot motioned Tailor to ignore his teacup in lieu of the double-sized mug on his desk.

Tailor left. The door closed.

Torrance lifted a cup and cradled it in his palm. The china was thin — the coffee warmed it quickly. He sipped, blowing briefly to avoid scalding. He wished he had eaten something.

"The World Council on Wormhole Physics is being held next week," Pinot said simply. "You will attend, and you will kill Emil Pentabill."

"If I refuse?"

Pinot gulped his coffee, then set his mug amid loose paper on his desk. "Neither of your ex-wives will care one way or the other, I'm sure — God knows I can vouch for the disinterest of ex-wives. I know you're not really close to your daughters, but surely they need their old man around, don't you think?"

Torrance squeezed his lips into a tight line. He loved Cassie and Mercy. But something had always gotten in the way while they were growing up — a conference to attend, or a seminar to facilitate. There was a war on, after all.

Men were dying.

There had never been enough time. He lost Marisa, his second wife, just as he had lost Adrienne before her. And he was gone while his daughters went from crawling to kindergarten to high school.

He had never felt like a very successful family man.

Pinot's threat, however, was clear and direct. Kill or be killed.

"I've known Oscar for years," Torrance said, calling Pentabill by his preferred name. "Why Pentabill?"

"The man is a confirmed traitor."

"I find that very hard to believe."

"Yet still true."

Torrance shook his head.

"You want evidence?" Pinot pointed to a brown data cube on the corner of his desk.

Torrance picked it up. The cube was small, its edges sharp and prickly.

"Read it at your leisure."

"What's on it?"

"Proof that Universe Three got to him years ago — before, even, your cruise with *Everguard*. Standard espionage stuff. Find a source, start early and small until they're hooked, then raise the ante. By the end, Pentabill sold them the star drive, several exotic matter-manufacturing techniques — specifically including solutions to throat tensors I might add — and, of course, Kransky-Watt."

Torrance grimaced outwardly.

Kransky and Watt were the first to demonstrate that the kinetic flow of a star's energy could be fed back into a wormhole's gate fields, thereby providing traversable stability. The throat tensors were needed to understand and build the most critical juncture in the wormhole system. It was this technology that had allowed them to draw energy from the interior of Alpha Centauri A to power star drive engines, and hence open up the galaxy to faster-than-light travel.

Universe Three was a terrorist organization — led by Casmir Francis, a flashy man now in his mid-fifties with a bold countenance and a slick delivery. The media portrayed him as ruthless, direct, and intelligent. People were drawn to his charisma, his passion, and the sound bite that had become the mantra of the entire U3 movement: "We will die only for those things we believe in. And we believe in the universe."

Without the information Pentabill had sold, Universe Three could not have developed their own wormholes. Without those wormholes, Francis could not have sustained a galaxy-faring fleet. And without a galactic-faring fleet, he could not have waged the war that had killed so many young men and women over the past three standard decades.

"Oscar is a very bright man," Torrance said.

"All the more reason to make an example of him."

"And you think I can attend the council without arousing suspicion in advance of the strike."

"A good assassin blends in."

"You're overestimating my status considerably."

Pinot gave a sarcastic huff. "You are no longer one of the scientific elite, Captain. If you ever were. I know this." He raised a pointed index finger. "But this is an advantage for you. Your compatriots will accept your attendance, but will keep you at arm's length. It should be quite easy for you to fade into the woodwork at an appropriate time."

Pinot's straightforward dissection of his standing stung.

He had gained celebrity within the scientific community as officer of record in setting the first wormhole. But when his passion for the idea of life on Eden was unearthed he found himself shunned cleanly and coldly. Nothing, it seems, ostracizes a man so fully as thinking outside the accepted.

"So I'm a Trojan horse?" Torrance said. "A wolf in sheep's clothing?"

"Trojan horse," Pinot said as he rubbed his goatee. A smile creased his cheeks with a series of abstract folds that made him look like a washed-out coconut. "That is good."

Torrance drank coffee and put the cup back on the tray. The liquid ate the lining of his stomach. The concept of killing in cold blood was suddenly very real. The coffee did not help his dry throat.

"I can't do it," he said. The pleading quality in his voice made him feel weak and somehow ashamed.

"Men are always capable of more than they think."

"It's not like that," Torrance lied too quickly. "I'm not afraid of it. I have a new project I need to look into."

"Really? I reviewed your assignments with Admiral Cash yesterday. She made no mention of new projects."

"It's..." Torrance looked at Pinot. The UGIO was enjoying himself. He was a fisherman who had set his hook, playing the game, letting Torrance run but keeping the line taut.

"Admiral Cash doesn't know about it," Torrance finally said.

"Then it cannot be important."

"Only the discovery of a new life-form."

Pinot sat back in his chair. "We're not going through this again, are we?"

"I've confirmed cohesive signals from Eden. No mistaking them."

"Don't waste my time, Captain."

Torrance clenched his jaw.

Their meeting was done.

The words *you can't make me do it* nearly came off his tongue. But that was wrong. Willim Pinot's entire career was about making people do things they wouldn't normally do. The parameters of his choice lay before him. Torrance looked across the table and saw confidence and certainty unyielding like an undertow.

Kill or be killed.

As he prepared for bed later that night, Torrance tried to convince himself that his decision to take the assignment hinged on the belief that he had more to do in life, that it was the only way to save Eden. But Torrance had never been very good at shielding himself from what he truly thought.

In the end it all boiled down to the simple fact that he was afraid to die.

***

A week after meeting with the UGIO Torrance found himself on Florecer, the innermost planet of the Cygni B system — a tiny type-K star some twelve light years from the solar system. He sat in the convention center conference auditorium, glancing nervously across the way at Oscar Pentabill. The chairs were large and cushioned, arranged in elevated circles around a central podium. The configuration made the conference feel more like a political debate than a scientific gathering—a fact that brought him a sardonic smile as he sipped chilled water and listened to scientists from around the galaxy argue.

"Alpha Centauri is going to run out of energy, and we've got to find a way to keep the spacecraft attached to it flying."

"It was supposed to last ten thousand years."

"That assumed the star fueled only a single spacecraft."

"So, we're supposed to trust the government this time, too?"

"Don't be an extremist, Vlad. The original estimate also assumed seventy percent flow conversion. Reality is closer to twenty-five."

"That's because Kransky-Watt is so horribly wasteful."

"The truth is their fault?"

"Would you suggest the missions not be flown, and the war lost?"

"There's the problem, then, isn't it?" Selene Runn said.

Heads nodded.

Torrance sat quietly, watching. Nothing positive was coming from the discussion but, ironically, he felt the bittersweet tingle of healing. He did not want to feel better right now. His assignment was cowardly and vile. It sat in his gut like cold oatmeal. It would change him forever, but he felt something important as he watched this bickering. This was only a stage, a place where names came to rub elbows with other names. Hermann, Yang, Jacob — pick a name, they were here.

But no truth was being discovered at this conference. No science was being performed. Science was done in labs and behind consoles. Science, at its core, was an endeavor one undertook in isolated groups, developing results to bring back to the entire community for review. It was the way of the world — the way of history. Bring hard data and you change the world. Bring ideas and you create spaghetti.

Now Torrance had data.

Late at night, between the seemingly never-ending briefings and training programs UGI agents had been stuffing into his head, he had been working to package information about the most recent Alpha Centauri emissions into a presentable paper. The effort left him tired and drained. His stamina dropped off earlier in the evenings than it once did, and he had not progressed as far as he wanted. But it was good work, and he was proud of it.

Most current estimates said that Alpha Centauri A would remain viable for something short of four hundred years.

It was all enough to make him sick.

But at least he was doing something about it. He was no longer certain he could say that about this collection of people he once thought of as friends.

"No." A wavering voice came amplified through the PA. "That is not the problem at all."

The room shuffled nervously as Fredric Parson stood on rickety knees, gripping a brown cane. His back was bent like a hook. His pate was bald and mottled.

Dr. Parson was 148 years old and living on his last telomere extension. He had been a leading figure in the development of the earliest wormhole models, and it was well known that Kransky wouldn't have gotten as far as he had if Parson hadn't solved the initial riddle that led to the confirmation of material with negative mass. In this way, Fredric Parson was, perhaps, the father of the wormhole.

"We are missing the forest for the trees, my friends. The problem has little to do with spacecraft. The problem here is that as we drain away fusing material, we leave the trash behind. It's only a matter of time before energy released by the star's fusion engine will be unable to resist the star's gravity. When that happens, Alpha Centauri will collapse under its own weight."

"Then we get a supernova," Kalista McKenna interjected.

Scientists across the room rolled their eyes to the ceiling as McKenna stood up. The young woman from Colorado University was brilliant, but she didn't know when it was best to be quiet. The membership had given her leeway for two years, but their patience was drawing to an end. Now McKenna stood like a corporate martyr in her white business dress with a scarf of pink and purple showing tastefully from her collar.

"That's a fanciful notion, Kalista," Parson replied. "Centauri A, however, is similar to our own sun. It will not go supernova."

"A star reacts differently when its mass is in flux."

"All theoretical."

"As is everything we do in this field — theoretical science backed up by computer simulations. I have a new solution that indicates pressure waves caused by transient masses act as pseudo mass. At the rate we're tapping Alpha Centauri A, its effective mass will rise dramatically. Alpha Cen will go supernova. The only question that remains unsolved is whether we'll get a black hole or a neutron star in its place."

The sound of clearing throats reverberated.

Chairs rocked backward.

Torrance nearly snickered aloud at the level of discomfort around the room. Admittedly, McKenna's idea was brash and most likely wrong. But it was also new and unexpected. Torrance could not help but delight in the ripples the mere suggestion caused this gathering of scientific minds. For the first time, Torrance was actually glad he had come to the council.

Parson's reed thin voice echoed throughout the center. "All we can really say is that never before have we had an opportunity to learn about this type of an event. We need to prepare. We need to push for new programs and more funding."

"Hear, hear."

A smattering of low-voiced conversations ensued. Torrance thought they were preparing to move to the next item on the agenda, which was to be a review of the less-than-glorious results of the Newton project.

"What if our fanciful friend is correct?" Benaj Ritta from Mars Colony Kasbian said. "A supernova so close to the solar system would be a catastrophe."

"Blast it, man! There will be no supernova!"

Torrance sighed and sat back to wait out the next cycle of the argument.

He glanced across the chamber.

Emil "Oscar" Pentabill sat quietly in a suit that matched the wiry gray of his hair, listening and not adding to the conversation. He sipped from a white mug, jotted a note or two into his comm system, and glanced around the room, pausing only momentarily to stare at the conversation.

Why? Torrance asked himself.

What would motivate a man of science turn his back on the people he worked for? What could take him over the edge of destroying everything with a single decision? The questions angered him. The whole thing was Pentabill's fault, after all. It was Oscar Pentabill's activity that had resulted in Torrance's assignment.

But Pentabill was not answering Torrance's questions.

***

The hotel hallway stretched ahead like a launch tunnel. The carpet was green and black with checkered patterns. Torrance looked for room 1512. Downstairs, the reception was beginning — cocktails and hors d'oeuvres at six, dinner at seven, and an informal presentation on FTL aging patterns at nine.

Pinot's agents had given Torrance more details about Pentabill than he felt comfortable knowing. Oscar had been married for twenty-three years but had no children. He was a quiet man who avoided the limelight. His habit at such gatherings as this was to eschew social drinks for quiet time with a martini and a trade magazine. He would arrive for dinner a fashionable five minutes late, eat a vegetarian plate, and play with his dessert. Then he would excuse himself to turn in.

The number 1512 stood out in relief against the door.

Torrance pulled a magnetic locksmith from his jacket. The glass vial in his pocket was solid against his thigh. Bionites swam in its clear liquid, ugly critters — creepy crawly things half organic, half machine designed to systematically attack a man's nervous system then dissociate into the cellular realms of his biology.

Torrance palms were clammy.

The scent of fear mixed with the dry odor of the door's latex paint.

The locksmith clicked against the wall. The processor spun numbers. Flickering digits fell into place. Torrance turned the knob.

The room was beige and yellow — bathroom to the left, bedroom large and comfortable. A Netvision rumbled from the far wall. Sheer inner drapes fluttered in the breeze of the open sliding door. The city splayed over the horizon below, a dirty tapestry of gray and blue as Cygni set on the opposite side of the hotel. Pentabill sat on a chair facing the city, his legs propped against the banister. The drapes obscured his shoulders and head. An iced drink sat on a knee-height table — a martini, complete with a local dashtar fruit skewered on a green swizzle. A portable reader lay propped on his lap.

The door shut with an audible click.

Oscar peered around the drapes, his expression more confusion than fear. A nested mat of his hair caught in the breeze.

"Torrance," he said jovially, collecting his drink and standing.

Pentabill must have seen something on Torrance's expression because he froze, one hand on the doorway's frame, the other dropping the reader mechanically to his side. His shoulders slumped. He was tall and slim, probably an athlete when he was a kid.

He swayed as if the drink was not his first.

Torrance put his hand in his pocket. The vial was cold and smooth, its cap small and ridged. The automatic hypo would react to sudden pressure. The injection would be quick and nearly painless.

"I'm sorry it's you, Torrance."

Pinot's evidence left no doubt that Oscar was guilty. He had to know it was only a matter of time before the United Governments would strike back.

"Why did you do it, Oscar?"

Pentabill's hand shook as he drank. "It's worse than you think."

"What do you mean?"

"Universe Three."

"Yes?"

Pentabill smirked, and tossed the newsreader onto the bed.

Torrance gave him time.

"Do you ever notice how we talk about decisions in the name of organizations — but organizations never make decisions."

"I understand that."

"I thought Casmir Francis would lead us in the right direction, but he's no better than the rest."

"What are you talking about, Oscar?"

Pentabill waved his drink around. "Doesn't matter, I suppose. Dead men tell no tales, eh?" He chuckled to himself and glanced at Torrance with an impish grin. "I did it, Torrance. Everything. Kransky-Watt. Exotic material."

"Tell me something I don't already know."

"I sold them Newton."

Anxiety was a moth under Torrance's breastbone. Pinot's cube said nothing about Newton. "Why would they want a failed program?"

Oscar pointed a bony finger. "UG would be best served to not underestimate Universe Three. Bright folks there—some of the best. Catazara went to their side, you know? He did you one better, too. Figured out how to set a remote link. It's trial and error, but within a probability range U3 can create and destroy wormholes anywhere they want."

"You're kidding me," Torrance said.

Oscar's response was a wry curl of his lip and a shake of his head.

This meant Universe Three was ahead of the game. The star drive gave human beings the ability to travel faster than light. But remotely configurable wormholes would provide the ability to instantaneously step from, say, the Cassiopeia system where Casmir Francis was rumored to keep his home base, directly to, for example, Earth. And nothing could keep him from bringing along an army of an additional ten thousand men.

"Are you sure?"

"It's not reliable, yet. But I've seen the work." Pentabill took a slug from his drink. His face was shadowed and drawn. He looked tired.

"There's more, isn't there?"

"Black holes." Pentabill's knuckles became white around his glass. "It took a few tries, but Castenades has planted the end of a wormhole in the middle of a black hole."

"Holy Mother of God."

"The other end is going into Alpha Centauri A."

Torrance was taken totally aback. "I don't understand."

"He's trading spacecraft. Alpha Centuari fuels ten spacecraft. *Icarus*, and nine UG craft. Kill the star, kill the spacecraft. Simple math."

Icarus was one of the spacecraft involved in the Cassiopeia incident, the event where the Universe Three rebellion first manifested itself. They had captured *Icarus*. A year later, powered by Oscar Pentabill's treachery, U3 was a bonafide wormhole power.

"It could be worse than that, too, right?" Torrance said. "The physics of that configuration gets calculated as if the black hole were actually inside the star, and we have no way of knowing the mass of the black star Universe Three is connecting to Alpha Centauri. A massive black hole so close to the solar system could be dangerous."

"Like I said — no better than the rest." Pentabill breathed through his nose. "The world protects its own, though, Torrance. I used to believe Francis truly wanted the holistic world he talks about. But he's just another card sharp. When U3 activates the trigger, every United Governments spacecraft attached to the star will be destroyed. Who knows what's next? But one thing I do believe with all my being is that Casmir Francis will deserve whatever happens to him."

The handle to the door jiggled. Oscar's face went pale.

"Who is it?" Torrance asked him.

Oscar looked at Torrance with a pallbearer's grimace. This was a man putting his burden down and accepting his fate, and Torrance found the expression made him angry in a place down deep inside.

"Do me a favor?" Oscar said. "If you get a chance, tell Glory I love her."

The door swung open. A man wearing waiter's white blew past Torrance and collided with Pentabill. Oscar grunted. His glass smashed against the wall with the smell of gin. The man was big and quick — maybe juiced. He lifted Pentabill in stride and rushed to the balcony.

Oscar disappeared over the edge.

He did not scream. Did not even speak.

Torrance anticipated the thick sound of a body hitting the ground, but the impact was not audible.

"You're with Universe Three?" Torrance asked.

The waiter looked up. He was maybe twenty, with brown hair and an angular face. He flexed his hands, bent, and reached toward his pants leg where Torrance could see the bulging shape of a weapon.

Torrance kicked. The waiter pivoted away and Torrance's foot crashed against the bed railing. His momentum carried him. His body twisted, losing balance, bouncing off the mattress and sprawling to the floor with a lung-crushing thud.

The waiter spun and locked onto him.

The gun was small—a laser weapon with charge enough for two or three good shots.

Torrance raised one hand.

Kalista McKenna, he thought.

Supernova. It was the only idea he had.

"If you kill me, U3 will be making a big, big mistake."

"Tell it to the bosses."

"Let me."

"What?"

"Take me to your bosses, and let me tell them about the mistake."

The waiter put his gun against Torrance's forehead.

"My name is Torrance Black. I'm a scientist from the Newton project. U3 is working without critical information. If you do what the man you just tossed off the edge of the world said you're going to do, U3 is liable to blow away most of the civilized galaxy."

The agent's face was impassive. The weapon's muzzle was cold against the front of Torrance's skull. He hoped his bluff was convincing enough.

"I can't leave you splattered here anyway."

Torrance released a breath he didn't know he was holding. He knew a bit of how this game was played.

Soon the nets would carry headlines about Oscar Pentabill's suicide. Another body in the room would ruin that story line.

"Get up and let's go."

Torrance complied, straightening his pants and jacket as he went through the doorway.

The hallway was still quiet. Their footsteps were heavy against the carpet. The waiter strode behind Torrance, the fabric of his pants rasping with each stride.

They came to the elevator.

"Get in slow. Understand? No collateral."

Torrance nodded. "I understand."

The doors opened. Four people stood in the compartment. The doors were burnished bronze, reflecting images as blobs of color. The air smelled of humid carpet and light cleanser. The waiter edged behind him, the blunt point of the weapon like a fist against his kidney. They stopped on the tenth and took on another passenger. Two more on the third-floor mezzanine.

Sweat pooled on Torrance's brow.

What should he do when the doors opened? Should he run? Should he turn and punch?

How many people could die with a random laser shot?

The doors opened.

"Left," the man said quietly into his ear. The lobby was large and open, but still crowded. "Outside." He walked across the pavilion. An automatic door opened as they approached the exit. The air at ground level was hot and stagnant. A gravcar pulled up and the back door opened to reveal a man in a business suit. Torrance could not see his face, but his hand showed another laser. "Get in," the waiter said.

Torrance didn't hesitate.

The door slammed. The man was slim and smelled of soap. His hair was long and tied tightly behind his head. He reached across the bench seating.

A pinprick burned on the back of Torrance's hand. His world went dark.

***

Somewhere in the deep swirl of dreams, Torrance decided that the question is not whether or not God plays dice. The question is what game he plays.

***

"Welcome to *Icarus*, Captain Black." The voice was distant and vaguely feminine.

"Wha—"

Bright light stabbed his temples.

His eyes burned.

A row of fluorescent lights lined the ceiling, ringed with halos of silver and blue. A pallet was hard against his back. Shadows with human form glided through his vision, shifting light like a kaleidoscope.

He was hungry.

Icarus? Why was that name familiar?

The man. A laser weapon. A car. Oscar Pentabill falling.

He took a full breath. Oxygen refreshed his body. Memory returned. Blinking brought things into better focus. A man in a blue medical uniform stood against the wall. A woman with auburn hair sat in a chair beside the bed.

"Get yourself cleaned up," the woman said, standing. "I'll order you something to eat."

The man leaned forward to read numbers from the monitor over Torrance's head. A guard came into focus on the opposite side of the room. The woman turned to the man in blue. "I'll report he's awake. Make sure he is presentable."

"Aye, ma'am," he replied.

***

Water rushed over him. The smell of soap was something normal to hold on to. The warm sting against his chest and shoulders made him feel human. He was stiff and sore, and the water brought him simple comfort.

Icarus was a carbon copy of *Orion*, a ship Torrance had toured with for three years. The two were among the first star drive spacecraft ever designed, each built in cookie-cutter fashion to save cost and development time. They had been made with maintenance in mind—with service nodes placed at key junctures on every level. Each node provided access to the systems command center through sleek, holographic interfaces, the first to utilize such controls.

If Alpha Cen A was going to be tied to a black hole, he was sitting on a ghost ship.

He wrapped the towel around his waist and stepped into his quarters. His clothes were gone, replaced by a pile on the foot of the bed. The pants were baggy and gray, tied in front with a drawstring. The shirt was blue polyfiber that hung below his hips.

Breakfast was cornbread and freeze-dried apricots in the officer's mess. A carafe of coffee sat in the middle of the table. An armed guard stood outside.

The food did wonders for the clarity of his mind.

"Good morning."

Torrance sat up straighter.

The woman was middle-aged — no more than sixty — with yellow blonde hair and a dark complexion that spoke of Latin heritage. She wore black trousers and a zippered sweatshirt with the Icarus logo sewn into the left breast. She was thin to the point of frailty. Her eyes were watery blue with dark half-moons beneath. Her lips turned down at the corners.

He took a swig of coffee and wiped nonexistent crumbs from the corner of his mouth.

The woman took a seat across from him. "I understand you have something you want to tell us?"

"I haven't decided whether to tell you or not."

"Choose your game carefully, Captain. Personally, I don't believe for a second that you have anything useful to say. And I resent the acrobatics we went through to rendezvous with you. But some people think you know something. They think you might actually be able to prove we're making a mistake. And unlike the United Governments, U3 actually cares about the galaxy."

"Sure you do. You care just enough to put a black hole right in the solar system's neighborhood."

"The solar system is not the galaxy, Captain. Besides, the people of the solar system will have quite a bit of time to find someplace else to go."

"But what if they like where they live?"

"Then they can stay until the end."

Torrance stared with disbelief at the woman. "Who are you?"

"I am Katriana Martinez, first officer on *Icarus*. More relevant at this point, I am responsible for forming the black hole link."

"I see."

"And you are Torrance Black, captain in the United Governments Space Force and one of the chief engineers on the Newton project."

"Your data is good."

"You have two ex-wives and a pair of daughters: Mercedes, who is currently stationed in a cryo research lab on Europa, and Cassandra, who graduates this spring from Canal University with a degree in accelerated-growth bioprosthesis. Your first marriage failed at least in part due to certain—" She paused and raised her eyebrow. "— deficiencies. Due to these same deficiencies both daughters from your second marriage are adopted. They both tell you they live alone. Cassie is actually holed up with another young woman who is studying multidimensional mathematics. Mercedes is preparing to get married, and has been living off and on with the man of her choice."

A chain reaction of images clouded Torrance's mind. Mercy was getting married, and Cassie — who had always had such a painful shyness about her — had someone special in her life. Why hadn't they told him? He never thought he was overbearing about such things. Maybe that was the problem.

Martinez's stare was filled with accusatory sternness.

She reached into a sweatshirt pocket and set a small vial on the table before her. It was the bottle Torrance had taken to Oscar Pentabill's room. Cold light from the ceiling reflected from its surface. Martinez put it on its side. It made a hollow sound as she rolled it from hand to hand.

"Do you know what's in here?"

Torrance shrugged, trying not to concentrate on the shiny bottle of microsized death.

"Bionites, Captain Black."

"Really?" Torrance said with innocence.

Martinez was having none of it.

"Are you threatening me?" Torrance said.

"I don't need to threaten you, Captain. You're already a dead man."

Torrance stared quizzically at her.

"You've surmised that *Icarus* will be destroyed when the black hole is set."

"Yes."

"What you don't understand is that *Icarus* has been given the honor of actually creating the link itself. We are nearing launch now."

"We're in the Centauri system?"

"Yes."

"I thought you could set links remotely."

"We can."

"Then why send Icarus?"

The first officer smiled. "I'm the one asking questions. You gave us a cryptic warning about blowing up half the galaxy. I want to know what you've got."

Torrance thought of Oscar Pentabill. He had said U3 could set links in any location they wanted to within a ring of probability. But…

"You can't control the mechanism yet," Torrance replied. "Your remote capability is fine when you have enough space to cast about. But now that you've got a black hole attached to one end, you can't afford to drop the other end willy-nilly, can you?"

The intensity of Martinez's gaze let him know he was right. "Doesn't matter either way, does it?"

"So, you'll set a link like *Everguard* did."

"Almost."

"What do you mean, almost?"

Martinez's entire face lit up in a maniacal smile. "Icarus herself will be part of the final mission."

"I'm not sure I …"

Sudden understanding made his skin contract. He sat, staring dumbly at the ship's first officer. "You're going to set the pods by flying *Icarus* into the star."

"It fits our sense of poetry."

Torrance stared at the glass vial Martinez was still rolling on the table. *Who was this woman?* he thought. What had her life been that she was willing to give it away so freely?

"*Icarus* is not designed to withstand the heat of a star's core like the pods are. We would burn up before reaching the proper trigger point. But the ship will get sucked into the wormhole as soon as the pods are activated anyway. So we'll get as close as we can before we launch."

"Launching from that close should reduce your probability of error," Torrance said.

Martinez grew smug. "This might be a good time to talk to me, you see, because if you are bluffing you will die with us and disappear into so many particles blowing on Centauri's solar wind."

She held the vial still with the fingertips of one hand.

"Besides that, U3 has operatives on every inhabited station around the galaxy — specifically including Europa and Mars. It would be a tragedy if a vial just like this dropped into a young woman's breakfast cereal." She paused, rolling the vial once. "If you have something to tell us, now might be a good time."

He set his jaw.

He had nothing to tell them that they hadn't heard at the conference, but this was no longer a simple game. He had to do something to stop this mission. There was no other answer. He had to disrupt the launch, and he had to destroy their communications system before Martinez could give any order in regard to his daughters.

The first step, though, was to get out of here.

He looked at the vial. It still had its injection cap.

Torrance waited until the vial was in mid roll.

He lunged.

Martinez's fingers tightened, but the vial slipped away, wobbling and clattering across the white tabletop. Four hands scrabbled after it as it dropped over the edge. It hit the floor with a solid thunk. Torrance leapt from his chair and grabbed it. He followed his motion, standing and wrapping an arm around Martinez's waist. He turned the vial in his hand and put the injector to her neck.

His elbows and hand ached with the pressure of his grip. The room seemed to suddenly contract. "I want out of here."

"This is a mistake, Captain."

"Let's go," he said, prodding her with his hip. "Now!"

"Where?"

He thought.

"Pod Engineering."

***

As they stepped toward the doorway, the enormity of what he was doing closed in on him with the crushing weight of the ocean.

He had always heard that a man's life flashes before him when he is about to die. Torrance saw images of Cassie and Mercy. Fresh-faced, clear-skinned men and women marching into battle cruisers. A star exploding, burning tracers of plasma spiraling into vacuum like twisted arms of jellyfish under Europan seas. He saw Alexandir Romanov, his captain from *Everguard*. Admiral Hatch, the man in command who had never known the risk he had taken in ordering a wormhole set.

And he saw Eden, a cloud-covered planet floating in this same churning sea like a long-lost island overgrown and ugly, unworthy of second thought.

***

The door slid open.

The guard glanced over her shoulder.

Torrance pulled Martinez closer and pushed past, holding the vial to her neck. "One step and she's dead."

The woman raised her weapon. She was young, with dirty-blonde hair and round brown eyes. Red energy flared. The odor of fried brains and scorched hair was everywhere at once, and Martinez's body was dead weight in his arms. Torrance's gaze went to the metallic muzzle of the weapon that had just put a fist-sized hole in the first officer's forehead.

The guard gave a gap-toothed grin. She was short, with smooth muscles that showed through her uniform. Her face was set and hard, his eyes showing humor at Torrance's confusion.

"I told 'em again and again there weren't no reason to play your game," the guard said.

Torrance dropped Martinez's body, tore the lid off the vial, and held it like a knife. "Do you know what this is?"

"I don't care."

"You should. If these critters touch you, you'll die quicker than you can pull that trigger."

The guard shrugged, but her gaze locked on the vial.

Seizing this advantage, Torrance threw the open container at the guard and bolted for the corner. She screamed and jumped back. Ten meters to another corridor. Footsteps came from behind. He ran, confused by the lack of foot traffic in the corridors — *Orion*'s hallways always seemed to be teeming. His joints ached and his muscles were putty.

The girl was probably in shape.

In a flash of insight, Torrance understood the empty corridors. This was a suicide mission. Icarus was being piloted by a skeleton crew — just enough to keep her flying.

He came to a maintenance alcove and entered a standard service code. A control holo spun before him. He toggled the fire systems. Carbon dioxide foam hissed in the hallway. The guard's surprised yelp echoed from around the corner.

Torrance did not look back. He raced to the lifts, each of his seventy-one years weighing in his lungs like lead.

"Central Ops," he said.

And he waited.

The lift's hydraulics creaked in the silence.

The sound of the guard's footsteps drew closer.

She coughed and said something that Torrance assumed was a call to whatever crew was aboard.

The lift arrived. The door opened. Torrance stepped in.

The guard rounded the corner, her hair soaked and dripping, her gray top matted to her body. She raised her weapon, but the door closed before she could get off a shot.

The lift dropped.

His heart clattered in his chest. The system hummed around him. He looked at his empty hands. Never before had he felt such a terrible understanding of what it meant to be defenseless. The lift doors opened. Torrance ducked in anticipation of other guards, but there were none.

Pod Engineering was around the corner.

The deck's power system was to the left.

He could do some serious damage by playing with the power grid — maybe create a diversion that would leave him free to work the pods. The system's security, however, was tricky. If he didn't get in, the advantage of his head start would be gone. To hell with it, he thought. No time to play games.

A light flickered from atop the lift, indicating the platform was nearing its destination. His time was short.

Torrance found a service bay near the lift. He pressed an entry code and accessed the lighting system. The hallway went dark. Luminescent rows of crimson emergency lights flickered on along the hallway. The controls on the maintenance panel glowed dimly. He looped around to take a path to Pod Engineering that wouldn't lead him past the lift. He heard the door open. Silence was palpable.

He followed the crimson dots.

The hallway was arched above him. The air was thick, and he found it difficult to breathe for fear of making so much as a wheeze.

A crossing corridor loomed ahead. It should take him to Pod Engineering.

Torrance glanced around the corner. Empty hallway. The double doors to Pod Engineering were dead ahead, on the opposite side of a corridor making another T with this one. The hallway behind him was empty, too. The guard was somewhere, though. The lift door had opened. She was on this floor, weapon at the ready. But which way would she come?

He had to choose. Fifty-fifty.

He took a breath, turned the corner, and strode with long, heronlike steps toward the double doors. By the time he neared the T, he was nearly running. He stepped like a shadow across the open expanse of the hallway, then knelt in the alcove outside Pod Engineering's door.

Voices came from a distance. More crew.

The hallway leading to the lift was empty.

She had followed him around.

He pushed an entry pad. Both doors rasped open. Light from inside extinguished the hallway darkness. Torrance stepped in and pressed the panel on the opposite wall. The door closed.

He ducked down and sidled up against a barrel painted blue. The place felt huge and smelled of electricity. The barrel was cool against his fingers. He rested his forehead on the barrel's surface to catch his breath. He was sore and tired from running. His calf muscles felt flayed.

Pod Engineering lay below him, the open "pit" and row upon row of drone pods several meters down. The second-floor control center looked out over the pit from its perch, its walls consisting of a belly-height wall and plastiglass extensions that rose to the girded ceiling.

Three technicians worked on a pair of wormhole pods in the pit. Torrance counted eight tubes closed and locked.

Staggered rows of olive-coated ion torpedoes lined a distant wall. A gritty calm spread over him. Every torpedo had a detonation sequence that could be programmed to provide a sequenced time-on-target capability. If he could detonate a few torpedoes, they would certainly destroy the pods. If he could get to the entire rack, it might well be enough to take out the entire ship.

He ran his tongue over his lips, tasting sweat and grime.

A pair of engineers hunched over a holographic display in the command center, probably loading navigation parameters into the pods. The weapons calibration station was in there.

Destroying Icarus here would stop U3 from planting the black hole and keep them from radioing home. It was enough for him.

It had to be...

...or did it?

The shuttle bay was a short jaunt from Pod Engineering. While a shuttle could never make it all the way home, it was certainly capable of sending messages back to the solar system. He would never live long enough for the message to arrive, but if he could launch himself before the blast, and if he was very lucky, a star drive spacecraft might happen upon his derelict shuttle in time to save him.

At worst he could make sure someone knew what had really happened.

It was as good a plan as he was going to get.

He crept along the curved wall toward the command center, trying to stay out of sight of the workers below. A minute later he knelt against the wall below the field of view of the windows.

The door was open.

"Pod nine loaded." The voice came from the communications system—a technician relaying status from below.

"Thank you," one of the engineers said.

Nine pods loaded. The tenth would be complete soon. Eight was enough to set the link. He had to move.

"How long until we go black?" the other engineer said. He was nervous. Not surprising. Torrance would be nervous in his shoes, too.

"I don't know."

"Pretty close. One more."

"Maybe fifteen minutes."

It was quiet.

"Probably less."

"Then there's flight time."

Torrance peeked through the plastiglass. Guidance and launch control lay directly ahead, maintenance to the left, inventory to the right. The weapons calibration station was just out of his field of view.

If he could draw the engineers near, he could catch them off guard. He positioned himself at the edge of the door, then scratched quietly against the metallic edge of the frame.

Neither engineer reacted.

He scratched louder.

"What is that?" the nervous one said.

Torrance stopped.

"What?"

He scratched again.

"That."

The floor was tile. Footsteps drew near on the other side.

Torrance sprang forward and threw his shoulder against the closest engineer. The *whumpfh* of air leaving lungs accompanied them as Torrance fell, tangled atop the engineer. He rolled forward, stood, and caught the second engineer with a right cross that sent shivers of pain up his wrist and forearm. The man fell like a sack of potatoes.

The first engineer raised to one knee, his hand rubbing the back of his neck. "What are you doing?" he said.

Torrance took two steps and kicked.

His foot struck the man's jaw and sent him spinning away. The back of the man's head hit the corner of a desk with an ugly thud, and he fell limply to the ground. Torrance stared at the man with a surrealistic sense of the absurd. Had he just done that? Was the man dead?

The second engineer groaned but did not move.

Torrance went to the weapons station. It was active.

He paged through screens, his fingers shaking with adrenaline. Too long — it was taking him too long. He found the screen entry system, selected a torpedo, and set the detonation time for seven minutes. The next he set at seven, and the next, and the next. The work went smoothly once he had the rhythm. When he had keyed them all he reset the system, closed the screen, and opened a security layer that locked the display against manipulation.

It would be almost impossible to find and fix them all, now.

He started the system counter.

That was that. The code had been sent. The torpedoes armed. He had seven minutes to find the shuttle bay.

A footstep sounded behind him.

The area lit up in scarlet flame. The weapons station exploded. Torrance leapt away. The woman stood in the doorway, her gray uniform streaked and smeared with grime, her hair dangling in short ringlets. She trained her glowing weapon on Torrance. Her eyes, dark and cold, told him her first shot was no accident. She had taken out the station to keep him from completing whatever work he had been attempting.

She was too late, of course. The code was in the torpedoes by now.

But he was her next target.

A ventilation grate was mounted on the near wall. The grills were plastic, about three meters long and one high, mounted a bit off the floor.

Torrance half dived and half leapt at the duct, rolling to strike the grating with his shoulder. Plastic splintered around him. Laser ozone cut into his nose and throat. He crashed into the duct, slipping on the dirty floor. Pain lanced his ankle — was he hit? He crawled, scrambling on his hands and knees into the darkness like a psychotic crab. His leg throbbed but he kept moving.

Clamoring echoed from behind. Metal reinforcements of the ductwork bent and popped.

The woman was following.

He was afraid then, afraid with a frozen fear — a sensation like falling. He wanted to live. Maybe it would be for only one additional breath, maybe for only a minute more—maybe for a mere week in a dingy shuttle floating out in space. But there in the darkness of Icarus's ductwork Torrance knew that more than anything, he wanted to live.

His fingers slipped in the grime. The place smelled like oily linen. He crashed painfully into a wall ahead. His ankle felt like a railroad stake had been driven through it. His ragged breathing echoed with reverberations that made the world small and claustrophobic.

Raw fear pushed him onward.

He took the left passage, thinking it the most likely to lead to the shuttle bay. A flash colored the duct crimson. The smell of hot metal brought a stifling pall to the chamber.

Torrance crawled over a heavily buttressed segment of the flooring — vacuum containment element — that marked the perimeter of the bay area.

A grating loomed. He threw himself into it. The ground knocked the wind out of him. The world swam. He thought he might pass out from the pain in his foot. Three shuttles sat in a line like massive green insects. Men raced in from the main bay entrance. Laser fire was suddenly everywhere. He crawled behind a landing strut to avoid being an open target.

The closest shuttle's ramp was open, maybe two meters away.

Gritting, Torrance launched himself. Something bit his thigh.

The rubber pad lining the ramp burned with an oily reek.

He dragged himself into the shuttle.

His pants were charred and smoking. His leg burned with pain. The shuttle airlock was still open. Footsteps scrabbled below. He dragged himself to the cockpit, each move making him suck air against knife-sharp pain. He pulled himself to the captain's chair and keyed the hatch system closed.

The craft shuddered.

Holding a nervous breath, he commanded the bay doors. They irised into six elements, dilating away.

He almost cried with relief.

Rockets on. Firing. Docking release made. Yaw commands steady. Right attitude. Trimming thrusters active and warmed. He pointed the craft out the doorway and crammed the engines.

The shuttle slid forward.

Zero-g took over as he left the ship's autograv field. Torrance nearly choked on raw emotion. He was in the umbra of *Icarus* against Alpha Cen. The blackness of vacuum was an open horizon in every direction. The stars glittered like pinpoints of glorious, glorious freedom.

Icarus fell away.

The brightness of Alpha Centauri A burned through the windshield. Torrance deployed a protective screen and looked at Icarus.

Would he be far enough out when the torps went?

The briefest flame roared from a launch tube.

At first Torrance thought this was the explosion of torpedoes. But instead, a black silhouette belched from the flame, a needle-shaped figure Torrance would know anywhere.

A wormhole pod.

Then another and another until there were ten pods flying, rocket engines engaging, turning, looping about, before taking a course toward the blazing star.

A hole formed in Torrance's gut.

Somehow, through the confusion and the turmoil, with two engineers knocked unconscious, somehow *Icarus* had launched the pods.

He pounded his armrests, cursing aloud, feeling powerless and shrill.

Then the torpedoes blew.

The explosion started at *Icarus*'s forefront, fragments peeling silently from the surface, debris racing haphazardly into blackness. Flames spouted and died. The ship buckled. Torrance watched with detachment.

When it was over, *Icarus* looked like a trick cigar, one end charred and serrated, the other slim and perfect. This bird was dead, its guts ripped by pyrotechnics and vacuum.

Torrance closed his eyes. Deep space was obliterated by proximity to Alpha Centauri's brilliance, but he knew it was out there. He thought about wormhole pods. He thought about black holes. He thought about Willim Pinot smiling. He thought about *Icarus* floating breached in space.

And Torrance was struck by the thought that perhaps human beings really were alone — that perhaps there truly was no greater power left in this world than the men who had created the wormhole pods that were flying at this moment so very close to the sun.

***

Now that he had time, Torrance stared at his leg. It was burnt and goopy. A small laser hole was burned through the fleshy place between his Achilles heel and the bone of his ankle. It felt like he had been skinned, then dipped in rubbing alcohol. He tried to prop it, but moving it brought tears to his eyes. He tried to pull the cloth of his pants away, but merely touching it was razor on bone.

Finally he decided merely to rest.

He gathered his senses.

This was it. He was floating four light-years from home without an oar. The pods would make Centauri A in a few hours. He twisted to check the freezedry. Enough food for two weeks if he skimped — maybe.

He knew what he had to do.

He flipped on the radio. The message would take over four years to arrive at the solar system, but radioing home was all he had left, so he did it.

"*Icarus* is dead," he said. He explained U3's plans for a black hole. He warned of their threat to kill his daughters, and he asked for someone to look for them. He described the flight of wormhole pods and what that might mean. He gave them his coordinates, then finished by telling Mercy and Cassie he loved them. "And do the same for Oscar Pentabill," he said, remembering the man's last wishes. "Tell his wife ... tell Glory ... that he loved her."

He clicked off the message and set it to replay every thirty minutes, casting each upon the turbulent waters of the vacuum to drift in its own invisible bottle of time.

"Maybe," he said aloud, "someone is close enough to —"

He stopped.

He remembered the icon flashing on his wrist. That moment seemed so long ago. So far away. He looked at his fuel monitor. There was enough.

He flipped the radio back on. "Strike those coordinates," he said, as he punched up his navigation screen.

Inertia shifted as the shuttle came around.

The planet came into view, a pinpoint of light against the black sky. The ship computer indicated something over twelve standard days to make it there. He hoped the atmosphere would support him. He hoped whatever life was there would help him.

In the end, though, he was surprised to find it didn't matter.

His chest welled with a new sensation.

After all this time, at least he would know, and this knowledge alone was enough to bring him a sense of peace he had never before felt. This was it. This was what his life was about, perhaps what God had made him specifically to do.

He commanded the engines on full, then toggled the radio again.

"I'm going to Eden," he finally said. "If it's still possible, come and get me."

And he flew toward the planet, a man encased in the cocoon of his spacecraft like parchment in glass, preparing to wash up on a distant shoreline — a message unto himself.

Or, perhaps, an answer.

Ron's Afterword

There was a time when I got into a brief internet discussion with a friend of mine who suggested that you cannot learn to write a novel by writing short stories. I don't agree with him, but acknowledge his argument has at least a leg to stand on.

After Dr. Schmidt accepted "Parchment in Glass," I wrote him a fourth story. Alas, he responded with a rejection and a note that read "I think it's time to write the novel."

Have I mentioned how much I enjoyed interacting with him?

I did, of course, write the novel.

In fact, I wrote nine of them.

Thanks to Dr. Schmidt's suggestion, I set my thoughts toward how the book would have to go, and pretty much immediately upon starting to plan things out had an image of exactly how the series ended. At the time, I thought the task then was to finish it in three books.

Silly me.

The writing of these nine books sprawled out over some time, and eventually ended up with the events that happen in "Parchment in Glass" being scattered mostly across books four and five. Strange how that happens, right? Turns out that a novel and a short story, though related, are actually different beasts.

That said, I'll stand pat on the idea that you can most definitely take your learning on how to write short stories and apply them to novels.

RON COLLINS

The opposite, to me, is probably harder—which is something I wrote about in considerable depth in my book *On Writing (And Reading!) Short*.

Just Business
ANALOG MARCH 2003

Here's the facts.

In 2025, Alphonse "The Glob" Calidino took over the nastiest crime syndicate in New York City. In August 2026, Frankie Morena, a boyhood pal of mine and a guy I call "The Man," ordered a hit. Three days later the Glob became one with the loading docks on Manhattan Island after lying down on the wrong side of an asphalt spreader. Go there today, and you still see the oily stain.

My pal Frankie took over within twenty-four hours.

Two weeks later he called me to his office. I showed up promptly. If I know one thing, it's that promptitude is always good when you're dealing with the Man, don't matter that you're good buddies or not. Frankie was an early riser, so the sun was still under the ocean when I made it to his high-rise. He stood beside his mahogany table, in a pressed gray suit and a crisp blue tie. Panel windows gave a darkened view of the city, which I suppose is okay if you like the city but gives me the willies seeing as I'm afraid of heights and all. A leatherbound planner and a single sheet of paper sat on his desk next to a half-eaten muffin.

Vin and Krueger were sitting in opposite corners of the room, both hidden in shadows. Vin's pupils blazed with an infrared tint, and Krueger flexed a hand so slowly that I could almost hear the microhydraulics inside.

"Hiya, Frankie," I said. "What's with the goon squad?"

Frankie jumped like he hadn't seen neither, then gave a nervous wave of his hands. Vin and Krueger left the room. I can't say as I missed 'em.

"Mick," he started once the door was shut. His $600 Ferragamos left imprints in the shag carpet as he paced. "I've got a problem."

"Then I'm here to help."

He ran his hand through slicked hair. There was something wrong about Frankie today. The lines on his face were deeper than normal and brown rings clung to his eyes like an old widow to her inheritance. His hands shook as he wrung them together.

"We've been friends for how long, Mick?"

"Since grade school, Boss."

He nodded. "We go back a long way."

"You know you can count on me," I replied, feeling an unpleasant sensation below my breastbone. "We're blood brothers, right?"

"Yeah, Mick. Blood brothers." Frankie looked at me. His hands shook as he retrieved a Partagas cigar from his breast pocket.

"You okay, Boss?"

"I need you to do a hit."

"Whatever you say," I said. "Who's the stooge?"

"The Glob."

I chuckled. "He done been hit."

"Then you'll hit him again."

"Should be an easy job," I said with a smile.

"Don't bet on it."

Frankie lit the cigar and the room filled with the smell of the Dominican Republic's finest. A bluish cloud of smoke surrounded him as he sat down and pulled his chair close to the desktop. I sat down with him, and he leaned forward so that the tip of the cigar was only a few inches from my face.

"He's back," Frankie whispered.

"The Glob?"

He nodded, looking both ways like he was afraid someone might be behind him. "He's here. I never know when he's coming or when he's going, but things will be really quiet, then boom! Suddenly he's here."

"I don't believe in ghosts, Boss."

"Neither do I."

"But you just told me—"

"I just told you the truth."

He clenched his teeth so hard his cigar broke in two. I only had to be hit over the head a couple times to see Frankie was serious.

"You need a hit, I do you a hit."

He sat back with a sigh of relief, and put the cigar into an ashtray he pulled from one of his desk drawers. "I knew I could count on you, Mick," Frankie said. He poked his finger at me. "You stay right here with me and watch for the Glob."

"Sure, Boss. Want I should take a spot over there in the corner?"

He shook his head violently. "Stay right here. Right here beside me." He drew a calming breath. "Just in case."

Sweet Mother Mary, I thought. Frankie's done gone over the edge. But I sat there all quiet-like because I figure it don't never do a guy no good to tell the Man he's running light on motor oil. The phone rang. I tried to pretend I wasn't hearing nothing.

"What?" Frankie said too forcefully as he answered. "No. No. I'm not going nowhere today, Annie. No. Sorry, babe. No." He hung up the phone.

The sun came up and the water reflected all red and orange. The day turned to afternoon. We ordered meatball sandwiches in. Frankie finally dozed into a dream that made him twitch like the little cocker spaniel I had when I was a kid. My mama, Lord rest her soul, used to say

Peppy was chasing rabbits. I watched Frankie chase rabbits all afternoon. Gave me the friggin' chills.

He woke with a start.

"Jesus, Boss. You're white as a sheet."

"Did he come?"

"No. Ain't been nobody here."

Daytime faded to evening. The chair was wearing sores in my backside regions, and the skyline twinkled with lights against the black sky. Then it happened. Sure as I was sitting there beside Frankie — the Glob stepped out of a dark corner. Frankie gave a yip. I grabbed my gun out of its pocket, and proceeded to put four bullets right through the Glob's heart. These were .45 caliber shells with hollow points capable of stopping a charging bull at fifty paces.

The Glob didn't fall, though.

He stood there, all shimmery and gray and transparent as a three-dollar bill. I never believed in ghosts before, but I got to tell you the idea was growing on me.

The Glob looked in my direction. "Now whadja go and do that for, Mick?"

I glanced over at Frankie, who shrank deeper into his chair.

The Glob shrugged. "I see. Just doing your job, eh?"

He walked in a half glide, half waddle until he stood right in front of Frankie's desk. "Hello, Frankie. Sorry to be away for so long. You'd think that things would be all harps and angels feeding you grapes in the great beyond, but even here it seems like there's always something ya gotta do."

Frankie just stammered and sank even lower.

"So, what's it gonna be, Frankie?" The Glob peered into Frankie's face.

"I, uh, well..."

The Glob gave a hollow sigh. "I may be immortal, Frankie, but I only got half the patience I used to. I told you once, I told you a thousand times — turn your territory over to my boy Pauley, or I do you and your family a few extra nighttime visits." He put his vaporous hands up to his neck. I swear I felt a graveyard chill run up my back. "Those visits won't be near as nice as these."

Frankie gave a choking sound.

The Glob faded back into the shadows and was gone.

Frankie ran a handkerchief over his brow, and panted like a dog. "You got to help me, Mick," he said. "We're buddies, right? You're the only guy I can trust now."

"Sure, Boss," I said.

"We gotta get rid of the Glob once and for all, or we're dead."

"I see that," I replied, though I wondered about the *we* part, seeing as I hadn't noticed the Glob threatening me.

"What you gonna to do?" Frankie asked.

I thought a minute. "Don't know. I suppose the first thing is to figure out how you get rid of ghosts."

"Good idea," Frankie said, standing up and pacing.

***

Not certain of exactly what to do about such a thing as a ghost, I went to see Sister Lisa Michelle.

"Sister, I need your help."

"What's wrong?"

"I got a ghost I need to exorcise."

"Have you tried McNally's gym? They're just down the street. Sister Gloria's been going the past six weeks and you should see her abs. I hear they've got a deal right now, too."

"Not that kind of exercise," I said. "I mean I got to do the old deep-six, if you get my drift."

"Yes." The sister grimaced. "I get your drift. Can't a guy take a joke?"

"So, can you set me up?"

"We don't do that anymore."

"What?"

"New Vatican directive. We don't believe in ghosts—"

"But I seen it with my own eyes."

"—and, as I was trying to say, even if we did believe in ghosts, which we don't, then they would be people, too, and we wouldn't participate in such abusive treatment."

"But ..." I stared at her, certain that my eyes were bulging out of their sockets.

"You might try the Baptists," the sister said. Then she leaned in and whispered. "Or you could go to one of those shops downtown."

"Voodoo?" I said with unsettling visions of tiny heads sitting on broad shoulders.

"It was just a thought. Or, you could do it yourself."

"I could?"

"Don't see why not. Just because we don't sanction it, doesn't mean a parishioner can't try."

"I see." I rubbed my chin. "How would I go about doing that?"

"I don't really know. But I'm sure there are a billion books that might tell you."

I gave a halfhearted nod. Books and I don't never get along, but in a race between Cordellia the voodoo priestess and a piece of paper, you don't have to guess too many times to know where I'll head. "Okay," I said. "I'll find a book."

***

"Tell me again," the librarian said. "What exactly are you looking for?" She was getting up in age, and wore her hair pinned back like a pair of Victorian curtains. Tired lipstick ran up into the little wrinkles around her pursed lips.

"I told you, I want to learn how to kill a ghost."

"Isn't that a bit redundant?"

"You calling me stupid?"

"I said redundant, not ignorant."

"Lady," I said, pausing to stare for all of three seconds. "All I need to know is how to kill a goddamned ghost, all right?"

"You don't have to be so frosty about it."

"You been goin' on for fifteen minutes about the do-he-or-don't-he decimal system, and playing twenty questions about the computer this-an-that, and I ain't yet to see a goddamned word about ghosts. I think I'm due a little frost."

"Well, all right. Follow me." She grabbed me by the elbow and sashayed toward the back of the library. The bottom of her blue skirt swayed this way and that as she walked. Holy Mother, I thought, this old dame likes me. It took a full minute to shake off the creeps from that idea. I mean, yeah, I'm a single guy and getting a little long in the tooth myself, and my belt size is edging up closer to my age every day, but ... I shivered and followed her along past a rack of data cubes and digital disks. I never knew a library could be so damned big. We went past wide-screen crystal panels that were all being used by kids playing the latest Zeta Blaster game. And we went past rows and rows of computer terminals and data discs. In the far corner, a guy was using a holoprojector to look at the way muscles laid over a body. Call me sentimental, but the sight of a skinned stiff standing in the library was enough to make do a double-take.

Finally we made it to the back of the library where they still had books.

"You've got your medieval mythology," she said, sweeping her arms this way and that. "And your religious structure, and then over there is all the old New Age material."

The wall of books was like a freaking tidal wave.

I pried one out of the row, afraid that the entire rack might crumble. It was old, with a black cover and pink lettering. *Ghosts and Goblins: Halloween Treats from the Old World.*

"Have I told you how much I hate books?" I said.

"That one explains the origin of Halloween mythology," the librarian replied.

"Doesn't sound very interesting."

"You might be surprised."

I put the book back.

"Here," she said, pulling a title. "How about this one?" *Exorcism: A How-To Manual.*

"Hey, that sounds good."

"Can I get you anything else?" She batted her eyes and waited there, all expectation and excitement.

"No. I'll just go over there and read a little."

"Oh," she said. "All right. If you change your mind, you know where to find me." She stepped past in short, quick steps and turned at the end of the aisle. Then she was gone.

I went to a desk in the corner and started to read. Fascinating book, really. Who would know there were so many types of ghosts and demons? I skipped the chapters on possessions and poltergeists, and went straight to hauntings. A half hour later, I knew what I needed to know. I was worried I might forget it all, so I figured to take the book with me.

"Excuse me." The voice came as I reached the door. It was the librarian.

"Yes?"

"Are you planning on checking that out?"

I looked at the book. "Oh, yeah, sorry." I put the book on the tall table between us. She picked it up.

"Can I see your card?"

"My card?"

"You need a library card to check this book out. I can get you one now if you need it."

"Great."

She stared me straight in the eyes and clutched the book close to her chest. "Dinner, Friday night. Pick me up at seven."

"Excuse me?"

"I said you can pick me up at seven."

Damn. She had me. So I made the deal. What the hell, eh? Who knew what was going to happen in the future. I might not even be drawing oxygen come Friday. She wrote her address on an index card and slipped it between the pages of the book.

***

So I bought frankincense and myrrh and a few candles. I scarfed a set of blessed crosses from Dooley's Pawn Shop, and paid a little extra for a nice incense holder. A few hours later I found myself down on the dock where the Glob got splattered — just before midnight, hanging the crosses and smelling the pot of incense burning away. The smoke mixed with the salty ocean and the odor of seaweed and sewage rotting under the pier to make a combo that's pretty far out of this world.

Once that was done, I looked around to see if anyone was watching. Not seeing no one, I started the process with a little prayer.

"Holy Father," I said, waving the incense about like it was a flare. "Look down upon this ground with your fav—"

"What the hell are you doing, Mick?"

I jumped with a start and rolled to the ground, coming up with my gun pointed straight at the man's heart.

"Didn't we already try that?"

"Alphonse," I said. He was standing all silvery by an old crate. I looked at the Glob's oily stain, then glanced at the book I had set on the dock. "You wasn't supposed to show up until I got past the prayers."

"Can't believe everything you read, Mick. Don't you know that the pope frowns on knocking off ghosts these days?"

"I heard that," I said. "But he also says something about knocking off regular guys, and I think we both done that."

"That's just good business, Mick. The Big Guy understands business. Knocking off ghosts, though ... That's something altogether different."

"Guess I don't see it."

"It's all about the soul, you see? A regular guy is a helluva lot more than a soul. You squinch a geezer who done wrong, you get rid of his body. His soul just goes on to the next place. A ghost, though — someone like me — well, I ain't nothing but a soul, so you go about squinching me and you ruin my eternity."

I laughed. "So you're saying that knocking off a regular guy is kinda like a service."

"Depending on the situation," the Glob said, his smile bending at his translucent lips. "Truth is, though, the best thing you can do for a ghost is to let him free, too."

"I don't get it."

"What's that book say about why ghosts get stuck here in the neverworld?" The Glob looked at me with one of those parental, I'll wait forever kind of expressions. I figured he meant it literally.

"Unfinished business?" I said.

"That's right. Unfinished business."

I didn't like where this was going. "I'm not so good at guessing games, so how about you just say what you're thinking so we can stay out of the night air too long."

"It's Frankie," the Glob said.

"I figured you might say that"

"I always said you was a pretty smart guy."

"So, you're suggesting I hit my own boss?"

"Makes sense, don't it?"

"Not in no book I ever read."

"Think about your future, Mick." The Glob glided over and put his weightless arm over my shoulder. Hair prickled on my neck, and I started to stammer. "You want to be right with the Big Guy, don't you?"

"Sure," I said, moving out from under his arm. The whole conversation was like riding one of those spinning cups at Coney Island — it made me feel like I had to puke, but it was too late to get off now.

"You hit Frankie, and my soul will be free. The Big Guy would like that. He would see it like doing him a favor. I mean, Frankie's not a really good guy, you know?"

I stared at him slack jawed.

"Look at me, Mick. I'm a freaking ghost. You think I don't know what I'm talking about?"

That's when I saw it. At first I thought I was missing something, but there it was — a little flicker off to the Glob's right. Something was wrong here.

"What's the matter?" the Glob said.

I stared at him, feeling my eyes widen. "Nothing," I said. "It's just that this whole thing gives me the creeps — you being a ghost and all."

"Just think of it as doing your job, you know?"

I dodged the question while I gathered my wits. "Squinching a boss has never been a good way for a man to do his job," I said.

"Get serious, Mick. Frankie told you to make me go away, right?"

"Just business, right?" I said. I tried to look nervous — which wasn't hard seeing as I was worried that I couldn't figure out what I had seen and I had a dead mob boss trying to get me to work for him.

"Oh, I understand. Believe me. But you're a smart guy. If you squinch Frankie, I'm free. And Frankie's free to move on to the next life, too — probably feeling a whole lot better since I won't be hanging around his neck all day. Think about it that way, and you see that hitting Frankie is just doing us all a big favor."

"You got a point there."

Waves lapped up against the pier, and moonlight reflected off the oily sheen that stained the dock. I looked through the Glob and thought really hard. Maybe my eyes was tricking me, but I thought I saw another flicker behind the Glob, and that got me to thinking even harder. I got a shiver right in my freaking spine when it hit me. Maybe the Glob ain't been hit after all.

The more I thought, the easier it all seemed.

The Glob just stood there, waiting like he had a few centuries to kill.

"All right," I said. "I'll do it that way."

***

If nothing else, I'm a man of my word.

The first thing I did was to pick the librarian up at seven the next evening. Her name was Jude. We had a good time at dinner, talked forever, and capped it off with popcorn and a flick. By the end of the evening I was singing that old Beatles tune, and she was giggling like she was fifteen again.

When I explained the situation, she volunteered to look up the stuff I needed without me even asking.

I like that in a woman.

***

Then I went to Frankie's and took care of business. News hit the street right away. Frankie Morena was no more. It was clean and easy. Professional all the way. Just business, you know? I went home feeling pretty good about myself.

The phone rang right on time that next afternoon.

"Mick, is that you?"

It was Two Sticks Casey, a friend in Frankie's family. I worked with him a couple times, mostly shaking down bartenders for their security donations. He's a good guy on the job, but skittish as a rabbit the rest of the time.

"Yeah, Sticks," I said. "What's the matter?"

"It's the Glob."

"What about him?"

"He's done taken over Frankie's place."

"You don't freaking say."

"I seen him with my own eyes, Mick. He stepped right outta the limo and went up to Frankie's office. We're screwed, man."

Bennie kept on yacking.

"Thanks, Bennie," I said. "Gotta run."

I love it when I turn out to be right.

***

I'll admit I was worried the Glob might want me squinched, but seeing as no one knew where the Glob kept hisself, I had to do something to get closer. I tailed him all day.

He stopped at Expressimo's Rotisserie for a plate of veal parmesan and spaghetti, pausing every few minutes to greet another shocked waiter or bartender and smiling as he explained the rules of business now that Frankie was gone. The same show played out at Gino's bar and at the Southside Laundromat.

Turns out I didn't have to worry none about how to get together with the Glob. I was down at Morelli's Ribs taking in a plate of my favorite baby backs when Goosey Jones slid into the seat across from me. Goosey got his nickname for getting slapped upside the head by a woman he pinched. I looked at the scar that ran down his cheek. Funny as hell at the time.

"Alphonse wants to speak with you," he said.

"Can't you see I'm eating?"

"He don't like to wait, you know what I mean?"

I looked at the ribs. They was only half gone. "Think he can wait as long as it takes the both of us to finish these off?"

Goosey smiled and grabbed a rib. "What he don't know won't kill him, eh, Mick?"

I didn't say nothing. Ten minutes later I paid the tab, and Goosey took me down to the Glob's headquarters. He took my gun while we were in the elevator. "Orders, you know?"

"I understand," I said, thinking about the knife in my ankle sheath.

"Mick!" the Glob said as I stepped into the room.

Alphonse Calidino's office was the opposite of Frankie's. First of all, it was in the basement. It was also old and cluttered — old as in antique, cluttered as in three guys were there with more hardware hanging off their belts than Batman. I recognized them all — Three Face Kennedy, Johnny Colletta, and Simply Maurice. All The Glob's favorite goons. The place smelled like cheddar cheese and cold cuts, which wasn't surprising seeing as there was a plate spread out on the table to one side of the room. The far corner was filled with a contraption that looked like a cross between a forklift and an electric chair.

I looked at the Glob. No doubt he was real and in the flesh. "I thought you was dead," I said to keep appearances up.

The Glob laughed so hard his gut jiggled. "I been running into people all day who made the same mistake, Mick."

"Whose guts are splattered over the dock?"

He leaned out over the desk, almost spilling the Styrofoam cup he had been drinking from. "First rule of business, Mick: Don't ask questions when you don't want to know the answer."

I decided to drop it. "You're moving on Frankie's territory," I said.

"Don't look like he's using it."

"Maybe he'll come back, too."

"I don't think so." The Glob stood up and waddled toward the metallic platform in the corner. Both his shoes and the floorboards squealed with distress.

"Do you know what this is?" he said.

"Looks like a shower stall."

"Doctor Frenelli?" the Glob said a little louder than he needed to.

A nerdy little guy who looked like he was made of toothpicks emerged from the dark corner beside the contraption.

"Tell my buddy Mick what's up with this."

"It's a holographic projector," Nerdboy said, pointing to the contraption with his thin finger. "But it's a better one than you've ever seen before. It creates patterns of photons where you are, then maps them to photons anywhere within range of the receiver. Even better, we can program it to sense wave patterns, too."

"Sa-weet," I said. "So what exactly does that mean?"

The Glob laughed. "It means I can send images anywhere I want, or have full conversations through it, or even take a gander at anything that strikes my fancy. Hell, I already found Sonny McLellan skimming his pony card, and T-Wreck cutting dope deeper than he ought to know better. Operational two weeks, and it's already saved me three hundred grand."

I looked at the machine. "Jesus Mother Mary," I whispered. "Where did you ever dream that up?"

"Cornell, actually," the little guy said.

"So you tricked me into squinching Frankie by pretending to be a ghost," I said to the Glob.

The Glob shrugged. "Just business, right?"

"Right," I said. "Why'dja bring me here? Why not just plug me and be done with it?"

"Gotta be honest with you, Mick. I considered that." He put a meaty hand on my shoulder. "Then I thought, you know that Mick, he's a pretty smart guy, he knows what side his bread is buttered on and he's damned good with a gun. I figured maybe you could be useful to a guy like me."

"You want I should work for you?"

"Thought I would give you the option, anyhow." He smiled so big I could see his capped teeth.

I looked at the three goons and Nerdboy, then back at the Glob. I looked at the projector. "I don't know that's a very good idea, seeing as I work for Frankie and all."

"Frankie's eating six feet of dirt," Simply Maurice said.

"Well ... maybe not," I replied.

Footsteps rumbled from the stairs.

I felt the Glob's fingers close around my shoulder. "What are you telling me, Mick?"

Kennedy and Colletta made for their utilities. Simply Maurice simply dived behind a table. Nerdboy stood there shaking. The door burst open, and the guys poured in. The blaze of Vin's crimson eyes flared, and an energy beam took Kennedy in the shoulder. The Glob wrapped a big arm around me so tight my collarbone hurt — but when Krueger got him by the neck and closed that mechanical hand, the Glob seemed to think better and let go of me.

A second later everything was quiet.

Frankie stepped in, draped in a dark trench coat and fedora, smoking a Partagas like something out of a hundred-year-old movie.

"Good evening," he said.

"What the hell?" the Glob squeaked in a hoarse voice.

"What's the matter, Alfonse? Did you think you was the only guy that could play dead?"

The Glob stammered.

"This is all mine, now, Alphonse."

"Bullshi—"

Three more people stepped in. The three amigos — Jack "the Ripper" Francis from the financial district, Perilous Pauline Tedero from upper Manhattan, and Guido "Mozart" Tchaikovsky from someplace deep in Spanish Harlem. None of these folks were big enough to run the city, but a guy needed to control all three if he intended to make a real buck here.

Frankie smiled. "I've got more, Globby. The whole city's on my side of this one."

Pauline's red hair caught the light from under the hat she had slanted at a hard angle. "We seen it all, Alphonse."

"We can't work under those conditions," the Ripper said.

"Da machine's got to go," Guido added.

Frankie nodded to Vin, who put his crimson eyes to work at turning the projector into a slagheap.

Nerdboy gave a stifled cry, but was too scared to move.

The Glob struggled to speak, and Krueger let up on the pressure. "I don't understand. How did you know?"

Frankie gave me a look that said it was my story to tell. That's something I like about the Man.

"I saw your projector flicker when we was on the docks. So I got a friend to check up on it. She tracked it to Nerdboy's school, and Frankie took it from there."

The Boss blew a stream of blue smoke and looked at the melting holomachine, then at Nerdboy. "Did you know it takes only a few million dollars to rent one of those from your buddies in Cornel?"

"You've got a projector?" the Glob said.

"That's right. And we been listening in," Paulina said.

"We don't like what we hear," Guido said. "Frankie runs his business on trust — so that's who we're backing."

"I own this city now," the Glob growled. "I'll put you all out of business."

A siren blared in the distance.

"I don't think so," I said smugly. "That recording of you talking about watching your guys run games and dope was piped straight to the Feds' computer system, complete with a location tag." That last part was Jude's idea, and I found myself enjoying the thought of her quite a bit right about then. A woman who knows as much as she does is a damned fine thing, especially if she's a hoot to be around when she lets her hair down.

The Glob got red in the face and struggled to run, but Krueger put the pressure back on and Globby stopped in his tracks. The other guys got the Glob and his gang all tied down.

"You were right about Mick, though," Frankie said as he put his hat back on. "He's a pretty smart guy. We woulda never found you if he hadn't have had the idea to use hisself as bait." Then he and the three amigos ducked out.

I was the last one to leave.

"You were right about something else, too," I said to the Glob as I stood in the doorway. "I know what side my bread's buttered on."

***

Frankie, he understands.

He offered a long vacation at first, but I told him I figured I was done with the squinching game. It's like the Glob said back on the dock — you got to figure the Big Guy understands business, but all these goings-ons with ghosts and souls and everything done got me to thinking about who I was and all that, and I decided I couldn't handle it all no more. Not a big deal, I suppose. I was getting too old for it anyhow.

I asked Jude out again for Saturday. And Sunday church. And Monday. By Tuesday evening we was headed out to a ranch she inherited from her father. It's in Wyoming somewhere, and she says it's got sky so big you can see to Mars on a clear day. Sounds like a nice place where a guy can make sure he's all right with the Big Guy, if you know what I mean. I've got a little cash stashed back, and we can both do piece work if things get tight. We should be all right.

Maybe life is just business, and maybe business really is just who you know. I'll always love Frankie like a freaking brother, but I decided I'm taking care of my ownself now. So I got Jude sitting in the car beside me and I'm riding 230 horses toward a clean future.

Feels pretty damned good.

And that's a fact.

Ron's Afterword

I had a writer friend look at this one after it was finished. I recall her having a fun expression on her face as she said she was enjoying looking at it from the perspective of Mick being both an unreliable narrator and a relatable character, despite his job as a hitman.

That made me happy, because I admit I do so enjoy Mick, and I like his relationship with Jude in the end. We're all redeemable, right?

For me, though, lighthearted as it is, "Just Business" is more a story about the use of technology to blur what's real—and that has a direct comment on what's happening in tech today. The use of large language models to make media (or art, if you're so inclined) means that all of us poor consumers are at a nexus where it's probably wise to take a moment to question just about everything of any import we see.

That's a stressful thing.

It's hard.

In Mick's case, he's an unreliable narrator simply because he's going by what he sees. He's relatable because he's loyal. Sensible in his way. But without questioning himself, he's easy to lead on. In the end, though, he's the rare individual who, when he does finally get around to looking at his own life with a bit more distance, can change his mind about who he is.

Perhaps we could use a few more Mick's around these days.

Survivors
ANALOG JUNE 2014

It was warm for early September, but Daytona Beach would have been busy even if the sun wasn't blazing down. Hiram lay on a towel, propped up by his elbows, watching girls walk by. Waves slid up the beach, then slipped back toward the ocean like silent curtains. The half-moon drapes of wet sand left in the aftermath erupted with dimples made by mole crabs as they dug their way toward China.

"Look at 'em, man," Taylor said, burping as he threw another can of beer into the trash at the trunk of the car. Taylor was a junior at USF, majoring in something that would almost certainly lead to a life selling insurance. They were together with a group of guys — all friends at from back at McKinley North high school, each enjoying a last blow-out before retreating to the hallowed halls of their chosen facilities of higher education, none of which would be populated with women in bikinis.

This was not what Hiram would have chosen to be doing. He had picked this host, however, and had learned long ago that making a host avoid things it would normally do was a bad idea.

"Them bugs always make me laugh," Taylor said.

"Not always," Hiram replied. He hated absolutes. "For example, you're not laughing now."

"You know what I mean."

"Yes," Hiram said. "I know what you mean."

What Taylor meant — according to Hiram — was that he, Taylor, was too damned stupid to see the crabs were just doing what they were supposed to do, that they were a species whose entire universe was contained in the top hundred centimeters or so of the crust of the earth, and whose existence relied completely upon the unrelenting waves and the constantly shifting tides to keep them in places where the water broke and helped them collect the plankton that fed them. What Taylor meant was that he was too damned stupid to notice a life-and-death struggle even when it was happening right before his eyes.

It wasn't Taylor's fault. He was a human being. Their lives are too short, their connections too slight. They did not feel things as deeply or instinctively as Hiram could.

It wasn't fair, though. Why do these humans live, while his people pass into the realm of galactic history?

Using his hand as a visor, Hiram peered over the late afternoon wash to where the constellation Taurus would soon appear if it weren't still daylight.

"You wanna go to The Drop tonight," Taylor said, fishing another can from the cooler. "Those girls said they're gonna be there."

Hiram sipped his own beer, feeling an all-consuming sense of resignation at just how deep the need to procreate is in any species.

"Sure," he said. "The Drop sounds fine."

***

He had left his home star some eight thousand years ago, traveling in a stasis cocoon designed to give him comfort. It had not been bad, not really. The field worked for the most part, and he woke only three times or barely a year or two each.

He was also lucky that the first time his field broke, his home star had not yet been destroyed, so he was able to enjoy the ultrahigh frequency of the Pentali music they piped to him. He also received a steady stream of newsfeeds that told him of the final preparations his people were making for their star to go nova. It made him weep to know that everyone he left behind was going to be gone soon, but he could not deny that listening to the feed also gave him a sense of pride larger than his body could contain. His were a noble people. They faced extinction with such beautiful dignity.

He, along with thousands of other chosen survivors, was their hope. Each of them, the survivors, had been feted, and worshiped. Their memories had been loaded with every element of information about their culture and their history that could be stuffed into them. The survivors would carry the genetic content of their species wherever they went.

They were all his people had left.

So, with the stasis pod working mostly as designed, and flying at near the speed of light, the seven thousand year flight — give or take a few — was easy. Then his cocoon's analytical programs deemed the third planet of this remote solar system to be inhabited, and its piloting routines guided him through the atmosphere, providing him a fiery entry made in a golden blaze one evening late in a month the indigenous people called August. It took him some time to dig out, but when he did he quickly gathered his first host, a young man named Kanji who had come to investigate the fire in the sky. Kanji was a thin, wiry man who had worked in rice paddies his entire life.

It was through Kanji's eyes that the traveler got his first view of the nebula that had once been his home—a bright spot, visible even in daylight, that would eventually become known to human beings nearly 800 years later as the Crab Nebula.

Something had gone wrong, though. There were supposed to be more of him on this planet, but he had searched for a thousand years across hundreds of hosts and found nothing. No signs of other survivors, no signs of other crashes. So over the years, Hiram had come to the staggeringly heavy conclusion that he was the only traveler who had landed on this planet that humans called Earth.

Until now.

***

Hiram was so shocked he nearly dropped his beer mug.

She was on the dance floor all by herself, moving to the beat of a Maroon 5 song that was, thank the human Gods, most definitely not that thing about Jagger. Her dark hair was cut short, or he might have missed the telltale red dot at the nape of her neck even though the strobe lights pulsed at a marvelous quarter-second interval that helped him see it glow slightly. She wore a pair of white jeans and a striped top. When she raised her arms over her head, that top lifted to bare her naval.

The red dot was mesmerizing.

It was a twin to the one at the base of his own neck. It was a scar left when they took a host — the place where they entered the body and then drilled upward into the host's brain. For an instant he wondered if he had taken this girl as a host earlier — if the dot was one of his own making. But that couldn't be right. She was young, like Hiram's current host. He would not have forgotten something so recent.

He ran his palms down his pant legs. Was it possible? Seven thousand years in a cocoon, and a thousand scouring the planet, and he had never found another survivor. But he felt her. He sensed her presence with something humans might consider smell, but was really more of a warmth, or a tingle against the membranes of his host's nostrils. The red dot spoke to him, and the girl danced amid sound waves that rolled over him like a hot shower.

Yes. It was possible.

Taylor noticed his double-take and screamed into his ear as he put his hand on the small of Hiram's back. "She wants you, man! Get'er done!" Then he launched Hiram out of his seat.

He nearly crashed into the girl, but she had her eyes closed and didn't seem to notice.

He took a step back.

The girl turned in place, arms stretching up to the sky.

He wanted to reach out and touch that red dot. He wanted to feel the scar to make sure it wasn't just a tattoo or a birthmark.

"Are you gonna stare or are you gonna dance?" the girl yelled. She had consumed considerable quantities of alcohol.

Hiram was no dancer to begin with, and had only been in this host for a few weeks. So he just kind of bounced on his feet. The heat of the kids on the floor made him sweat. Another song replaced Maroon 5 — a mash-up this time, Pink, D-Jive and MoTzart KZ.

The girl's skin was milky. Her eyes were blue — not unheard of, but a bit of an oddity on one with such dark hair. His host body responded to hers. This close, he could smell the red dot.

There was no doubt.

She was a survivor. Another of his kind.

His head nearly exploded with questions. Every cell in his system wanted to link. His human eyesight grew wavy as his eyes teared up. Could it happen? Could the two of them be the ones to make their civilization whole again? Hiram struggled to find words. What do you say in a situation like this? Where have you been all my life? Do you come here often? When were you launched?

He reached out to her with his need to link, but she was vacant, a wall of silence.

"Do you want to go to the beach?" he asked when the next song transition came.

She ran a hand over his shoulder and up to cradle the back of his head, drawing him closer as if to kiss him. Her finger grazed his red dot. Her eyes grew suddenly wide, and she stopped moving as she was just now sensing him for the first time.

"No," she replied.

Hiram pressed closer, putting his hand on her waist. He felt her stiffen. The pressure of his hand seemed to keep her rooted in place as waves of sound played over them like surf.

"Can I get you a drink?"

"No," she said again. "I'm going to the ladies room." And she bolted through the crowd.

Hiram waited for nearly thirty minutes before asking another girl to check on her.

It was no use.

She was gone.

***

He felt a sense of loss deeper than any he could remember, a loss that shredded him as certainly as if she had exploded and sent stardust shrapnel across his universe.

Why had she run? What had he done wrong?

He tracked her, of course. To connect was ingrained in him, and knowing there was another survivor on the planet gave him renewed hope. She wasn't hard to find the first time. It took only a few dollars placed in the right palms and bit of asking around in local hot spots.

But she ran again, and then her apartment was empty.

The next time he found her she was in Arkansas.

Then Vancouver.

Then she was tending bar and waiting tables at a pub in the tiny Scottish town of Pitlessie. Each time, she ran.

Then she went dark. Nothing. Was she dead?

Sixty years passed before he saw her again.

He was on a vacation tour of Africa, wearing a host named Kanady, a body that was thirty-five years old and that lived in the Caribbean. He worked at fishing docks and dealt genetically refined cocoa extract on the side. She was wearing a guide, a woman of Norwegian descent who had come to the veldt country when she was eight. Her name was Brita. It was a purely random happening, and it took her days before she recognized him and slipped away, this time escaping while their troupe was out camping, leaving her co-workers with the task of taking care of them, and trekking back on her own.

He sent her a notice, then, passed through the safari company.

"I thought you would like to know that I am through chasing you," he said. *"Live a good life. I wish I knew you."*

***

He was back home in Nassau, two weeks later, when she sent him the note that asked him to join her for dinner.

He put the paper into the pocket of his work shirt, and kept it there the rest of the day, thinking about Brita as he worked to mend nets and watched over a contractor who was up-fitting a power boat for a rich client. It was simple work, work that kept his mind occupied and left him feeling like he had accomplished something at the end of each day.

The Shanty was an open restaurant with a roof made of thatched palm leaves and a touristy view that looked out over emerald waves. The aromas of warm crab and cold fruit laced with alcohol drifted on the late afternoon breeze. The sun neared the horizon, and lit Brita's cheeks, which, since her Nordic skin was fair, seemed to be in a perpetual state of sunburn.

She was seated at a table overlooking the beach, drinking something orange. He sat down and ordered rum. They looked at each other over the distances of three feet and a thousand years. The waitress left a plate of papaya.

He reached to connect with her, but received only a cold, empty vacuum.

"Why don't you love me?" he finally said.

She stared over the surf and rolled her straw between her fingers.

"I'm broken," she finally said.

"What do you mean?"

"I can't be with you. I don't ..." her voice broke. She took a deep breath through her nostrils, then drew on her drink, taking half of it down at once.

"I know what we are here for," she said. "I know what you expect. But I am blank. Don't you see? I cannot connect."

Suddenly it was clear. She had not been blocking him — not shunning him at all. Instead, she was damaged and unable to fulfill her purpose for being here on this planet. Maybe radiation in deep space had taken its toll. Maybe it was something else. All he could say for certain was that he looked at Brita and knew she blamed herself, and that she felt the weight of her people on her shoulders.

She didn't cry. He was impressed by that, though maybe he shouldn't have been. She didn't seem to display any emotion at all. Perhaps that was part of the problem. Or perhaps at one point Brita had despaired over her condition, but the years had left her with nothing but this cold resignation that radiated from her like a beacon.

He didn't say anything at first. Just reached out and touched her hand. How would he feel if he were the one damaged? How crushed would he be? He cleared his throat.

"You run because you're embarrassed."

"No."

He waited.

"I run because every time I see you it reminds me that I am a failure."

Kanady, who had been Hiram before that, and who had been many others prior to Hiram, sat back.

"I see," he said.

She pressed her lips, then sighed and reached for her purse.

"I wanted you to know why I can't see you again," she said.

He nodded, trying to comprehend this more fully as she slid off the stool and moved away, leaving him behind once again, passing the bar to walk out the door.

***

"Look at those two," said a man at a table across the dining area. "I think they're breaking up."

"Tell me we'll never be that way, all right?" his partner replied with a hint of snark.

"Never, love. We'll never be that way."

If Kanaday had overheard them he might have told them how humans are flawed, how their lives are too short to feel connections as deeply as those whose lives span millennia. Or maybe he would have just nodded and told them how lucky they were to live in such a condensed moment together, holding hands and connecting for only a few scant years, how lucky they were to have each other even if it were only for this brief moment in time.

But he did not hear them.

Instead, he put money on the table, and he left to follow Brita down the beach where she was walking away.

As he walked across the beach, waves rolled over the sand to leave clear, dusky patches that erupted in mole crabs digging their way toward China.

He needed to tell her he understood, and that he would always be here if she changed her mind. He needed to tell her she would be all right. But mostly he needed to tell her he didn't care about tomorrow, that he had long ago stopped worrying about whether he would be one of the parings that might extend their species. He had learned that life isn't about tomorrow. Life is about today. Kanady needed her to know how lonely he was, how much he yearned for someone like her, someone who understood his pain and who he could understand in return. He needed her to understand how much it had meant to his life merely to know she existed.

Ron's Afterword

It was the day before a writer's workshop was to begin, and Lisa Silverthorne and I had gotten to our hotel a little before most everyone else. "Let's write a story," she said. So, we proceeded to do just that. As fodder, I selected something for her to use as a prompt. She selected for me a little crab that had been painted on the wall of the hotel.

He was a happy little crab. Painted a vibrantly red shade of orange, with his claws raised upward.

Not a crab you would guess would inspire anyone to write a story about yearning, loneliness, and loss, better yet yearning, loneliness, and loss that plays out over galactic spans and generational lives. And yet, that's what came out. When I closed my eyes and thought about crabs, I got the image of sitting out on Daytona or Cocoa Beach and watching waves roll in. Seeing that, as they slid away, entire spans of wet, flat sand would erupt in pinprick fields of crabs that had been exposed digging down deeper to hold onto their little spot of land.

That's a hard life, isn't it? And it's a life that plays out before our eyes as we watch, never really seeing it for the struggle it is.

Unfolding the Multi-Cloud
ANALOG OCTOBER 2014

I am waiting. I have made myself pretty for you. I know you will be tired, but I have done up my hair in the curls and tints I know you like, and I have bathed in warm, perfumed water that has left its aroma across my skin like an invisible tattoo. My body is smooth and warm. And, I admit, it is hungry. We have taught my body so well that now it reveals me, despite my desire to seem aloof and distant. It has known almost on its own that tonight is the night you will return.

So I lay on the bed, draped in our sheets, waiting.

***

I was anxious the first time you left.

I knew the rumors — that the pure vastness of data could change you, that its boundless realms could stretch a person past the edge of their sanity. I worried you would return with parts of your fingers missing, or with your mind blown, or some other such thing. Months later, when I confessed this, you laughed. But I did worry about all those things. I heard them often about data miners. Folders, as they are called. I still cannot fathom the name, folders. Perhaps I will ask you about it again tonight.

Or not. It no longer matters. Not really.

After you left, I did the normal things people do, acting as if I expected to be alone, as if it were normal, as if you were working just around the corner like other husbands, wives, or lovers. But while I went about this normal living, I imagined what you were doing. When I was at the grocery site, I picked up a jug of virtual yogurt and spun it on its axis, wondering if you were there somehow. Could you feel me?

I'm sure you weren't there. The chances of you mapping the specific bits of ones and zeros that just happened to make up the yogurt tub at that special moment when I just happened to be touching it had to be so small as to be nonexistent. But I loved the idea that you *might* be there, that I might be putting bits that represented me against bits that in some distant fashion *were* you, and it made me smile so hard that I cried for a long while after I left the store.

You were so happy back then, so I didn't feel I could complain. But I worried.

I worried you would come back from the multi-cloud somehow less, missing the parts that are you, missing the William-ness of your being. But mostly I worried you would find the world of infinite data to be so expansive, so engrossing, and so attractive, that you would choose to not come back.

I should have known better, I suppose.

I should have known there were worse things than to be spurned by a lover.

You returned, though. And you seemed fine.

***

I lay in bed, now, remembering the night of your first return, replaying each moment as it happened in realspace and realtime as if it were happening now. My shoulders throw themselves backward, and my lungs ache for air. I feel the thread of the sheets like electric fire against my perfumed skin. It is a cool, dry anticipation everywhere except one place that is not so very cool and not so very dry.

I remember your smell tinted of the multi-cloud, coarse and wooly. The muscles along your back and your forearms. I remember the frame of your body. It felt like you had been gone for years and I wanted to absorb everything that had happened to you in some physical way.

I wanted to know what you had done in the multi-cloud. Yet, I was afraid to really know. I asked, of course, in a partial, superficial way, and you said it was like being everywhere at once, which immediately made me think of my yogurt at the grocery. Had you actually been there?

Your job is to know data, to live in it, to find patterns that pure algorithms can't hope to find, and to bring them to your employers so they can leverage those patterns into new ideas — or merely resurrect old ideas that have been forgotten through the years.

"It's a job," you had said when I asked how you felt about it. "And it pays a fortune."

I told you I didn't care about money or about where we lived. I said we could get regular jobs selling tomatoes or washing offices, but you wanted more so I said that I, too, wanted more. Our house, bought with your first paycheck, is lovely. The bathing room is fit for a princess — which is how you thought of me. We have our food brought to us, and I have time to work on my jewelry, my fashion, and my occasional dabbling into oils and watercolors (though my talent in those arts is so poor as to make me laugh). But as each cycle passed with you in the multi-cloud I could not hide from the fact that you are all I want, you are all I have ever wanted, and that this, unlike almost everything else about our lives, has not changed.

***

It is cliché to say the eyes are the windows to the soul. But clichés, like stereotypes, exist because there is truth in them.

The first time I realized something was missing was when I looked into your eyes. We had just made love, as we always do when you return. You rolled away, chest rising, a sheen of sweat glistening from your shoulder, which was newly colored and writhing in green. You looked at me and smiled, but my gaze was drawn to the vacuum hiding behind your eyes.

You were still working, weren't you?

Still in the multi-cloud — just a piece of you.

I learned exactly how true that was later. I would have seen it in your next pay check, anyway. Leaving part of yourself in data to keep working brought bonus pay enough to afford the crystal pool we put out back, and after you began leaving even more of yourself behind, we added a dream room — a self-configuring space where we could imagine ourselves to be anywhere or do anything.

You called it the holodeck, laughing as if it was your own inside joke. It smelled of plastic.

I slapped you playfully on the cheek that night to bring you out of your distraction, tickling you and telling you to focus on me. You laughed, and grasped my wrists, and you asked if that was what I really wanted, if I understood what I was getting into, asked it so forcefully as you smiled and pinned those wrists to the mattress. And I said yes, that is exactly what I wanted, and yes, I most definitely understood. I said yes. I remember you that night. Focusing. Fully. On me. And I remember wrapping myself around you, engulfing you, spreading myself over you so fully, so continuously, so completely, that I thought you could not possibly get away.

***

But you cannot cage a bird that has already flown.

***

The last time you returned you were tired.

When we were finished, you slept a deep, though not peaceful, sleep. I watched as your chest rose and fell. I watched as your arm jerked and the muscles that wrapped your stomach flowed like waves. I was hungry, and I had with me a plate of casserole Lanie had made before I sent her and the rest of the staff away for the next three days.

They know your cycle better than I, the staff.

When you return it means seventy-two hours liberty. I pay them, of course. We can afford it. I pay them to be gone because that is the time I have with just you.

I sat the plate down, thinking I would wake you and you could tell me of your adventures. I enjoyed hearing your stories, though your jargon of restriction gates, and meta-flows, TG-props, and other such things made them hard to follow. I didn't care, though. These things were you, so they would be me.

I slipped into bed, smiled at your warmth, and ran my fingers down your chest to your stomach, and then farther until I came to where there had, at one time, been hair that was soft and would have been wet from our previous exertions.

That was when you hit me.

***

It was not your fault.

I saw in your eyes exactly how afraid, and exactly how embarrassed you were as I cowered against the bedpost. I saw you were ashamed. You towered over me on the mattress, braced on your knees in the half-dark of the room, your fists clenched. Your breathing came in long, rasping streams that sounded like a snake's hiss. My arm throbbed where you had grasped it in your grip like a vise. I held my hand over my cheek, which blazed like it was freshly burned, my skin felt stretched over the hard rock of my bone. It would bruise the next day, turning darker before eventually fading.

You apologized, of course.

It wasn't you.

I had caught you while you were dreaming. It happened without a thought. A simple reaction, you said. You told me you loved me, only me, and I believed with all my heart, and we made love again, and again, and you seemed so much like you were there. Until...

Until afterward when again you fell asleep, and again your body moved in quirky ways as if something was inside you. But I knew the opposite was true. It was not something inside twitching your arm. It was your body missing something that should be there, perhaps aching for that part of you or those parts of you still floating out in netherspace, your biceps lamenting the loss of corpuscles or sinew or some other element it felt affinity to, your thigh needing a twine of muscle or missing the touch of one most special red blood cell.

I understood what it was feeling.

I lay next to you that night, nursing wounds. The ache in my arm made the sheets feel like they were made of lead. My cheek burned such that I felt I had been branded.

Who were you? I thought. What had you become?

***

So tonight I wait, knowing so much more than I once did.

I wish — so hard I wish — that I had studied the multi-cloud before we decided to take this path. When this started, I would have said you made this decision. But I know better. I could have stopped you then, before you left the first time. I could have told you I was afraid, or that the money didn't matter — I could have told you all the truths I had to tell, and you would have listened. Back then. You wouldn't have liked it. You would have pouted. But you would have listened, and we would have made it through whatever hardships we were destined to face together.

But I didn't say any of those things.

Instead I listened to your passion, and I believed in your love for me — a love I know was strong, but was also the wrong tool for this job. Your love for me and the need to provide is what moved you to become a folder in the first place. You needed a job, and they were scarce. I tried to support you after each rejection, but we were both so young and I was afraid and you were embarrassed. So when this opportunity came you took it.

It turned out you are good at this. I see it. I hear it in your voice. You are a good folder.

So now your love for me (that was once so strong and beautiful) has as its greatest competitor your pride as a man doing things you see as manly. It has to face your success, your position, and the ancient allure of adventure that has forever tempted men toward what they see as their greatness. It has to defeat your utter competence.

I have learned, though.

I have learned the multi-cloud steals a person a few bits at a time — slowly, yet certainly. It's even acknowledged in the contract, though folders are not generally the types who read fine print. I have learned of the esprit de corps of the few who give their lives to this, I have learned of the addiction that folders have to the sense of wrapping themselves about the universe, spreading themselves across oceans of context, across galaxies of data. "It's like you breathe in everything at the same time," you told me back in the days when you shared.

You have changed.

I have learned that in so very many ways.

And yet, I still need you. I feel that need in a place buried so deeply inside me that no doctor could ever uncover it. Can you come back? Can you be the man I knew before the multi-cloud came, the William who has faded away? I do not know, but I must find out.

I hear the sound of your return. The crash of a ceramic mug on the floor. I hear your groan, and I picture you picking yourself up off the floor. You know where I will be. I hear your footsteps. I smell the odor of the multi-cloud before the door is fully open.

Then you are here.

***

"I want you to stay here forever," I say on the second day of your return. We are at the pool, me lying in the sun, you hanging at the edge and catching your breath after lapping for what seemed to be hours. This is as close as I get to telling you what I want. It is as close as I can get. It should be enough. If your heart beats against mine as firmly as mine does to yours, it should be enough.

You smile.

That's all.

But it's your beautiful smile, and for a moment I pretend that every part of you is here — and that I haven't seen the way your gaze still slides away and how your hands move of themselves. I pretend that the new image of the serpent scrawling up your calf is not a sign that the multi-cloud has taken full hold of you.

But though I pretend, a part of me sees the truth, and I feel ... out-gunned.

***

You are due to leave again tomorrow morning.

I feel your anticipation.

Your cheek twitches and I sense annoyance as I run fingers through your hair. It is a jealous flinch, I know. If data has a soul, I'm sure the multi-cloud hates me as much as I despise it.

I should leave now.

I should get up and walk away. I would find ways to go on, though I would always wonder if you were there with me in the digital read-out of my sleeve or the automatic coloring of my wall. I would feel your presence, and I would cry.

I am strong enough to do that.

But I cannot be the one to walk away. Not from you.

So I wait one more time, wrapped in this sheet as you come to our bed. This is our last chance, I think as I kiss you and you kiss me back, our last chance to see who we are.

Our bodies intertwine and I reach to you with everything I have.

"Please don't leave me," I whisper to you later, as you sleep, watching your arms shake and your shoulders shiver.

"Please," I whisper. "Please."

I whisper it because I love you. I whisper it because I need you. And I whisper it because I know in my heart that if you leave me tonight, I cannot let you ever come back.

Ron's Afterword

Ten years ago, when this was first published, maybe this story was a little too ambitious. All I can say for sure is that, at the time, reviewers seemed to be kind of nonplussed by it. Opinions ranged from disappointed, to intrigued, to horrified by its sense of loss and its view on relationships and love. I use the term *horrified* there as (I think) a mostly good thing.

I wonder if the reviews would be the same now.

Because at its core this is a story about how spending a life too deeply embedded in the digital world can strip a person of who they are, and it's a story about how that stripping might change the lives of all the people around them. That's the modern take, anyway.

As I was writing it, I was also looking backward across time.

I remember thinking about how the daily grind that comes from needing to scratch out a living at a series of jobs that a person simply hates can change them. My grandfather worked thirteen days out of every fourteen—putting in very long hours to eke out his living by running a service station (back when they provided such things as service). He seemed happy enough to me, but I was just a kid. Did he really want to do that? Did his job fulfill him? Did he wake up every day thrilled to be digging into carburetors and oil pans? Did he love patching blown-out tires?

I don't know. But I'm sure it changed him.

And I'm sure those changes impacted everyone around him. Including me.

The Day the Track Stood Still
JOHN C. BODIN AND RON COLLINS
ANALOG MAY 2003

Indy's like no other racetrack – four turns, all left handers on nine-degree banks, each with its own little personality disorder. Turn 1 is narrowest and fastest. The grandstands tower above it, lending a claustrophobic aura that makes racing feel like you're pissing yourself back into a toothpaste tube at 481.532 miles an hour. Turns 1 and 3 follow the front and back straights, so you brake like a sumbitch there or the safety crews get to scrub skin off concrete. You can accelerate through turns 2 and 4, but 1 and 3 take your respect one way or the other.

Yes, Indy is like no other track.

But then Babs is like no other car. Long and sleek with a flash-molded titanium body, a Banshee 250 q-drive power plant, an effective IQ of 245, and a drive-by-wire neural net that sucks beta-blockers like sugar pills, Babs just begs to be driven hard.

"Drive me hard," she purred as I connected up and strapped into the cockpit. "We've only got four minutes, six and thirty-seven hundredths seconds to get to the grid, and I need a warm-up lap." The skin around my neck grew warm as she ran the serotonin check. I suddenly smelled fuel and rubber and the tantalizing aroma of cool asphalt warming in the late morning sun. Most cars on the circuit love to run, but Babs takes it to a totally different level.

I tried not to think about what was at stake. The pressure was bad enough without telling her this was for all the marbles: if we lost this Indy 500, she was gone. Sayonara muchacha. Hasta la bye-bye, and good night, Babs. That's the way it is when you race the B'arada. They put up a piece of tech, you put up a piece of tech. Winner takes all, Indy 500 style.

Turns out Babs was the only thing humanity had left that the B'arada wanted.

I flipped the ignition, and a quarter-million horses rumbled from the back. Babs hit a couple switches that doctors from around the globe would give their Hippocratic oath to know about, and the endorphin-meter inside my brain snapped to attention.

"Hear about the B'arada swap in the number 11 car?" Sparky screamed from my left earpiece.

"What?"

"Just a Foyt clone. Not a big deal."

Sparky's a helluva of a simchanic, but sometimes his sense of reality isn't torqued to spec, if you know what I mean.

"Not a big deal? Four minutes till race time and you're just now telling me about a driver swap? Whatthahellduya mean, not a big deal?"

"Put your rockets on simmer, man. There's a bunch of clones running – Mears, Fittipaldi, every Unser and Andretti in the catalog, even an old Parnelli Jones from what I heard. Don't worry, though. The Foyt is probably a late model. No competition."

"I'm glad you're not a clone, Buddy," Babs murmured. "They're so cold and unfeeling." The entire chassis vibrated with harmonics I'm certain had never been invented until then. "I need a warm-up lap, Buddy. Ready to lay a little rubber and heat up the tires?"

"Hold your quarks a sec, okay, babe?"

Her proton splitter roared displeasure, but I needed time to think about this.

Number 11. Latest design from Lockheed-Reynard, ion-plasma drive with the latest fusion intercooler technology. It was outside-front-row fast, and that was with a B'arada behind the console. A Foyt clone, even a late '80s model, would beat crap out of a B'arada.

Damn.

If there's anything I'm good at (besides driving Babs), it's sniffing out rats, and this one suddenly reeked particularly rodentile. We were on the pole, though – fastest qualifier and all that. So bring 'em on, I thought.

"I'm not waiting any longer," Babs said.

The engine screeched like the banshee it was so-aptly named for. The intake manifold sucked matter-antimatter pairs from the quantum foam and fed them into a pair of supercooled synchrocyclotron coils Lawrence would have been proud of, which in turn spun up the gravity downforce generator.

Next thing I knew we were scrubbing rubber at the Brickyard. If there's anything more uninhibited than an overrevved 500-mile-an-hour hot rod with 1800 megawatts of power at her disposal, I've yet to meet her. The gravity-gen downforce system sucked enough power to run Chicago for a year as we dove into turn 1, picked it up around 2, and hurtled down the backstretch. Babs moaned with ecstasy as I hit the brakes in turn 3. Friction melted my mind. Everything from the tips of my toes to the ends of my hair tingled with electricity. Babs has this habit, you see, of getting a little, uh, enthusiastic in the early laps, and being netted means I've resorted to wearing rubber knickers under my g-suit.

Let's just say it's never too hard getting corporate sponsorship to ride shotgun in neural-link position, if you get my drift.

But I'm a professional and I had a job to do.

I kept us on course and feathered the throttle through the short chute. Babs burned mass in 4 and we were back at the bricks in what the pylon said was an unofficial track record. The crowd went white noise.

Yes, Babs is not your average car. She could, of course, run code that would do all the driving, but the Galactic Racing League quickly found that no one paid to watch a bunch of nuts and bolts whiz around a track like grown-up slot cars. Losing a couple advertising contracts was all it took for them to institute the human-in-the-loop rule that ensures jobs for lead-footed neural jocks like me. Every now and again, I kid her about being an overgrown riding mechanic, but it never seems to bother her any.

"That was beautiful, babe," I said with a grin.

"Thanks," she purred in reply.

A car flashed by us. The pylon lights flickered. Our lucky number 13 moved down to the second slot.

I didn't have to guess twice to know what would be there now.

Number 11.

***

"Are you okay?" Babs said into my cerebral cortex.

We were sitting in the pits, waiting to go back to the track for the start of the race. My features must have darkened. The smile slipped from Sparky's face. I was the one treated to Mr. Toad's Wild Ride the day we faced the Foyt Mk V in his Intel-Penske, but Sparky had been there, too. He remembered same as me.

"Is it Lucy?" he said.

"Who's Lucy?" Babs asked, suddenly awake.

I just stared at the number 11 car. She was different. No doubt about it. They had changed her aerodynamics, wiped her memory banks, reprogrammed her personality center, and painted her up like a Market Street hussy. But there was no doubt it was her under that Lockheed-Reynard facade. Given everything I could see that they had tinkered with, I glumly wondered what the B'arada had done that I couldn't see.

"Wasn't your fault, Buddy," Sparky said. "And it's just an A.J. clone. It's not like it's even *the* A.J. clone. Those things don't last more than a race or two. Besides," he continued, his voice lower, "it was a fluke, Buddy – just a mistake. It's in the past, and you've got a race to win."

"Absolutely," I said. "Let's do it." I didn't feel any better, but Sparky was right. It was time to pick my chin off the floor and get to work.

"I asked you a question," Babs said in a tone cold enough to pass for a naked shoulder in Siberia.

"What question was that?"

"Who's Lucy?"

I did my best imitation of a guy shuffling his feet. "Uh ... it's a long story," I said. "And we've got only two minutes to get to the grid."

"We're not going anywhere until I get a straight answer."

Dammit, I thought in an unguarded moment. I should have told her before.

"Told me what?"

This is the biggest problem with neural linkage: It takes a lot of concentration to keep a thought to yourself. Babs and I have been together a long time. I was lucky to hold it this long. I looked at the system clock, feeling her virtual foot tapping in the background. This had better be fast and convincing, or we weren't going to be doing any racing today.

"All right. You win."

"That's better." Her collider manifold settled into a gentle rattle.

"Lucy was my first big-time ride, my first shot at the circuit. She was an early Lockheed-Reynard – state of the art and very, very fast. We were unbeatable for a couple years."

"Yeah," Sparky chimed in, "all the way until Indy in '34."

"You had a girl before me?"

"Give me a break, babe. I was a two-time champion before we paired up. You knew that."

She was quiet for a nano. "So. What happened?"

I sighed, watching the seconds slip away.

"Like I said, we were fast. But what I didn't say is that we were fast because Sparky was the first electron monkey to perfect the neural link."

"Ah. You used B'arada technology against them," Babs said with admiration in her voice.

"More or less," Sparky said proudly.

"Pretty slick."

"Very slick," I agreed. "The B'arada were baffled at first. To make things even better, Sparky's modifications messed up B'arada physiology when they tried to use them."

"Boy-howdy were they ever pissed," Sparky hooted.

"Nobody likes to lose," Babs replied.

"B'arada like it less than most," I said.

"So you pissed them off and they took you and Lucy out by planting you in the wall with some kamikaze move?" Babs guessed.

"I wish that were the case. But what they did was far worse than that."

"What could be worse than that?"

"Ever wonder how clones came to be a part of racing in the first place?" Sparky asked.

Her gauges brightened as she thought. "The B'arada used them so they could exploit Sparky's interface?"

"Bingo!" Sparky said.

"Okay. So, what's the big deal? Buddy's been beating clones for years."

"I'm a better driver now than I was then, and they were sneaky about it. They didn't reveal their first clones until after they arranged a less-than-friendly wager," I said bitterly.

"A wager?"

"You know how the B'arada love to gamble."

"Well, sure."

"They let Lucy and me rack up the wins while they laid a line of ever-increasing bets. Then at Indy they brought out the big kahuna – interstellar hyperdrive technology."

There was silence for a moment, then Babs asked, "What did you have to put up in return?"

"Lucy," I replied.

"You bet your girlfriend?"

"We thought we couldn't lose," Sparky said, his head hanging like a whupped hounddog's.

"The first A.J. clone was an early '60s vintage. It beat us easy."

"I can't believe you lost your girlfriend in a bet."

My hesitation was, perhaps, just a moment too long. Sparky cleared his throat.

"Don't tell me," Babs said. "This time it's my proverbial butt on the line?"

I couldn't look her in the console. "You don't understand, Babs. Hyperdrive technology will advance humankind by centuries, and it's not like I had any real choice in the matter. The president of the United Earth herself made the deal."

Silence hung heavy in the air. The countdown to the parade lap drew toward zero. Suddenly Babs's power plant spun up.

"You're gonna owe me big time for this, Buddy."

"Huh?" was all I could muster.

"You've beaten A.J. clones before, right?"

"Yeah."

Her tires squealed, and a cloud of dust rose in the air behind us.

"I don't want to spend the rest of my days in a B'arada dustbin, so get your ass out of the dumps and drive me hard."

***

The Jim Nabors clone sang the song. The Golden Girl threw the baton. Mary George IV said the famous line "Ladies, gentlemen, and all you other things ... start your engines."

The green flag fell, and Babs screamed down the front stretch and into turn 1, the A.J. clone fading in her rear-vid mirror.

"So that's Lucy, eh?" Babs said as she flipped a neuro-transmitter, and a gazillion sensations raced through my brain. "Doesn't seem so hot to me."

Let me tell you, there can't be anything more frightening than turning megarevs while strapped into a suicidal lover who's just learned you've risked selling her into slavery on a bet that might let humankind do the Star Trek boogie. Her first lap was a new track record. Her second was faster. Her third faster still.

You might say she was a little pissed.

I just let her run and tried to concentrate on the track. I experimented with getting on the brakes a little later in 1 and hitting the throttle quicker on the way into the short chute. I guided Babs into the high line, and pulled her away from the wall down the straights. Ten laps into it we were working together like Rogers and Astaire. It was almost enough to take my mind off the number 11 that suddenly seemed plastered to the rear-vid.

"Don't worry," Babs moaned as we swept through 3 and 4 for another lap.

I gave a tension-filled laugh.

They say worry is a stainless-steel rat that gnaws through neural interfaces to short-circuit your persistence by defecating on your survival instinct. But I know better. For me worry is a car and a clone and a set of circumstances from my past. Worry is an A.J. strapped into a Lockheed-Reynard lurking in my mirrors and waiting for me to make a mistake.

Don't worry, she says?

What the hell did Babs know about worrying?

***

We led for a while, then backed off while lesser drivers tried to win the race before it was halfway over. A yellow came out while they scraped a Rutherford off the wall. A three-car inferno erupted on the restart, causing the B'arada contingent to file a claim that the Galactic Racing League commission ignored or lost or otherwise failed to rule upon.

Other than that, the first 190 laps were uneventful.

***

We were running a strong second with ten laps to go – right behind a B'arada, believe it or not. Lucy and the A.J. clone were nearby but hadn't shown the ability to take us all day. Babs was writhing in ecstasy with every turn. I was burning with that fever that comes when your butt's three inches off pavement and you're traveling at something approaching the speed of sound. We were, as they say, in the groove.

The B'arada was dead meat, and everyone knew it.

We passed the start/finish line, and the B'arada's machine slowed to enter turn 1. I waited on the brakes as long as I could, and we blew past him. The crowd cheered and shot to their feet to get a good look at the massive wreck that would undoubtedly occur when we hit the wall. I jammed the brakes. Babs responded with split-second timing, cutting in for the turn and taking advantage of the oversteer that had snuck into our setup after the last pit stop.

I kicked the proton gun and pulled on the antimatter coil like it had never been tapped before. I would have blacked out if it weren't for my g-suit and Babs' insistent presence echoing through my cranium.

We rocketed through turn 1 and thundered down the short chute with less than ten laps between us and victory. I glanced in the rear-vid and was surprised to see a car there.

Number 11.

Damn.

Apparently Babs and I hadn't been the only ones holding back. Sweat broke out all over my body. "Come on, babe. Time to hit the afterburners." I rolled a finger over the gearshift and dropped down a gear. She seemed to jump out of her skin – as fresh as she had been at the beginning of the day. Amazing. I had never seen a car like her before, and probably never would again.

Number 11 grew smaller in the mirror.

"You weren't worried, were you?" Babs asked in her smokiest voice. A shiver went down my spine. "We're the unbeatable ones today, lover."

By lap 199 the margin was comfortable.

It was going to take more than an A.J. model and an old flame to stop us today.

Lady luck is a fickle wench, though.

Had I been listening to the radio better, perhaps I would have been able to avoid the situation. But as fate would have it, I missed the announcer as he said, "And *another* Mario is slowing down."

We barreled into turn 1 and there it was – a Mario unit loafing along at 200 miles an hour, smack in the middle of the racing line. Braking would have been disastrous, so I fired off a quick left-right-left. Babs swerved toward the unforgiving wall. Her tail slewed, and she grunted as the right rear brushed the concrete. A 495-mile-an-hour rugburn brought tears to my eyes.

The maneuver was successful, though, and we flashed past the slowing Mario. I allowed myself to resume breathing about halfway through turn 2.

A red blur flashed past us. My heart skipped a beat. Number 11 – Lucy and the A.J. clone – raced ahead. Babs screamed from all synch-cycs and poured it on, but we had scrubbed too much speed in the Mario event. The A.J. clone's lead stretched to several car lengths by turn 3.

Lucy may have been my first great car, but I realized at that precise moment that it was Babs who was my real soulmate. Tears welled in my eyes as I thought of losing her. What had I been thinking? What was I going to do without her?

"Buck up, lover," Babs said through gritted circuits. "T'ain't over till it's over."

I owed her. We weren't going to win, but I owed her the nobility of this effort if nothing else, and I was determined that Babs would at least know what true love meant before she was carted away to languish in some dirty old B'arada tech lab. So I screwed on my determination, cranked up my resolve, and brought her down under the racing line. Her quantum foam drive roared and scooped particles through turn 3. She raced out of the short chute and into 4. My view narrowed and darkened as acceleration brought on tunnel vision.

The distance between us shrank. The A.J. clone saw us looming in his rear-vid and ducked even lower on the apron, all four wheels under the line. We were two lengths behind coming out of turn 4.

It was a drag race to the end.

The A.J. pushed Lucy harder than ever. My synapses commanded the particle accelerator through the floorboard, and Babs screamed like a rocket. We were gaining. Inch by excruciating inch we were hauling them in.

But I saw clearly that we didn't have enough track left.

We were giving it all we could, but we were going to come up short. I pounded the console. "Dammit!"

Babs's voice came from all directions at once. "Hang tight, Buddy." She swung out from behind the A. J. and into that massive wall of air.

Then my stomach turned a loop, my ears crackled, and I swear I saw stars. The finish line receded like I was looking through the wrong end of the binoculars. Someone dropped a concrete block on my chest, and my view became a pinpoint of light.

Did I see a checkered flag waving?

Number 11 crossed the finish line ... racing toward us?

Yes. That's what I saw.

We were sitting at the entrance to turn 1, facing backward. Somehow we had come to rest beyond the finish line.

"What the ...?"

"We won, lover," Babs said in a dreamy, faraway voice as her engines wound down to a steady purr.

***

The rest of that afternoon happened too fast. The victory lap, Sparky pounding me on the back as I accepted the traditional bottle of milk, hefting the Borg-Warner trophy in the Winner's Circle, the interviews, the phone call from the president – it all disappeared in a blur. It wasn't until later that night in the quiet of the garage area that Babs and I got a chance to talk.

"I don't understand what happened today," I said after linking into her net.

"We won."

"You know what I mean."

"You really didn't know that hyperdrive units are just tweaks of the same technology that went into my engines?"

"No, uh, I didn't. What does that mean?"

"Hyperdrive. Think about it. I came up with it just before the race started."

She spread a little serotonin enhancer across my wet-net and my vision ran clear.

"We created a temporal displacement?" I asked in disbelief.

"No," Babs chided. "*I* created a temporal displacement. You just sat there trying not to vomit."

I swallowed hard. "I don't think the rules committee is going to like this."

"Maybe. But I don't think the B'arada are going to protest."

"Why not?"

"You've been too busy playing hero to the sponsors to hear the news, eh? When they lost, B'arada had to fess up because they couldn't pay the bill. They never had hyperdrive capability in the first place."

"I don't understand."

"They were betting tender they didn't have."

"They can't do that."

"They defended themselves by saying they didn't think they could lose."

I was suddenly embarrassed. Knowing that Babs could feel my embarrassment made it worse. Damned neural interface. "I'm sorry," I said. "I shouldn't have allowed them to bet you."

"That's all right, lover. You're forgiven."

I felt better.

"Don't think that means you're off the hook, though."

"How can I make it up to you?" I said, not certain I was going to like where this was going.

"I put a call in to the president and offered her a deal," Babs replied. "Hyperdrive technology for unlimited access to every racetrack in the world."

"Cool."

"Only one catch."

"Yes?"

"I don't pay up until you agree to a lifetime contract."

I grinned. "The first man/machine marriage?"

"You got it, lover. I was thinking Monte Carlo for the honeymoon, then maybe Sebring. I hear they do some endurance racing there."

"It's a deal," I said. I was more than a little concerned with my ability to keep up with her for twenty-four hours of rugged road racing, but that was an issue for another time. The connection between man and machine tingled in every nerve I had and a few that I'm certain hadn't existed until now.

"I still don't understand, though. If you knew you could do the hyper-thing from the very beginning, why did you even bother to run the race?"

"Oh, Buddy," Babs said with a hushed breath catching in her neural circuitry. "It's all the laps in the middle that make a race worth winning."

Ron's Afterword

This was the first of my collaborations with my friend John C. Bodin, and it led to the very fun project that finally completed at "Seven Days in May." I say that because the project was (or, should I say, is) evergreen. The concept included adding a new story every year and then re-releasing the volume.

It was a good deal of fun.

We had a bit of a go-around with Dr. Schmidt before he took this one. His problem, you see, was that he understood his readers, and he knew they'd go with future technology as long as it's plausible. And when we first wrote it, the quantum drive engine wasn't even in the ballpark. So we did a little more thinking and a little more theorizing. What we ended up with is obviously not here now. Not even close. John and I are both of engineering mindsets, though, and can report that the ideas behind using fluctuations of the quantum foam and a few other bits do make proper sense. So check marks on that.

What I love the most about this one, though, is the base relationship between human and car, and the core mindsets of gamblers no matter where they come from.

Everything is always so clear when you figure you can't lose, after all.

ABOUT RON COLLINS

Ron Collins is a best-selling Science Fiction author who writes across the spectrum of contemporary and speculative fiction. His short fiction has received a Writers of the Future prize and a CompuServe HOMer Award. His short story "The White Game" was nominated for the Short Mystery Fiction Society's Derringer Award.

With his daughter, Brigid, he also edited *Face the Strange, An Anthology of Speculative Fiction*.

Follow Ron at: http://www.typosphere.com
Twitter: @roncollins13

Get Free Books!
Join Ron's Reader List
http://typosphere.com/newsletter

Glamour of the God-Touched
(Book 1 of *Saga of the God-Touched Mage*)

STARCRUISE
(a short story in the *Stealing the Sun* universe)

Other Work by Ron Collins

Novels

Stealing the Sun (9 books)
Saga of the God-Touched Mage (8 books)
The PEBA Diaries (2 books)
The Knight Deception
Wakers

Fastballs and Fairies (3 Books), with Brigid Collins

Collections

Collins Creek (3 volumes)
Tomorrow in All the Worlds
Picasso's Cat & Other Stories
Five Magics
Seven Days in May, with John C. Bodin

Poetry

Five Seven Five

Nonfiction

On Writing (And Reading!) Short
On Creating (And Celebrating!) Characters

Special Appreciation

I want to give special thanks to all the Amazing People who supported the early release of this book on Kickstarter. Your help was immense, and so greatly appreciated!

AGB — Alexander H. — Alexander Ourique — Andy F
Annie Reed — Bill Kohn — Bradley — Baker
Céline Malgen — Christa Concannon — Christian Meyer
Colleen Feeney — Craig Garvie — David H. Hendrickson
GhostCat — Greg Levick — Ian Carmen — James Palmer
James 'The Great Old One' Burke — Jim Gotaas
Joe Gillis — John Lamar — Joseph Procopio
Judy McClain — Justin Alexander Dorsey — Kal Powell
Kari Kilgore — Kate MacLeod — Kelly Washington
Laura Ware — Lisa Silverthorne — Mark Leslie Lefebvre
Mary Jo Rabe — Michael A. Burstein — Michelle Yvon
Patrick Hay — Pierino Gattei
Rajasekaran Senthil Kumaran — Rebecca M. Senese
Richard O'Shea — Risa Scranton — Robert D. Stewart
Rowan Stone — Ruth Ann Orlansky
Ryan M. Williams — Tony Hernandez — Ultra Bithalver

Acknowledgements

I would like to thank the two editors Stanley Schmidt and Trevor Quachri, as well as Emily Hockaday and every other member of the staff at *Analog Science Fiction and Fact* over the years. They have been and continue to be eminently professional and a joy to work with. I would also like to thank *Analog* readers through those same years, especially those who have taken the time to send me notes of encouragement regarding one story or another, as they saw fit.

It is such a pleasure to see my work in this publication, and that would not happen without their support.

I thank, also, Lisa—the true love of my life, and the greatest copyeditor and typo crusher who ever existed. She is the best of everything. I guarantee that *any* errors found in any of my work have been created after she got her hands on it.